TAKING CHARGE

Diana jumped as if he'd slapped her. The pistol came up. "Take off your coat," she said.

James stared at the pistol, then slowly let out his breath.

Her eyes narrowed. "I said, take it off."

He could easily take the gun. But it might be more enjoyable to oblige her. James unbuttoned the two buttons that held his coat closed and shrugged it off over his shoulders. As was his habit, he wore no shirt beneath.

Diana's lips parted, moistened with her breath, as she looked him over. "Unbutton your trousers," she said.

THE PIRATE HUNTER

JENNIFER ASHLEY

LEISURE BOOKS NEW YORK CITY

LEISURE BOOKS®

May 2004

Published by

Dorchester Publishing Co., Inc.
200 Madison Avenue
New York, NY 10016

ISBN 0-8439-5280-6

Visit us on the web at www.dorchesterpub.com.

ACKNOWLEDGMENTS

Special thanks to Glenda Garland for her gallant, last-minute critiquing and splendid, solid advice. Also thanks to Trudy and Al and the whole Ashley clan for their continued and enthusiastic support. And of course to Forrest for his unceasing willingness to brainstorm, critique, and proofread, stand in line at the post office, and offer loving support.

THE PIRATE
HUNTER

Chapter One

James Ardmore opened his eyes. He lay facedown in the sand, arms outstretched like he'd tried to climb the pale beach at the last desperate moment. Sun warmed his hair, his coat was drenched, and his boots were full of water.

He wanted to roll over, sit up, get his bearings, find out where he was. Except his body would not move. He lay for a long time, sand grating against his cheek, willing his muscles to do something. A finger twitched, and that was all.

A seagull landed next to him. It cocked its head, studying him nearly eye to eye. He could see the red dot on its beak, the stark white of its head, the black feet on the sand. They stared at each other with the mild curiosity of strangers in a traveling coach, until the seagull, bored, turned and waddled away.

Some time passed. The sun grew warmer. After a while, James lifted his head.

The first thing he saw was another body, a man limp

1

on the sand not five feet away. The man had hair the golden color of batter-fried chicken and wore the uniform of an English naval lieutenant.

The lieutenant had brown eyes, James knew, though the man's face was turned away from him. He knew because the lieutenant had loosened James's chains on the frigate when it had started to go down, giving James a fighting chance. In return, James had pulled the man onto the piece of longboat when he'd floated by. The lieutenant had been barely conscious then, and he might be dead now.

More time passed. A small crab crawled by. A wave snaked up the beach, scooped up the crab, and pulled it back into the sea.

The land smelled clean, the wind, fresh. Another look up revealed that he lay on a small strip of beach surrounded by black rock filmed with succulents of green, yellow, and scarlet. A hill reared above him, black against the bright blue sky.

He knew he was not in Tangier, which would have stunk of human waste and coal fires, and besides, someone would have robbed him of his boots and the knife he could still feel in his pocket. This was not Gibraltar because the rocks looked wrong, and some efficient soldier from the garrison would have already dragged them to safety, arresting James along the way.

He might be in some remote part of Spain or down the coast of Morocco, where they would lie until a farmer happened to venture to the beach. If this was Spain, the English lieutenant would be taken to an army camp, and James would be arrested. If this was Morocco, they would both be arrested for breaking the monarch's edict that foreigners were allowed only in Tangier. Not a happy thought, he mused, as his eyes drifted closed again.

The next time he opened them, the sun had moved higher, and he heard voices. A high-pitched voice and another, a woman's, answering. The farmer's wife and child.

He wondered if the farmer followed. Would he see a man in a Moroccan *galabeeyah* and pointed leather shoes or a Spanish farmer in breeks and shirt and worn boots? Both men would wear dour, weather-beaten expressions; neither would be happy to see two men needing assistance.

The clattering of rock on rock obscured a child's prattle. Then a woman spoke. "Isabeau, have a care, for heaven's sake."

In surprise, he cranked his head around to look, but they were still out of sight. Her tones had been those of a high-bred English woman. Not a Spanish peasant farmer's wife, unless that Spanish peasant farmer had some damned good luck.

Or— Memories slid through his head. It couldn't be. Could it? He'd been trying hard to find Haven, and then the frigate that held him prisoner had broken up, and here he was. Pain tingled through his fingers and laughter through his head. It was too good.

Or maybe this was Gibraltar after all and she was not Diana Worthing, the woman he'd abducted a year ago. Maybe she was some officer's wife who would fetch her husband to drag James off to the garrison and prison.

Two tiny boots under a crinkled skirt stopped in front of him. A little girl stooped to look him in the face, just like the seagull had. She had round, pink cheeks, inquisitive blue eyes, and bright red flyaway hair. She was perhaps eight or nine years old. She emitted a breathy squealing sound, for all the world like she was asking if he was all right, but didn't know the words.

Another pair of feet stopped beside the girl's. Identical boots under an identical cotton skirt, but these ankles belonged to a woman. A shapely woman who smelled of fresh wind and soap. He could see under her skirt the way she held it, and that was no bad thing. The worsted stockings and breeches underneath molded to her fine body. If she were his woman, he'd tell her not to bother with the skirt.

She stooped down and turned him over. Her fingers held strength and warmth.

She had an oval face tanned by the sun and framed with the child's same fiery red hair. Gray-blue eyes widened in sudden recognition, and James felt an impossible joy.

The last time he'd seen her, her hair had been carefully coiffed, her skin creamy white. She'd dressed in a high-fashion silk that hid none of her charms. Little rubies had dangled from her ears. Now her lobes were bare, and she wore the worn cotton of a farmer's daughter. Her lips then had been reddened by cosmetics, but now they were pale and pinkish brown. He imagined they tasted the same.

Her eyes had not changed. They flashed now, just as they had one year ago on the south coast of Kent when he'd so boldly kissed her, and she'd so boldly kissed him back. That is, after she'd thrown the potato soup at him.

She stared at him, frozen, shocked. He dimly wondered what the hell she was doing here, but his curiosity was smothered by a wave of mirth.

"Hey, darlin'." He let his Charleston vowels take their time. "I said I wanted to get to know you better, remember?"

Her shocked look turned to one of pure rage. Her lips parted. Her voice was just as warm and contralto and just as dripping with scorn as Diana, Lady Worthing, could possibly make it. "James Ardmore," she bit out. "I never wanted to see *you* again."

He chuckled grimly. It hurt. "Thought I'd surprise you," he said.

She bent over him, her cool scent covering him like a sheet fresh from the line, her blue-gray eyes wide and beautiful. She drew breath to say something else, likely something sarcastic, but then her face blurred and her voice blended with the waves, and he lost consciousness again.

Chapter Two

Diana looked about for something to throw. Nothing presented itself, so she made do with kicking the sand.

James Ardmore lay at her feet, his black hair matted with water, his hands bloody, his clothes torn. And he laughed at her. Still.

Hadn't she had Fate's surfeit of his sardonic drawl, his arrogant calmness in the sticky heat of the previous July when he'd abducted her and carried her to his ship? Of the utterly cool way he'd stolen her from the house party full of English admirals, and equally as coolly, deposited her back again. But not before he'd frightened her, baited her, turned her ideas inside out, made her cold and ill and angry, and stripped her of her illusions about herself.

That and he'd kissed her. He'd kissed her to mock her, and he'd succeeded in shaking something loose at the bottom of her soul.

For the first time, she was glad Isabeau could not hear, because Diana's epithets were very unladylike.

She sent Isabeau off for help and worked to save the life of the arrogant bas—the life of James Ardmore and that of the man who had the misfortune to be with him. A lieutenant she guessed from his uniform.

Visions of the decadent house on the south coast of Kent, the tedious, weeklong house party given by Admiral Burgess, which she had attended with her now deceased husband, rose like the smell of fish entrails on the kitchen slop heap. She remembered the dripping days, the heavy nights, the admirals and their wives trying to be fashionable, the young men-about-town invited so that all would think Admiral Burgess was à la mode, the local earl's son, a man who lisped and dragged the maids, one by one, into his bed whether they wanted to go or not. Diana had played whist with ladies who cheated, conversed with gentlemen who openly looked down her bodice, and danced with admirals who tried to grope her on the ballroom floor. She'd pasted a smile on her face and pretended to enjoy every minute.

Another guest, an American named Ronald Kinnaird, was the only person Diana could tolerate. He was polite and affable and never whispered indecent suggestions while they danced the cotillion. So, of course, it turned out that he was a spy.

Even so, Diana might have been content to play out her role as wife of the famous Sir Edward Worthing, if she had not had to leave Isabeau behind. Sir Edward had firmly refused to bring her, though Diana had argued until she was hoarse. No one, Sir Edward had snapped, wanted a deaf child who talked by squealing and fluttering her hands. It was bloody embarrassing when she started making those noises. She would stay in London with her nurse, and that would be that.

Diana had become furious, but Sir Edward's eyes had glittered with the beginnings of one of his violent rages. Diana hated to be separated from Isabeau and usually arranged for the little girl to accompany her wherever she went. But this time Sir Edward was adamant. He wanted to show his best face to the admiral because he might finagle a promotion to commodore. Diana tried to feign illness at the last minute, but Sir Edward was having none of that.

So Diana went, though she saw no reason not to let her husband know precisely what she thought of a man who was ashamed of his own child.

"What about a man ashamed of his own wife?" Sir Edward had retorted. "Do keep your licentious nature under control this week, Diana. I am trying to be made commodore, and my wife discovered in the bed of one of the admiral's guests will not help me."

Diana replied sharply that she had never betrayed him and never intended to do so. Sir Edward just gave her one of his skeptical looks, and Diana had spent the rest of the journey in furious silence.

The house party had worn on in disgusting frenzy. Sir Edward pretended to be proud of his beautiful wife, while Admiral Burgess pinched Diana's bottom when he thought no one was looking. The ladies whispered about her behind their fans or made blatantly rude remarks. Diana slept alone and missed Isabeau.

She hated every minute of it, but she'd had no idea how much worse it could become until she turned the corner of a walk in the admiral's vast garden and found a man there. A small, leathery-faced man who was neither a guest nor a servant. She could not help noticing that he held a pistol, for he pointed it straight at her.

This walk was screened by a line of large trees on one side, a high hedge on the other. No one could see her, or the intruder, from the house. He was brown-skinned and had wiry black hair and wide black eyes. His smile was just as wide.

"Don't be making a sound," he said in a broad Irish brogue. "I hate to shoot a lady. Especially one as beautiful as you."

Diana thought rapidly. It was not unheard of for an Irishman to try his hand at assassination in retaliation for the English who held their island in thrall. After the '99 uprising, things only had become worse. Had he come to murder one of the admirals, or perhaps the much-decorated Sir Edward Worthing?

"There are too many military men here for you to prevail," she said, surprised at her own calmness. "Leave now and I will say nothing."

The impudent grin widened. "I believe you misunderstand the situation, my lady."

Before she could ask what he meant, someone loomed up beside her and a very large, very strong hand clamped over her mouth. She'd struggled, only to find herself pulled in a firm grip against a tall man's hard body.

His breath was hot and smelled of coffee. He had a hard face, tanned from the sun and sea air, a long nose, a pale mouth, and eyes so light green they might have been made of ice. Long black hair, unruly and loose, brushed his shoulders. His grip held so much strength she feared her jaw would break.

A voice holding the slow heat of the American South trickled into her ear. "Not a sound, Lady Worthing. Not a move."

"She nearly walked into me, she did," the Irishman said, apologetic. "Five minutes either way, she'd never have found me."

The green-eyed man did not reply. He just looked at Diana. He was too strong to fight—too strong, period.

His fingers bruised her mouth, and his arm pinned her like a band of steel. She felt the slow beat of his heart, the rise and fall of his breath, the hard muscles of his thighs pressed right into her hips.

"It doesn't matter," he drawled. "We've got him."

Got who? Admiral Burgess? The slimy Lord Percy, the earl's son? Her own husband?

Footsteps approached, walking rapidly, assuredly. "Good Lord," a very English voice said.

Perhaps one of the dandies had come to investigate. Perhaps he would show uncharacteristic bravery and rescue her. Perhaps the sun would rise backward and Sir Edward would fetch Isabeau to dance a jig in the street.

Two men came into her line of sight. She knew one but not the other. The Englishman who had spoken was a stranger to her. He wore a dark, very well-tailored suit and gold spectacles. His hair was blond, and he sported a fine beaver hat of the latest fashion. He looked very much like the puerile dandies at the admiral's party, except that his astute gray eyes showed that he might actually possess an intelligent thought or two. "Who the devil is she?" he asked in amazement.

The gentleman with him was the American, Ronald Kinnaird.

Kinnaird went with them willingly, proving he was no captive, and he made no objection when told they'd have to drag Diana along. Diana had been furious.

And they'd taken her. Just like that.

So had begun her two-day ordeal with James Ardmore, the pirate hunter. She'd spent most of it on his ship, the *Argonaut*, a vessel as proud and arrogant as himself. Those two stormy, brief days had changed her life forever. So short a period, and yet it was a lifetime.

Now in the bright spring sunshine of Haven, she remembered every humiliating, embarrassing, infuriating moment. She remembered his fierce kiss and their sharp quarrel in the private room of the public house. The incident had involved flying bread and butter and potato soup before he'd seized her wrists and backed her into the wall. His hands had bruised her arms, his lips had bruised her mouth.

She remembered the darkness of the English lane before at last he'd let her go, the biting pressure of his fingers on her arms, the warmth of his forehead against hers, his hot breath on her skin. He'd said, "Come with me, Diana." His voice had cracked, but his Southern drawl had still warmed her.

In her frenzy of emotion, she'd almost agreed. She'd almost run away with him in her pink silk frock and beaded slippers, disgraced herself by becoming the mistress of the legendary James Ardmore. London would simply consider it the final outrage by the scandalous Lady Worthing and pity her husband.

In the midst of her agitation, she'd had one calming thought. *Isabeau.* She'd thought of Isabeau and of Sir Edward Worthing, and she had made her lips form the word "No."

It had been the hardest word she'd ever said.

She'd thought herself strong, but James Ardmore proved her weak; thought herself worldly wise, but he'd shown her ignorance; thought herself decadent, but he'd proved she didn't know the meaning of the word. She was proud of doing her duty by her husband and daughter no matter how scandalous her behavior, but James Ardmore had nearly shattered that adherence to duty with one intense, bruising kiss. Only the fear of abandoning her daughter to Edward's mercy had stopped her.

James had interrogated her, mocked her, grown angry

at her, argued with her, berated her, helped her, and kissed her. When she'd at last reached the relative safety of Admiral Burgess's house, she'd collapsed in her chamber and wept for a night. The house party, at first alarmed by her disappearance, had assumed she'd eloped with the American Kinnaird and that he'd abandoned her. She did not contradict them. Vicious gossip ensued, and Edward did not get his promotion.

"You stupid hussy," Edward had hissed. "You've ruined me." Admiral Burgess had been furious. She supposed that if she'd slept with the admiral instead of getting herself abducted, Edward would have made commodore.

She'd never told a soul what had really happened. She'd gone to her father's house soon after, seeking peace.

Now James Ardmore was here, on Haven, at her feet. Hurt.

When her father and the hired man Jessup arrived in response to Isabeau's frantic summoning, they parted his coat and found a long gash cutting his abdomen. That cut had been made by a thick blade, a sword or a cutlass. It oozed blood, and James Ardmore's face was ashen.

The man with him, an English naval lieutenant, was hurt as well. Blood covered his blond hair and they could not wake him. Using makeshift litters, Diana, her father, Isabeau, and Jessup dragged the two survivors back to the house.

James opened his eyes. It was bright daylight, he lay in a narrow bed, and his back hurt. Whitewashed walls, clean as though a hundred sailors had scrubbed them, surrounded him in a tiny room. Beams dark with age bowed toward him like the ribs of a ship. A small black insect crawled languidly along a crack in the wall to the open window. Fresh wind and sunshine poured through this window, wooden shutters flung open.

The room, neat and bare, held nothing but his bed and an armoire that looked about a hundred years old. All was quiet, tidy, unhurried. Even the insect behaved with the decorum of a Southern lady strolling off to tea.

He knew where he was. The island home of Admiral Lockwood, one hundred miles southwest of England, the place he'd been trying to find for a long, long time.

He lay still, savoring his triumph. It was short-lived. He was here, yes, but alone and wounded. His tired hand moved to his abdomen, where he found bandages and sticking plaster. He remembered the flash of the sword wielded by the frigate's captain, the bright pain in his side. It still ached.

James closed his eyes. For a moment he saw only the bloodred tinge of the inside of his eyelids. Then a wall of black water was rushing at him, and he heard the screams of men washed before it. Ironically, the chains had saved him, holding him in place while the deadly waves had swept sailors and officers past him in a hideous heap. The water filled his ears, its roar drowning all other sound, all thought.

His eyes snapped open.

A small girl stood next to his bed. She watched him solemnly, blue eyes fixed on his face.

James Ardmore had little experience with children. Cabin boys were not children; they were youths who grew up too fast, like himself.

"What is your name?" he asked. His voice came out cracked and broken.

The child blinked once, assessing him with the same unafraid gaze as her mother. The little mite was good at it. His own sister, Honoria, used to look at him like that when she wanted to let him know that his arrogance did not intimidate her. Come to think of it, Honoria still did look at him like that.

The little girl spun away and scuttled out the door. James closed his eyes again. In a few moments, they would come for him. Marines in red uniforms would fill the room. They would march him off to some English ship and transport him to a prison hulk to await hanging, and he would have lost the chance to complete what he'd come here for. Maybe the ship's captain would simply hang or shoot James straight away. Wouldn't Diana Worthing enjoy that?

But for the moment, he was free. The room smelled clean, the air from the window bringing the scent of sand and brine and woods. The mattress beneath him had a decided lump just under his knees, but the worn coverlet was soft. He heard nothing, only the breeze at the window and the shrill call of a gull beyond. Too bad he did not have the strength to leap from the bed, climb through the window, steal a boat, and scurry away. Escape would have to come later. For now, he could scarcely move his head.

The door opened. Steps whispered across the board floor, and then a cool hand touched his forehead. He opened his eyes.

Diana Worthing bent over him. Her red hair hung in a loose braid over her shoulder, soft wisps escaping. He liked her better like this, simple, mussed, no artifice.

The bones of her face and curve of her jaw were clean and strong. Hers was a fierce beauty, a beauty that could stir ancient mating desires in a man. She certainly had stirred them in James Ardmore.

He lay still and enjoyed her soft hand on his forehead

and his cheek, the scent of her skin. She behaved like she thought he was too helpless to leap from the bed and bite her. She must not notice his slitted eyes watching her.

He took a grating breath. "I'm surprised you let me live."

She nearly jumped a foot. Her lips parted, eyes wide behind red-gold lashes.

Then she mastered herself. Red brows drew down, and she tucked in his sheet with a sudden, vicious tug that sent fire through his wound. "My father is a kind man," she snapped. "He insisted we look after you."

She obviously hadn't shared his opinion. "My thanks to him."

"He admires you," she sneered.

He tried a laugh, but it came out cracked and harsh. "Doesn't work, Lady Worthing."

Her beautiful eyes widened. "What does not?"

"The lofty lady act. I know what you're really like. All fire and sparks and sharp edges. Nothing ladylike about you."

She gave the sheet another tug, and he spent a moment in a searing wash of pain. "I told you," she said in a hard voice, "I am not pleased to see you again."

"But I am pleased to see you."

Which was unusual for James Ardmore. He knew very few women he'd be glad to stumble over twice in his life. But Diana, Lady Worthing, was different. He'd never abducted and interrogated a woman like her. When he'd kissed her in that wayside inn, more to make her shut up than anything else, he'd learned that she had fine lips, and that she could kiss.

In the cramped private parlor, where he'd made the stubborn woman eat before she fainted and had to be carried the next five miles, James Ardmore had almost—almost—fallen. Like a mighty oak that had resisted storms all its life, only to be pushed over by the touch of a butterfly when it wasn't looking.

How prettily her bosom had risen against that thin silk bodice when she'd fled across the room, cheeks pink, eyes moist. She'd said that she was a married woman and knew her duty, even though he could see that she hated Sir Edward Worthing. Hated him viciously.

She'd wanted James with the mindless longing of one starved for physical touch. That wanting had radiated from her like sparks from a firework and had ignited his own response.

What he should have done was flung all the dishes from the table and tossed her onto it in the wild frenzy they'd both felt. They should have taken one another in a fierce storm of passion and gotten it out of their systems.

Instead, they'd degenerated into a long, ridiculous shouting match. He, James Ardmore, feared throughout the seas, bane of pirates, hated by navies, had been reduced to exchanging expletives and bread missiles with the wife of one of the most famous captains in England.

Captain Sir Edward Worthing was now dead, and Diana Worthing was free. God help everyone.

She was glaring at him like she had when he'd sat her backside down in front of the soup. "I will fetch my father."

"Surprised you haven't already. I'm sure he's sent for a naval ship to take me to my hanging."

"He's sent for no one. We're cut off."

James stopped, surprised. "Are we?"

"We keep only a gig," she said in a matter-of-fact voice. The one-masted rowboat would not be much good

17

for long distances. "We'll have to wait for a passing frigate, and this is not their usual route."

His tightened muscles relaxed. "Well, now, isn't that too bad?"

"So you are in our care until then."

"Why doesn't that make me feel any better?"

She rested her slim hand on the sheet, right over his abdomen. "Does it pain you?" She sounded like she hoped so.

She was too certain his injury made him helpless. He wanted to reach out and drag her to him just to show her he had the strength for it. He could tug her onto the bed, lift her to straddle him. He could kiss her firm lips and teach her to want him again. In this quiet place, before real life returned, they might steal a moment of happiness.

"It's not so bad," he answered.

She pressed down. Pain shot through him with a fiery vengeance.

"Jesus," he cried out.

She lifted her hand. The pain lessened.

"Damn you, woman."

She calmly scrutinized him. The sheet only covered him to his chest, baring half his torso and his arms. He wondered how transparent the sheet was, how much she could see of his legs and his belly and hardening arousal.

Whatever she saw, she didn't mind looking. Her gaze followed his pectoral muscles to his shoulder, the sinews of his throat. Any moment, she'd lick her lips. Any moment, she'd bend over him, knowing he could not fight her. Any moment, she'd steal herself a kiss, the one she'd refused to finish last summer in the sticky heat of the English night.

She settled for giving him an annoyed look, but his blood still ignited.

"Not fair," he said. "Me lying here all helpless."

He closed his hand around her wrist. Her pupils widened until the black nearly swallowed the blue. He thought she would pull away, flay him with the scorn she did so well, maybe look around for some kind of food to throw at him.

She watched him, her ample bosom rising and falling with her quickened breath. Her eyes were a fine color. Then, very slowly, she drew one finger across the bronzed flesh of his shoulder.

It was like a spark from flint had landed on his bare skin. Mating desires was right. This was a woman men would duel for. No, he corrected, dueling was too civilized. In London, they must fight over her like beasts. Drawing-room manners probably flew out the window; etiquette must mean nothing. A man would want to possess her, to control her, to mate with her. Nothing civilized about it.

She could play; he didn't mind. He brushed his thumb across the inside of her wrist. Soft, soft skin. Lovely Diana. Stay and play.

"I told you, remember," he whispered. "We'd do well together."

She glared at him in sudden, icy fury, and snatched her hand away.

"You started it, love." He tucked his arm comfortably behind his head. "What happened to the lieutenant?"

She gave him an odd look. "He is better. My father thinks he'll make a full recovery."

"Good. How long have we been here?"

"Three weeks," she snapped.

He stopped. "Three—" He lifted his hand to his face. No beard marred it.

"You have been very ill. We feared you would die." She sounded like that would have suited her.

Three weeks. Damn.

"You should rest now," she said, her voice ringing. "I'll call Jessup to change the bandage."

"Wait a minute. I want to talk to you."

She put her hands on her hips, her eyes flashing like southern stars. "Well, I do not wish to talk to you. I have said all there is to say."

"I remember. You said I should go back to the swamp I crawled out of. You didn't even use good grammar when you said it."

"I believe that was after you had thrown half a loaf of bread at me."

"Only after you fired it at me. You're a good shot."

She turned abruptly away. He started to laugh, at least as much as his throat would let him.

"I will fetch my father," she snapped. "And the lieutenant. They have something to ask you."

Probably a good many things. He was James Ardmore, an outlaw in England, wanted for numerous crimes against the Royal Navy, damn their rotten souls.

She almost ran away. Her hem lifted, giving him a nice glimpse of her long legs in boots and breeches. Her sloppy red braid caught on the back hooks of her bodice. He liked her better now than when she'd dressed as a fashionable tart, all silk and gossamer. She looked like a real woman now, one he could throw over his shoulder and drag off to have a little fun with.

She'd left the door open. Sunlight danced in the hall, and James sobered. Three weeks. Interesting. These people had healed him, shaved him, cared for him. For three weeks. They could have let him die, and the world would have been rid of James Ardmore the pirate hunter. Admiral Lockwood would have been praised as a hero again. Diana would have thought it a job well done.

His sister Honoria would put up a stone to him, as she'd done for Paul and their parents, then settle in to decline slowly in their elegant house on the Battery. Honoria would put every effort into playing the role of the last scion of the Ardmores. She'd so enjoyed all her other roles—obedient daughter, debutante, society belle, and finally, fading spinster. The only role she'd never quite grasped was that of dutiful sister. She'd made it quite clear long ago that Paul had been the preferred brother. James deserved no devotion, and Honoria would not give it.

But these English people who had no cause to love James Ardmore had saved his life and nursed him back to health. He wondered why. Was this kindness, or something else?

Heavy footsteps sounded in the hall, interspersed with Diana's lighter ones. Over those came the pattering footsteps of the little girl.

They entered the room, Diana Worthing, her daughter, an older man who had the same firm jaw and forehead as Diana, and the blond lieutenant who had washed up on the beach with him. The buttons on his dark blue coat had been polished, and his epaulets nearly gleamed. His brown-blond hair was neatly combed and trimmed, and his brown eyes were both watchful and frightened.

Hmm. The man inside the uniform of the most powerful navy on earth was frightened.

The lieutenant approached the bed, the watchfulness in his eyes turning to hope. "Hullo," he said.

James stared back at him. An officer in the British

Navy did not speak to James Ardmore in such a friendly tone. "Hey," he answered neutrally.

The lieutenant stopped, swallowed. "You do not know me."

"Not really."

The man stared at James for a moment longer. Then sudden tears appeared on his lashes, and he balled his hands and turned away. He moved to the window and looked out, his back straight and stiff.

"You do not know him," the admiral said.

"Should I? He was a lieutenant on the frigate."

Admiral Lockwood looked at him sharply. "And you do not know his name?"

"No. Sorry. I didn't get much to the quarterdeck."

Diana flicked her intense gaze to the lieutenant, then back to James. Her eyes could burn him up. He wasn't sure he'd want someone to douse him with water if they did.

"He does not remember," she said. She sounded angry, as though she blamed James. But then, she always sounded like she blamed James. "He remembers nothing that happened before waking up here. We hoped you could tell us who he was."

Chapter Three

Diana sat on her campstool on the ledge overlooking the beach, pretending to sketch. She tried to concentrate on the landscape she was drawing, but she was very aware that James Ardmore had left the house and now leaned on the garden gate, watching her.

A week had passed. Diana had turned over his nursing to Mrs. Pringle, the small woman who acted as their cook and housekeeper. Unseemly for her to continue, Diana had explained in a hard voice.

Coward, she had admonished herself. But she could not trust herself around him.

She'd come here, after a scene with her husband she did not want to remember, to console herself on remote Haven. Back in London, Edward had gone through with the legal separation before taking the voyage that had ended his life. On Haven, nothing touched her. Here she could pretend that nothing disturbing ever happened. She could regress to her childhood days of quiet happiness. She could enjoy walks with Isabeau and her father, the peace of puttering in her garden, playing on the beach with her daughter.

Now James had come to destroy her peace. He'd come looking for her father, but she knew he would not mind a side mission of driving her insane. He had laughed when she'd touched him as he'd lain helpless in his bed. He'd watched her with those knowing green eyes, and the sheet in the area of his thighs had risen the slightest bit.

The carnal reaction had startled her, just as it had when he'd held her in that dark room in the public house. Her admirers in London had liked to chase her about ballrooms or corner her alone or write badly rhymed poems to her, but true carnality had never entered the equation, despite what her husband had believed.

Overall, it was best that Mrs. Pringle took over the nursing.

Isabeau played in the waves below her now. The blond man they'd decided to call Lieutenant Jack helped her gather shells.

Lieutenant Jack remembered nothing, not the shipwreck, the ship itself, or anything about his life prior to waking in Diana's father's house. Diana pitied him. He covered his distress with determined cheerfulness, but she saw in his eyes, when he thought no one was looking, the blank fear of man who walked the edge of a cliff and wondered when he would fall.

He'd been so full of hope when Isabeau had run to tell them that James had awakened. James could tell Lieutenant Jack his true name and perhaps trigger the rest of the lieutenant's memories.

But James had claimed to know nothing. Diana wondered whether that was true. James had not explained what he'd been doing on a ship with an English naval lieutenant anyway. He'd only shrugged and said he'd been traveling. Very suspicious. James was a liar. Her father knew that, but he was strangely willing to let James tell his lies.

Haven was well provisioned for visitors, thanks to her father. Two more mouths to feed would not hinder them unduly, and both gentlemen had gallantly claimed they could tighten their belts with the best of them.

They both were far too capitulating, Diana thought darkly. Shortage of food was not the danger she and her father worried about. Haven had its secrets, her father's secrets. Upon discussing it, she and her father had decided that they should not worry unduly. The island could hide its secrets well, even from someone as ruthless as James Ardmore.

Diana's pencil poised on the clean paper clamped to her easel. She was supposed to be drawing the two below her, the waves, happy memories of Haven. But she was acutely aware that James Ardmore had left the garden gate and was strolling her way.

They'd mended his clothes, but neither her father nor Jessup had possessed shirts large enough for him. So his dark coat hung open, exposing his hard chest and abdomen and the white bandage across his waist. He'd offered no explanation for the wound, and oddly, her father had not pressed him for that either.

James stopped beside her. He could have continued down to the beach, helped Lieutenant Jack collect shells, but did he? Oh, no. He stood next to her, rested one booted foot on a rock, and forced her attention entirely on him.

Determinedly she slashed her pencil across the paper. The resulting line had nothing to do with what was in front of her.

"A fine day," he observed.

His voice had healed, the grating from near-drowning gone. He spoke with long vowels and silken consonants, and managed to make every word sensuous.

"We are always lucky in our weather." Diana's words were cold, clipped, very English.

He was standing too close. She suddenly envisioned herself drawing him, imagined the pencil strokes to outline his shoulders, his chest, the shading for the hollow of his throat. She was acutely aware of every ridge of his abdomen, of the slash of bandage across brown skin, of the line of black hair that dusted his chest.

Her pencil moved on the paper. She stopped, gripping the pencil so hard that it snapped.

"Careful," he said.

She slammed the pieces down on the easel. "I do not care for sketching. It is too windy." She nearly ripped the paper from the clasps and tumbled it and her pencils back into her sketch box.

She folded the easel, pretending to ignore James stooping to retrieve the box for her. Below her Isabeau dug fervently in the sand. Lieutenant Jack squatted next to her, showing her how to mold the sand with the small bucket she'd brought with her.

Diana softened a moment. "He so enjoys Isabeau's company. I wonder if he has children of his own."

James's gaze followed hers. "He won't know until he gets back to England."

"His family must imagine him lost." She glanced at James. "So must yours."

He looked at her coolly. She didn't think he'd ever forgive her for rummaging in his locker aboard his ship or for reading his brother's diary. She'd been searching, in the cabin where he'd left her alone, for James Ard-

26

more the man. She'd realized, as he'd interrogated her, that she'd already found him. James Ardmore the man was not a quivering mass of emotion hiding under a chill, ruthless exterior. He really was the chill, ruthless exterior.

She expected him to make some sarcastic remark about her prying, but he answered, "The only one left is my sister, and she'd be happy to see the back of me."

Diana remembered the pretty, black-haired girl who had stared out of the small portrait she'd seen in his cabin. A girl with James's green eyes. "Why do you say so?"

"Not all families are full of tender-hearted warmth. You ought to know. You hated your husband's guts, didn't you?"

She started, but realized she had not tried very hard to pretend otherwise. "Isabeau is waving," she said frostily. "I will go down to her."

He insisted on carrying her sketch box and folded easel. She sped nimbly down the path before him, wishing he'd go away. But he followed, navigating the rocky passage to the beach with no difficulty, even burdened, not to mention wounded.

Lieutenant Jack rose from the sand and beamed her a smile. She quite liked Lieutenant Jack. *He* was polite. He strove to hide his bewilderment with friendliness, and his gratitude for their help touched her. He was her own age and quite handsome. She wished she could fall in love with him, so that she could put James firmly out of her mind.

"Your daughter wants to build a castle the length of the beach," Lieutenant Jack said, flashing a grin.

"She would," Diana said darkly.

"How do you understand her?" James asked. "She can't speak."

"Oh, she gets her meaning across well enough," Jack said. "She and Lady Worthing speak in signs, you know. Very clever."

Isabeau had invented the signs herself. Over the years, Diana and Isabeau and Diana's father had added to them. Diana warmed still more to Lieutenant Jack.

Isabeau had been running through the waves, making the high-pitched squealing noises that she called singing. Now she hastened back to them and grabbed Diana's hand. "Be-lu?" she asked breathily.

"My father is preparing the boat for launching," Diana said to Lieutenant Jack. "He wants to fish 'round the leeward side."

Lieutenant Jack brightened. He liked sailing around the island with the admiral and had already done so several times. He would remember things, he said, such as tying knots and moving sails and navigating. The last time her father had taken the boat out, however, Lieutenant Jack had been laid low with a foul headache, a remainder of his original injury. He had been almost pathetically looking forward to another outing.

"I would be happy to accompany him," he responded. "Coming Ardmore?"

James made a show of considering. "Not today. My side still hurts a bit. Best I stay a landsman a while."

Lieutenant Jack looked concerned. "Then perhaps we'd better not desert you."

"Don't worry about me. I'll rest and be right as rain by dinner."

His countenance was neutral, looking for all the world as if he believed every word he said.

Diana shot him a hard look. She didn't trust him any

more than she trusted the island's cat not to shed on the parlor cushions. But she knew that she did not dare stay behind with him while Lieutenant Jack, Isabeau, and her father departed. Much too dangerous. She didn't fear him, but her own response to him. Jessup was here. Jessup knew not to let James Ardmore pry into things he should not.

"We will go, then," she said. "Come along, Isabeau." She held out her hand to her daughter.

Isabeau clasped her mother's hand and thrust her other toward Lieutenant Jack. Diana glanced back as Isabeau pulled them along the beach to where the boat would be waiting. James watched them go, holding her sketch box under one arm, her easel under another. She could not read his face, but she knew he was up to something. She saw it in every line of the blasted man's body.

Isabeau grinned at her, showing her missing teeth, and Diana reluctantly turned away. She felt a headache coming on.

James stood on the beach longer than he'd intended, watching her walk away. She was achingly beautiful.

The lieutenant with her was utterly English, pale skin under sunburn, aristocratic tilt to his head, brown-blond hair fashionably short. Probably he was a lieutenant because his papa had got him his midshipman's post and hired lofty tutors to help him pass his exams. Everything about him shouted English gentility.

The man inside James Ardmore did not like English Lieutenant Jack walking off with the beautiful Diana Worthing. But James Ardmore the pirate hunter welcomed the time to himself. He'd not had an opportunity to learn this island he'd been seeking for a year, and he needed to bring its secrets to light.

So far, he'd seen only the house and the small tract of beach on which he now stood. For verisimilitude, he walked back to the house with the easel. The house could not be seen from the cove where Lockwood moored the boat, which was to his satisfaction.

James had seen the boat, a gig with one sail, a fine little craft for sailing around the island and partway out into the sunny sea. He admired it as a seaman, and he blessed it now as a fugitive. It would take his keepers out of the way for a time while he got his bearings and made his plans.

The house was quiet. Jessup was way down in the kitchens, which were built back into the cliffs against which the house rested. Or, he suspected, the man had stolen away for a much-needed nap. Jessup worked hard, and the afternoon was fine and warm. The climate here was warmer than England's, with the temperature hovering around seventy degrees even now in March. A nap would be just the thing.

James deposited Diana's sketch box and easel in the airy ground-floor sitting room, then looked idly out the open window. The room had obviously been a man's abode—the furnishings had been chosen for comfort, not show. Nothing matched, and styles had been haphazardly mixed.

Then this bachelor's paradise had acquired a woman, Diana. Her touch showed in the workbasket by the fire, in the embroidered pillows placed on the faded divan, in the wheeled tea table neatly in its place. Every afternoon, Mrs. Pringle filled the table with cakes, and Diana deferentially poured her father his cup of tea. A picture of domestic harmony.

And yet . . .

James felt the undercurrents here, the worry, the tension. In the way father and daughter had broken off conversation when he'd entered the room. Diana watched James in sharp suspicion, and so did her father. They did the same to Lieutenant Jack.

James spied the small craft heading out to sea. The sail snapped and went taut. James wished for a spyglass so he could watch the admiral and Jack working the sail, to observe how they maneuvered the craft, but he did not have time for such professional musings. They would be gone only a few hours, which did not give him much time.

A quiet investigation proved that Jessup had indeed stolen away to his room behind the kitchens, and the cook herself snored on a settee near the hearth. Well, they deserved it. Diana had explained to James that this household made their own beds and generally fended for themselves while Jessup hauled wood and water and Mrs. Pringle created hearty and mouth-watering meals from the fish and crab the admiral—and Isabeau—caught.

James, used to taking care of himself most of his life despite having been raised in a genteel Charleston mansion, had no objection. Jack, a naval man, knew how to live neatly in a small space without complaint. They were a most congenial group.

And yet . . .

James let himself out the front door and strode through the sparse garden. Diana had done her best, but the ocean winds had destroyed all but the hardiest of plants. Succulents clung to the rocks through which wound a brick path. Pansies in pots struggled to find the sun, brilliant dots of scarlet against the greens and yellows of the succulents.

At the end of the garden, a gate and a path led to the

rockier side of the island. He'd never observed anyone from the household passing this gate.

The path led down a sharp slope, over black rocks thick with vegetation. But the path had been cleared. Tendrils that might naturally have grown over it had been pushed back and in some places, cut.

James opened the gate and began to descend. The path was steep. He placed his hands on the black rocks and eased himself down. Pain bit into his side, reminding him he was still far from whole.

He remembered the blade of the oh-so-honorable captain slicing him while he lay helpless and chained. Even as James's blood had stained the deck, the captain laughed. James called him a bastard, and the captain backhanded him across the mouth. Fine specimen of a man. Well, he was at the bottom of the sea now. The admiral and Jack had gone out to look for other survivors while James lay unconscious and had found none. The bodies, they suspected, had drifted far, and only small pieces of the wreckage remained near Haven.

At the bottom of the hill, a narrow path skirted walls of limestone and granite. James followed this path a long way, noting that it too had been cleared. On his left, the land sloped sharply down to the sea. Waves boomed high, the windward side of the island.

He slowed. He did not want to round a sudden corner and catch sight of the boat with his hosts and Jack; he'd be in plain sight on the rocks. When he turned the next corner, however, he saw that enough vegetation grew up the sides of the hills to screen him much of the time.

He must have walked a mile by now. He was tiring. The wound had sapped his strength, and three weeks of laying flat on his back had not helped. But the path went somewhere, and he was determined to discover where, even if it were only back to the leeward side of the island. Perhaps the secret of this island was that it had no secrets.

He knew better.

The path dipped sharply again, disappearing through a niche in the rock. At first he thought the path simply ended at the cliff edge, but he found, as he scrambled on, that it led down through the tiny opening to a strip of sand. And there, he found the caves.

They were dry caves. The sea raged far below, and the ground leading to the caves was covered with silky sand. James balanced on the rocks, eased himself down, and trudged across the sand. He reached the first cave and peered inside.

Rock clicked on rock behind him. He swung around to see a stream of pebbles sliding down the path he had just taken. He dipped his hand into his pocket and touched the cold hilt of his knife.

Slim hands hugged the rock, then down the last curve came Diana, her skirt lifting to show him shapely legs in breeches and boots. She was alone, no Jessup or Isabeau climbed behind her.

He walked to meet her, his hand still on his knife.

"Tired of fishing?" he asked, keeping his voice light.

She was flushed from the climb, perspiration curling tendrils of her hair. "I thought you wanted to rest."

"I did. Then I wanted a walk. I wondered what was down this path."

It was the truth and a lie. She lied too. They lied together.

"I found the caves," he continued. "Why don't you show them to me?"

Her gaze flickered. "There is nothing of interest. Only sand and rock. You do not need to see them."

The top two buttons of her bodice had come undone. Her agitated breathing made that fact delightful.

"I like caves," he said. "I always have a hankering to explore them."

"They are dangerous. Let us return to the house."

Her color was high, her eyes glittering.

"Only if we can do something interesting there."

"Whatever you like."

He stared at her a moment, studied gray-blue eyes that sparkled in fury. *Liar, liar.*

He turned away. He'd gone two steps when he heard her behind him. "James!"

He swung around. She stood right in front of him. Her lips hovered below his, and she flung her arms about his neck. "James," she said hoarsely. "Kiss me."

She crushed her lips to his before he could stop her.

Chapter Four

Not that he wanted to stop her.

He slammed his arm around her waist, scraped her to him. She smelled like sunshine and sand. Her lips were wet, her breath hot.

He remembered the dark public house in Kent, the hard kiss he'd forced on her, and then the still, stunned moment when she'd kissed him back.

This kiss was no less frenzied. *Oh, yes, this is what you are made of, my girl. Fire and desire, and you pretend to be so genteel.*

She was not genteel. Diana Worthing was a demon in his arms, and he loved it. Her attempt to keep him from the caves was obvious and clumsy. He'd thought her smarter than that.

But what did he care? They were alone, and she was savagely beautiful, and he wanted her. His plans flew to the wide winds.

He explored her mouth, enjoying the sweet velvet of her tongue. His lips bruised hers, taking what she was giving. *Darlin', I'll take it all day and all night.*

Her fingers gripped him hard, like she couldn't stand to let him go. He slowed the frantic kiss himself and finally, eased her away.

"Let's do this right, darlin'."

She looked up at him, panicked and flushed and wary-eyed, her hair snaking around her throat. "What are you talking about?"

"Gently, for once. I want to savor this."

She glared. "What for?"

"What do you expect, sweetheart?" He brushed her cheek. "I've lain awake nights since I met you, remembering you reclining in my cabin, all insolent and taunting me. I like that memory."

Her imperious brows arched. "I was not taunting you. I had nowhere else to sit."

"You were the one who commandeered my cabin. Sometimes I lay awake pretending that I went ahead and took you on that bunk, instead of being so polite."

"Polite?" She raked him with a scorn-filled look. "You call questioning me and sneering at me *polite?*"

"It was a hell of a lot more polite than what I wanted to do." He almost smiled at her outrage. "But I wonder, love, why you've decided to become a sacrificial lamb."

She looked confused. "Sacrificial—"

"Beguiling me with your charms." He stepped close to her again, pushed a lock of wind-torn hair from her cheek. "So I won't find the secrets in your caves."

"There is nothing in the caves; I told you."

"I don't believe you." He stroked his finger from her temple to her jaw. "But I thank you for letting me sample you. You taste like vanilla sugar, did you know that?"

Her face went scarlet. "No."

"Hasn't anyone ever told you? All those men chasing

you around that admiral's house and they never once talked about your charms?"

"They wrote poetry," she said coldly.

"I bet it was awful." With great reluctance, he at last lowered his hand, then made himself turn away. His breeches had never felt this tight before.

She called after him. "Where are you going?"

"To the caves."

The sand grew thinner as he walked, packing under the shadow of the dry caves. He heard her pattering after him. The sea roared and rushed below, the waves on the windward side showing their winter might. She reached him just as he stepped into the shade of the wind- and water-carved cave.

There was nothing there. The two caves ran together not ten feet back, and held nothing but sand and rock and a tiny crab that had crawled too far and died.

"You see," she said triumphantly. "Nothing."

Nothing visible anyway. But why had she not wanted him here? What did he not see?

The wind was not as fierce here, and his voice echoed hollowly under the rock. "You kissed me for some reason, Diana. Why don't you tell me about it?"

"I kissed you to discover whether you would behave as a gentleman."

She just kept on lying. She already knew exactly what he was like.

"There are easier ways of finding that out. Like watching if I quirk my finger when I drink tea."

She gave him a frosty look. "I have known plenty of men who have perfect manners but are not gentlemen once they are out of company."

"You mean once they are with you." He turned back to her, planted his hands on her waist. She still smelled good, like salt and wind. "And then all manners go to hell, am I right? Men did fight duels over you in London, didn't they? I can see why. You are quite a prize. A man might do anything to possess you."

She flinched and pulled away.

"What is it?" he asked mockingly. "You're done seducing me because I already found the caves?"

Her momentary confusion dissolved into pure rage. "I believe I know the answer to whether you are a gentleman," she said, her words clipped.

"I was raised a gentleman. I come from a very fine Southern family. My sister is a pillar of Charleston society."

"She would not like me, then."

"I think she would."

She gave a wild laugh. "She would not. Have I not proved how wicked I am?"

He watched her, half puzzled. She was angry, but not only at him. Everything she said held a trace of self-mockery. As though someone, probably her useless husband, had told her over and over how horrible she was.

"I think you don't know what you are," he said softly. "You started a game with me, Diana. Why don't we finish it?"

She wanted him. He knew that. Her nipples behind the thin bodice were hard little nubs. When she'd flung herself at him and kissed him, she had not expected to want him. She'd planned to use her wiles to lure him away from the caves. She never thought she'd light a fire that could swallow the island.

Not his fire. Not her fire. Their fire together.

He sought the buttons of her bodice. "When I first saw you facing down Ian O'Malley in that garden, I told myself you were dangerous. And I was right." Her buttons were bone, smooth white and chipped about the edges. "How many lovers have you burned up, darlin'?"

He parted the placket. She was bare beneath the gown. Her breasts hung round and firm, the breasts of a woman who had born a child. The tips were hard and dark, just begging for his fingers. Lovely, lovely. He could stand here for hours looking at her.

"How many?" he repeated.

She looked at him, her mouth wet, her eyes half-closed. God, she could melt stone. "None. I mean—only my husband."

"What about all the men who chased you? You just teased them? Played with them?"

"Yes." Her eyes flashed.

"I'll bet they were a pack of fools. I'll bet you held court over them like a little queen. No wonder you're hiding here so far from England. Once your husband was dead, they might have had thoughts of revenge."

Her jaw hardened. "It was not like that."

"Then they were a pack of fools. You should have had a lover who could tame you, who could fan your fires and then damp them down so you would not burn up your husband. Did he like your fires, Diana?"

Her breath came fast. "No."

"If your husband couldn't quench you, and you didn't have a lover to do it for him, you must have been a wildfire. You burned every man you touched, didn't you? I'm just sorry I wasn't there to catch you." He bent to her. "Oh, Diana. We could have lit up the sky."

Her moist breath touched his lips. His blood was pumping, his erection hard as it had ever been. She'd started something and he was going to finish it.

"You must have been incandescent," he whispered. "Waiting for your husband, who didn't know what to do with you. It pours out of you, Diana. You need loving."

Her eyes snapped open. She took a step back. Her bodice gaped. Windblown and half bare, she was the most beautiful thing he'd ever seen.

"I do not need you."

"That's not what I'm feeling."

Her eyes glittered with rage. "No. I have Isabeau. She is more important. Much more."

"She's a fine child. Pretty like her mama. But don't hide behind her. It's not fair to her."

Her glare could have peeled paint. "You know nothing about it. How could you?" She yanked her placket together.

If he took her now, he had the feeling she'd kill him and dance with joy about it. But what fires he'd taste on his way out.

She whirled from him and ran for the path. He let her go. Without looking back, she dashed across the sand, sliding on the slippery surface. Nimbly, she climbed the rocks, her dress bunching above her waist to reveal her long, athletic legs.

She disappeared from view. James let out his breath. His throat was dry. She had meant to sear him and render him a pile of ash. Instead she'd stirred a dangerous thing within him, one that wanted only her on the sand and nothing else. That dangerous beast would undo him, and he'd find his neck in a noose before he knew what had hit him.

And he didn't care. It would be worth it.

About time something was.

Diana had her composure back when her father, Isabeau, and Lieutenant Jack returned.

Barely. She tried to convince herself that no one would

think anything of it if she stayed in her room and pretended to have a headache. She'd invented one in order to remain home in the first place.

But Isabeau had rousted her from her room, laughing with delight about the boat ride with her grandfather and Jack. She had tugged Diana downstairs for supper.

Diana sat now, uncomfortable at the head of the table, while her father recounted what they'd found beyond the breakers—a few drifting pieces of board. Jack contributed to the discussion, his manner relaxed and even happy. James sat silently on his other side, eating the fish in wine sauce without comment.

Every time she looked up from her plate, she found his gaze on her.

She'd remained behind that afternoon because she'd feared what he'd get up to if she did not stay. He had too much intelligence in those ice-green eyes.

As she'd suspected, as soon as he thought the boat gone, he'd sought the path to the caves. She'd known simple persuasion would not work, so she'd tried her other weapon. Last year, James had desired her. Men always desired her. They fought to stand at her side, fought to dance with her, fought for her favors. They behaved like lunatics, glowering at friends and enemies alike.

At first, when she was a young and foolish seventeen, she'd loved it. Being the belle of the ball was a heady thing. She'd liked the gentlemen's attentions, the envious glances of the other ladies. She'd grown conceited, and she'd thought, idiot that she was, that these gentlemen had *liked* her.

She'd learned what they wanted soon after she married, once her taboo status of virginal miss had gone. She'd learned then that they'd not wooed her for her conversation or her cleverness or her wit. They had desired her. She had learned, still a fool, that she could wield their desire like a weapon. It had given her power.

James desired her. He had not hidden that fact. But he had not done what he was supposed to. He had not fallen to his knees, had not begged for her, had not quoted bad poetry to her. He'd laughed at her.

Because he had the same power.

He had turned her weapon around on herself and wielded it with practiced brutality.

When he'd pulled her into his arms, she'd felt the hunger she thought she'd never feel again come awake, just like it had when he'd kissed her in Kent. His kiss today had been skilled as ever—this man knew how to seduce.

Had she torn herself away, fainted in shock, scolded him for taking a liberty? No, she'd thrown her arms about his neck and kissed him back, delighting in his hard mouth, his fiery taste. She'd certainly not cared for propriety.

The only triumph she felt now was that she had successfully misdirected him. His attention had been drawn to the innocent caves, distracted from the real secrets that the island held.

As her gaze flicked to him again, she knew that he knew that she had tried to distract him from the caves. He knew that she knew that he knew it.

Her head began to ache. She stirred her soup.

"Come with us next time, James," the lieutenant said. "The sea was fair, and the view of the island is beautiful."

"When I heal," James answered. He sipped his wine.

"We found little of the wreckage. I can only hope the rest of the crew discovered as safe a haven as we did."

"How far can the craft sail?" James asked.

"A good distance in fair weather," the admiral said. "All the way to Plymouth, if need be, though I prefer a larger ship under me for that journey. But the seas are high here. We are more or less cut off, I am sorry to say. The odd frigate or merchantman calls, but we are effectively on the way to nowhere." It was a lie, and her father told it well.

James nodded, as though not very interested. "I took a walk today," he said.

Diana shot him a look. He returned it steadily. "Down through the back garden. To the caves at the end of the path."

Her father looked swiftly down, hiding his consternation behind lowered lids. "Did you?"

"Yes. They are not very deep, but worth seeing. Come with me tomorrow, Jack."

Jack nodded. "Certainly."

James looked at Diana. His green gaze burned her. She remembered, very precisely, the exact feeling of his erection as it pressed against her abdomen. Her face heated. He gave her a long look.

Drat the man.

After the interminable supper, Diana fled to the refuge of her father's study. The room had been built onto a wing of the house on the first floor. Three walls set with windows overlooked the sea, a beautiful room, one Diana had always loved.

She strolled to the west window, enjoying the last fingers of light that tore at the clouds on the horizon.

The admiral shut the door and came to stand behind her. "He found the caves?"

He'd found much more than that. He'd found the spark that had lit her again, just when she'd thought she had banished sparks altogether.

"Yes, he found them. The wretched man went exploring."

"What else did he find?"

"Nothing. He did not go beyond the caves."

"Thank God for that."

She turned. "What do we do if he finds it?"

Her father waited a long time to answer. "If he finds it he finds it."

"I do not trust him."

"Nor do I. But I have the feeling that Captain Ardmore can keep secrets."

She looked at him in alarm. "You do not mean we should take him into our confidence?"

"Of course not. But I worry far more about Lieutenant Jack than James Ardmore. James Ardmore has his own agenda. Lieutenant Jack is a member of the Royal Navy, and he will call on the Admiralty the moment he lands in England." He slanted his daughter a smile that always warmed her. "You know how untrustworthy we naval chaps can be."

She stood on tiptoe and kissed him on the cheek. "Oh, Papa."

He hugged her tight for an instant. "Have I mentioned how happy I am you and Isabeau joined me here? I thought I'd be content here alone, but Lord how I missed you."

"You never will have to be alone again, Papa."

He smiled at her, his eyes sad. "You are a sweet girl, but your cage will grow confining. You'll soon long for the world."

She shuddered. "No, indeed."

He did not answer, but his expression told her he did not believe her. "Kiss Isabeau good night for me. She ought to be tired. She was most—energetic—on the boat."

Diana laughed, her heart lightened a little. "She is a born sailor. I hope she did not drive you to distraction."

"A most welcome distraction. The lieutenant is a bit melancholy, and no wonder. He's frightened."

"I wish I could help him more."

Her father eyed her sharply. She raised her brows at him, but he only softened the look and kissed her cheek. "Good night, love."

"Good night, Papa."

When she reached the door, her father called to her. "Oh, Diana, please give Captain Ardmore the message that I want to see him."

She froze in the act of reaching for the door handle. "On the moment?"

"When he can spare the time. But tonight, yes."

She drew in a breath. She could speak to him. There was no reason why she should not speak to him.

There was no reason why her fingers should have gone all cold and shaking, either.

"Yes, all right." Her voice cracked, and she hoped her father did not notice.

Once in the hall, the door shut, she exhaled. She wondered if her father suspected the manner in which she'd dissuaded James Ardmore from searching beyond the caves. Her father had always taken her side, no matter what her husband had claimed. But that had been in England, when she'd been more or less innocent. Was she innocent now?

Squaring her shoulders, she descended the front stairs and made her way to the parlor.

* * *

James knew the instant she walked into the room. He had been standing inside the French doors to the garden, breathing in the fragrance of the bougainvillea and hydrangea. The scents brought with them a dart of homesickness. The gardens at the house in Charleston would be just beginning to bloom, early spring bringing a riot of blossoms to the Southern city. He had been gone a long time.

Her cotton gown made barely a rustle, but he turned, her presence tugging him like an unseen tether.

The lieutenant, absorbed in a book, looked up and sent Diana a smile. She acknowledged it with a nod, but James's idea that she was smitten with him seemed ludicrous now. She was a woman of powerful passion and what she gave the lieutenant was mere friendliness touched with pity.

She stopped at least two arms' lengths from James as though she did not trust herself to be near him.

"My father would like to speak to you," she said stiffly. "When you can give him a moment. Upstairs in his study."

James inclined his head. She was breathing hard. She wore a tidy blue frock now, buttoned all the way to her chin. The disheveled woman of this afternoon at the cave had vanished. But James knew that woman was still there, hiding behind this neat and sensible daughter like a nymph behind a rock.

"I'll speak to him," James answered. "Please show me the way."

Anger flashed in her eyes. He expected her to refuse, to stamp from the room, to leave him to find her father's study on his own. Then she hooded her eyes and nodded.

Well, he could pretend if she could.

"Good night," the lieutenant said to them. "I will likely

turn in soon. Sailing makes me tired nowadays."

James bade him a good night and followed Diana from the room.

She waited for him in the hall at the bottom of the stairs. "Up there," she pointed, her finger as rigid as his throbbing arousal. "Through the double doors to the end of the hall."

James looked up the stairs. Then he caught her wrist as she silently tried to slip away.

"Perhaps we should say good night before I go up."

She gave him a hard look. "Isabeau is waiting for me."

"It won't take long." He put his fist beneath her chin, leaned down, and kissed her.

Her mouth remained tight, firmly resisting. Then suddenly, she relaxed and kissed him back.

It was a brief, hot burst of passion. Their mouths locked for the barest instant, but it was enough for him to find again the heady taste of her. Damn, but he'd love to spend all night tasting her. Tasting her would be one long voyage of discovery.

He lifted away. He brushed the moisture from her lip with the ball of his thumb.

"Good night," he said softly, then ascended into the darkening house.

He had to wait outside the study door a good five minutes before his erection deflated enough so that he could face the father of the woman he wanted to ravish.

It had been a long time since James had been so intrigued and fascinated by a woman. Many women had tried to catch his attention, but he habitually held himself back. Not because he was cold, as so many believed, but because he was the opposite of cold. Whenever James

Ardmore fell, he fell hard. And so he'd not allowed himself to fall.

He could not fall now, much as the landing would be sheerest bliss. He had things to do, and at the end, he'd either be dead or forced to flee. Diana would hate him no matter what the outcome. This sojourn with her would become just another memory among the many in his past.

He raised his hand and knocked on the plain wooden door.

At the admiral's called invitation, he opened the door and entered the room.

The sun had descended, and the windows were dark. A fire roared in the grate, bathing the room in a scarlet glow, both comforting and rather hell-like. Admiral Lockwood turned from lighting a candelabra and motioned for James to close the door. James complied.

The admiral tossed the paper spill into the grate. The fire devoured it with a hungry crackle.

The admiral wore his white hair long and pulled back into a tail, no doubt the way he'd worn it all his naval life. He had the same blue-gray eyes as his daughter, set in a handsome face that age and the sea had hardened but not marred. Likewise, he was not bent with his sixty years but remained ramrod straight, his shoulders square.

"Captain Ardmore," he said cordially. "Tell me. What weapons are you carrying at the moment?"

James stopped for a heartbeat. He and the admiral studied one another across the dark room.

Then James slid his hand into his coat pocket and withdrew his steel-hilted knife. He displayed it in his palm, then laid it on a nearby table.

Chapter Five

The knife was plain, utilitarian, its iron-gray handle wrapped tightly with a leather strip. James had bought it long ago in Martinique.

The admiral looked at it. "Is that all?"

James let his hand drop. "Not really."

The admiral continued as though he were having a friendly conversation with a subordinate. "When I helped my daughter put you to bed, I was astonished at the number of knives you had secreted about your person. I found no pistol, however."

"I didn't have time to grab one," James said mildly. "The ship was sinking at the time."

"No doubt. And prisoners are rarely issued pistols, even to save their own lives. I wonder how you came by the knives."

James gave him a level look. The admiral stared back, unfazed. Lockwood was an experienced naval man. He had been a captain for a long time before being promoted to admiral after Trafalgar. He'd know all about James and guess what he was doing on the frigate. Likewise, James knew all about the admiral.

"The naval officers were lax about searching me," he returned.

Lockwood gave a nod. "No doubt so happy to have captured the famous Captain Ardmore that they grew careless." He paused. "I guessed the only way we'd have found you with an English lieutenant was if you'd been his prisoner. Or at least a prisoner on his ship. I saw you once before, you know. Only a brief encounter, but I could not forget your eyes." He looked into them, now. "They were the eyes of a man with no heart."

Before he'd arrived here, James would have agreed with him. Not anymore.

He touched his breastbone. "I have a heart. It's beating in there."

"So you say. I watch Lieutenant Jack. He has no idea who or what he is, and that terrifies him. He fears to learn what kind of man he used to be. You know who you are and what you are. And you've closed yourself to that truth." He traced the carved top of a scrolled-back chair. "But I did not send for you to tell you about your heart. I wanted to ask what you plan to do."

"I plan to recover."

"We cannot fight you, my daughter and I. I am too old, and she is a woman, though I must warn you that she has a hellcat's temper." He smiled fondly, and James stopped himself from snorting. The admiral didn't know the half of it. "For instance, if anything happened to Isabeau, she'd fight to the death. She loves Isabeau more than her own life. Understandable, because that is how I feel about Diana." He gave James a pointed look.

"I can promise that I had no intention of hurting any of you. I don't harm innocents."

"Yes, I have heard that said about you." He eyed James shrewdly. "However, I never knew if that was a declaration you made yourself, or whether it was an observation by others. All in all, I do believe you are an honorable man, even if you are a ruthless one."

"Then you aren't like any other man in the Royal Navy. I haven't met a captain or admiral yet who thought me honorable."

"I have followed your career with interest. One ought to know one's enemies, after all. You have brought down a considerable number of pirates on the Barbary Coast and in the Caribbean who were nothing but cutthroat murderers. I cannot condemn you for that."

"I do what I can," James drawled.

"You board English frigates for amusement. Do not look at me in feigned astonishment; I know you fully enjoy it. You release American prisoners and press-ganged sailors, and you enjoy terrorizing English captains." He actually smiled. "I cannot fault you even for that. I heard about you having Captain Langford flogged. He was an idiot, and it was long overdue. You embarrassed him out of his career, you know. He never lived it down."

"I do my best."

"And are proud of it." He gave James a long look. "But you are still young. Regrets will come later."

"Oh, I have regrets. I have plenty."

"When you are my age, you will have plenty more." For a moment, his voice saddened. No answering sympathy moved in James's heart. He knew what regrets the admiral had.

The admiral gestured to a chair near the fire. "Let us sit down, as friends. I know I am a fool and should have locked you up right away until another vessel arrived.

51

But this is Haven. And if you wanted to kill me, you'd have done so by now."

James walked to the chair, leaving his knife behind. "That is true."

The admiral moved to a side table, poured brandy for them both. He sat down facing James. "I hope that you will relate some of your adventures. It would pass the long winter evenings."

James swallowed the warm brandy the admiral handed him. "What have you told Lieutenant Jack?"

The admiral fingered his glass. "I understand why you do not want him to know about you. It would be his duty to recapture you. But he has his hands full simply trying to recover his memory. When he does—" He made a "we'll come to that when we come to it" gesture. "I will keep your secret from the lieutenant for now. But, in return, I want to know everything. Beginning with how you came to be on an English frigate in the first place."

"Now that," James said softly, "is a long story."

The admiral smiled. "Excellent. We have all night."

Diana thrust her trowel into the earth and tugged at the root that entirely refused to budge. A bead of perspiration ran down her temple from her mussed hair. Despite the cold wind, her exertions heated her.

Her father had taken her aside this morning and explained what James Ardmore had told him. He'd been a prisoner on the English vessel, her father had said. He'd been captured while helping the crew of a smaller vessel smuggle brandy past the British blockade. He had offered himself as a prisoner alone if they would let the other Americans go.

Diana did not think much of a crew that would sacrifice its captain and then not try to rescue him. Or perhaps they had tried and failed, or they had gone for help too late. In any event, the storm had broken apart the English frigate and only James and Lieutenant Jack had survived. Jack had unlocked James's chains out of compassion, and James had saved Jack's life. A tale fit for a ballad.

There were too many ballads sung about James Ardmore already. She'd no doubt the man had twisted her father around his little finger. Her father liked a man of courage and integrity, and he believed James had both. Hence he would not lock James in the cellar and throw the key into the sea.

She jabbed the trowel into the earth. Bits of hardened dirt broke apart and sprayed the leaves of the weeds she was trying to clear from the bougainvillea.

Her father had decided to trust him. The two of them had made a pact that neither would harm the other while on Haven. Then the two gentlemen had stayed up all night swapping stories and draining the decanter of brandy. That was men all over. Forget danger and betrayal as long as they could crony together over a bit of brandy.

The root came away abruptly, and Diana caught her balance with the trowel. She flung down the weed and began on the next one. While her father and James were becoming fast friends, she had dreamed of lying next to James the pirate hunter all night. She had envisioned his large body filling her bed, his large hands on her skin.

Last year, it had been months and months before she'd stopped dreaming about him. She never had the same dream, but the same thing always happened. He would kiss her, and she'd melt and they'd make love wherever they'd happened to be—on a beach, in an inn room, in a carriage. Now the dreams were back, vivid as ever. She gave the next weed a vicious jab.

Boots stopped next to her. Diana pretended not to notice. She cared nothing for the worn leather creasing his ankles, scuffed squared toes on the flowerbed, tarnished buckles resting on black leather. She cared nothing that he went down on one knee next to her, his strong thighs stretching the cloth of his breeches until it molded to every muscle.

Never mind that he rested a large, scarred, bare hand on his knee; never mind that the masculine scent of him clouded her senses; never mind that she felt the weight of his stare on the back of her neck.

She became suddenly aware that the top hook of her dress in back had come undone with her exertion, that her hair had escaped its braid, that her skirts were hiked to her knees.

Lieutenant Jack had taken Isabeau with him down to the beach to look for shells. The garden was otherwise deserted. She could say what she wanted.

"James Ardmore." She bit off the words. "And my father. Two legends swapping stories. You certainly swayed him to your side."

"Why shouldn't I?"

His voice sent warm sensations up and down her spine. Did he draw out his vowels on purpose, make his consonants liquid simply to distract and unnerve her?

"My husband was a legend," she said sharply. "My father disliked him."

He spread his fingers across his knees. "Your husband was much decorated, I hear."

She dug mercilessly. "He was a complete fraud."

"Really? Now, that's interesting."

She jammed the trowel into the dirt. It stuck. "My father *admires* you."

"Does he?"

She looked up. He watched her with the stillness of an animal assessing its prey.

"He does. I cannot think why."

He gave her an odd look. "Why do you say your husband was a fraud?"

She had never in her life voiced her speculations to anyone. She could not seem to stop the words now. "Because he tricked everyone into believing he was a great naval captain. Half his victories were won by subordinates, and he stepped in and took the glory."

"Is that so?" he asked slowly. "A man is a sorry thing when his wife despises him." He gave her a slow look. "On the other hand, all the stories about me are true."

"Are they?"

"Every one of them."

She wondered. She had heard accounts of him sinking pirate ships single-handedly with the small, sleek *Argonaut*. He had boarded English ships and reduced the captains to quivering mounds of fear while he freed press-ganged sailors and anyone else he perceived to be enslaved.

She had not really believed the tales, knowing naval men loved to spin yarns, but after meeting him face-to-face, she had begun to change her mind. He had something in his eyes that made her believe he would do whatever he wanted, whatever it took. Even a frigate, fully gunned, would not stand in his way. Were she a naval captain, and he boarded her ship, she too would swallow her pride and let him do as he willed.

Her mind conjured a picture of herself in knee breeches and a blue coat, eyes wide as he walked across the deck to her. After laughing at her for being a female captain, he'd drag her off to the cabin, where he would do—whatever it took.

She closed her eyes briefly as the vision segued to herself and him stripped of clothing, his mouth on her flesh, his hands stroking her. His hair would be rough beneath her fingers, like warm strands of silk.

She opened her eyes again. He watched her, as if knowing her thoughts. He reached out and smoothed one strand of hair from her forehead.

She clenched the trowel's handle, fought for breath. His fingers were strong, yet gentle. He knew how to tempt a woman.

He moved his feather-light touch across her temple, smoothing the already smoothed strand. She wanted to turn her cheek into his palm, to lean to its warmth. She wanted it so much she stiffened her muscles to keep her head from turning of its own accord.

He watched her, his eyes darkening. She had kissed him like a wanton every time she'd had the chance, and likely he knew she would do it again if he asked it. Women must makes fools of themselves over him all the time. And no wonder. To be touched by those large hands, gentled for a lady, to look into those green eyes and find them dark and fixed on you must be . . . well, like it was now.

He stroked his thumb across her cheekbone. It was no use. She turned her head, leaning into his hand.

"Darlin'."

She kissed the tip of his thumb. He held still, watching.

Her senses screamed for her to stop. Too late. She gently bit his fingertip. His gaze fixed on her. Those would-be suitors in her salad days, those gentlemen who had pursued her after her marriage had all been masqueraders, playing at passion. This was real.

Unpleasant memories flooded her. She remembered the night after she had returned home from her two days with James Ardmore, when she had entered her husband's bedroom and told him exactly what had happened. He had been inclined at first to believe she'd run off for an assignation with Mr. Kinnaird, the American spy, which had been bad enough. When she'd told him she had been abducted by James Ardmore, that had been much worse.

Edward had swung on her. "You little fool, he laid a trap and caught you, didn't he?"

"It was pure happenstance," she'd retorted, nearly sick with anger. "He came to rescue Kinnaird, who was a spy. I'm surprised you and your Admiralty friends didn't tumble to that! A spy, sitting in your midst. You are the fools."

Sir Edward had been so far gone in rage, he'd overlooked even this ferocious insult. "Do not be stupid. He must have watched the house for days, known who you were, what kind of an affront it would be to abduct Sir Edward Worthing's wife. I'm surprised he did not ask for ransom, but he must have feared that we'd be scouring the coast for him. That is why he let you go."

She'd wanted to laugh at his naïveté. "He never intended to kidnap me. I simply got in the way."

"Or perhaps he did ask for ransom." Sir Edward's eyes narrowed, glittering and mean. "What did you give him, Diana? Or do I need to ask?"

"I gave him nothing," she'd snapped. She hadn't. She'd stopped herself. She'd broken away from him, coming to a stop on the other side of the room, holding herself upright with her hand on the wall. "I am a married woman," she had told the pirate hunter. "With a daughter." Tears had wet her eyes. He had taken the answer for that, then made her sit down and eat the damned soup.

Sir Edward went on. "He did nothing? I cannot believe that."

Her fury matched his. She hadn't wanted to tell him the truth, but now she threw it at him to hurt him. "He kissed me. That was all. But it was enough."

He did not react as she'd thought. She'd been prepared for him to try to strike her, had been poised to flee. Instead, he looked thoughtful. "He only kissed you? What happened, Diana, did you not beg him hard enough?"

She'd slapped him. She felt the sting of it on her palm even now. Edward's eyes had filled with raw rage, and she'd found herself on the floor. She'd scarcely felt the blow. He'd stood over her, red-faced with fury, called her several colorful names, and snarled that he had started procedure for a legal separation.

Sir Edward had died a hero's death in a battle near Cadiz. There hadn't been enough left of him to bring home and put in the family crypt. Edward's mother had blamed Diana. Edward's mother blamed Diana for everything.

Diana found herself in the garden again, gasping for breath. She had fled to her father's island with Isabeau and tried to banish the memories.

"What is it?" James Ardmore's voice was strangely gentle.

Her eyes grew hot. He watched her, green eyes intense, and suddenly, she wanted to tell him the whole of it. "I hated him, James," she whispered. "I hated him so much."

She thought he would drawl a sarcastic reply, or ask

what she meant. "I know you did," he said, his voice soft. He smoothed her hair again.

Their gazes met. In that second, she knew he understood her rage and her helplessness.

His fingers were warm on her hair. Yesterday they'd thrown themselves at each other; today was this quiet tenderness. She could stay here all day, on her knees in the garden with him, while he stroked her hair and looked at her in that calm, assessing way.

She was saved from this fate by her daughter's piping voice and Lieutenant Jack's answering tones.

Chapter Six

James withdrew his touch, and Diana dragged in a breath of mixed disappointment and relief. He turned just as Isabeau came bounding into the garden, her hands full of shells. "Maa," she shrilled, then grinned at James. "Shoo," she said, making the noise that meant him.

"Let's see, sweetheart," Diana said, the mother once more.

Jack panted up behind Isabeau, looking cheerful. "We must have walked most of the way around the island. She found dozens of the things."

Isabeau knelt on the ground and spread out her findings. Diana bent over them, pretending her heart was not pounding like a rabbit's.

Her daughter began to sort the shells into piles: flat oyster shells in one, conch shells in another, fluted shells in a third. Isabeau had several collections of shells, which she kept carefully in lined boxes, sorted according to size and type. She would frequently open these boxes and pore over the shells, examining each with the seriousness of a member of the Royal Academy.

Diana had once thought to teach her how to make pretty trinkets from the shells, but Isabeau had not liked that. She wanted them to remain as they had been found.

Isabeau lifted the largest conch shell from its pile and held it in both hands out to James. "Joo."

Before Diana's eyes, James Ardmore softened. He reached for the shell. "Why thank you, Isabeau."

"Like this." Diana made a fist and touched her heart. "That is her sign for 'thank you.'"

James curled his thick fingers together. Bits of earth clung to his fingertips. He touched his breastbone. "Thank you."

Isabeau smiled. One of her upper teeth was growing in.

"What is this one?" Lieutenant Jack crossed his wrists, touched them to his breast, then opened them out. "I see both of you do that one all the time."

Isabeau giggled. Diana's face heated. "It means 'I love you.'"

"Ah." Jack grinned.

James absently brushed sand from the conch shell. He rose to his feet.

Isabeau waltzed back to her shells, pleased. James looked at the shell for a long time. He seemed mesmerized by its beauty.

He glanced up and saw her staring at him. Diana's heart beat faster. His gaze was so green. A tingle laced the tips of her breasts, pulling them to tight points.

Jack, oblivious, said, "Now what about these caves, Ardmore?"

The captain glanced at Jack. He gave Diana another long and nipple-tingling look, then turned and gestured for Jack to follow.

Jack made a polite bow. "Lady Worthing." He followed James down the path to the little gate.

Diana sank to her hands and knees again. She yanked the trowel out of the earth, slammed it back into the root of a recalcitrant weed. Isabeau began to hum.

James took the path more quickly than he had the day before. He knew the route, and his warm memory of Diana throwing herself into his arms sped his footsteps.

She was a puzzle. He sensed her wanting, but he also sensed fear. She was complex, layers and layers of her. He wanted to peel away those layers and find out all about her.

The tension in her had been palpable. The muscles of her arms and back had tautened as soon as she'd noted his presence. The tendril of hair trickling down her back had been irresistible. The button of her bodice had been undone, and it had taken all his willpower not to run his finger along the inside of her collar. If Lieutenant Jack and Isabeau had not come up, he would have continued the sweet seduction as far as he could have.

He wanted her. He wanted her with a deep, carnal wanting he'd not felt in a long time. She was a woman made for loving. She wanted him. She feared the wanting, but she had it.

Diana's daughter, when she grew older, would be just as beguiling as her mother. Isabeau had smiled with lopsided charm when she'd handed him the prize shell, the conch with its pretty designs. She'd wanted him to have it—him, not Jack or her mother.

James had slipped it into his pocket. It rested there, warming him a little.

"I think she fancies you, Ardmore." Jack's mirthful voice came behind him. The young man breathed heavily as they climbed and slid down the overgrown path.

"Isabeau? She's a little young."

He chuckled. "The lovely Lady Worthing, I meant."

James stopped before the vertical niche of rock that would take them to the sand. "She is lovely."

Jack's eyes twinkled. "Ah ha. The feeling is returned. The two of you, thrown together here. Better watch out, or you'll have your head in the noose."

James stilled. "What?"

"You'll get yourself snared into marriage. It could happen before you know it. But the beautiful Lady Worthing would be worth it, would she not?"

He looked a bit wistful. James put his back to the rock, folded his arms. The man's casual mention of nooses unsettled him. "What about you? You in love with her?"

Jack looked away. The sudden pang in James's heart surprised him. He and Diana might play in the sand, but it was a temporary thing. James had a more deadly game to play; he always did. Jack, on the other hand, was an Englishman, a naval man, one of them. He might never recover his memory. He could settle here with Diana as his wife, and the admiral would bless them. A perfect couple in an idyllic setting.

Jack looked back at him. His gray eyes were bleak. "I could lose my heart to Diana Worthing. Any man could, good Lord. But Ardmore." He paused. "I could be anyone." His words were tinged with fear.

"You could be a lieutenant on a British frigate," James said dryly. "Which is exactly what you are."

Jack studied a shoot of a succulent that clung to the rock near his head. "In the offices of the Admiralty my name is on some ship's manifest. As second or third lieutenant. Or perhaps I am an excellent officer, and I've been made a first lieutenant. But who is that lieutenant?

64

Do I have a wife, a family? Who is waiting for me to return? Or who is glad that I am dead?"

"You will know," James said. The rushing sea below crashed into the rock, receded. "A clerk will look at that manifest and tell you your name. He will know where you live. You'll know."

"But what will I know? Am I the cheerful gentleman I appear to be, happy I remember how to tie knots and move a sail? Or am I someone else? Someone terrible."

"Likely you're just like everyone else. Happy when you're warm in bed and annoyed when your breakfast is cold."

His lips thinned. "Do not placate me. You cannot know what it is like to have this—this blankness. I might love a woman who is good and beautiful. Hell, I might love a *man*. I—don't—know."

The sea crashed again, foamed. Tide was coming in. James said, "If you decide you maybe love a man, will you walk a little ways from me?"

Jack stared at him, brow furrowed. Then he laughed. "You're a damned hard man, Ardmore. Are all Americans as unfeeling as you?"

"Most of them, I think."

"I am glad of it. I do not need coddling, I need a kick in the pants. Thank you for obliging."

"Shall we go on?"

Jack nodded. James gripped the rocks and scrambled the rest of the way to the beach. Jack followed him nimbly.

James had never expected to feel sympathy for a lieutenant of the Royal Navy. As far as he was concerned, they were all bastards. British frigates strolled the seas with overweening arrogance, sweeping aside all in their paths. They blocked sea lanes from legitimate traders, and they blockaded islands in the West Indies to bar Americans from trade there. They accompanied East Indiamen, the huge ships of the East India Company, to Asia, not only to protect them, but in an effort to keep all Eastern trade British.

English frigates floated over all corners of the globe, and if captains felt peevish, they bullied American ships, which had no one to protect them. The American navy consisted of few ships. The British navy had hundreds, and they were getting to be damned nuisances. Worse than pirates. James Ardmore felt it his task to take them down whenever he could.

And now he was forced to confront two naval officers as human beings, Admiral Lockwood, hero of Trafalgar, and Lieutenant Jack, a bewildered and broken man struggling to retain his dignity.

And then there was Diana Worthing. Widow of the legendary Captain Sir Edward Worthing.

James slithered on the dry sand approaching the caves. She'd called her husband a fraud. Angrily. Anger had poured from every word. Her declaration of hatred for her husband had hurt her, and yet, she'd had to say the words.

Come to think of it, he'd never seen Diana Worthing not angry. But it didn't matter. Anger made her beautiful. God, she must have cut a swath through London and left a trail of violence behind her. Her rage told him this was true. Her confusion told him she did not understand why it had happened.

Because you are beautiful, that's why, darlin'. Beautiful and dangerous.

No way in hell would he stand aside and let Jack have her, no matter how sorry he felt for the man.

They reached the caves. James ducked into their shade. The air inside was cold.

Jack entered and looked about without much interest. "Shallow."

"Yes." James moved to the back of the cave, studied the walls and the shadows there.

"What are you looking for?"

"Whatever Lady Worthing did not want me to find."

Jack leaned against the rock wall. "There is nothing here."

"She worked hard to keep something from me. Damned if I know what."

James scanned the surface of the dark wall, trying to see within the shadows. He'd hoped for some crack or other opening that would take him to a farther cave, or perhaps show him something stowed here. Diana had certainly been eager to steer him away.

She was a careful woman. He saw that in the little things she did, from the sharp way she watched her daughter to how she helped Jessup clear the plates after supper. She ran this household for her father, and despite the paucity of servants, she ran it well.

She was not the sort of woman to lose her head and fling herself at James in a burst of lust. She hadn't, to his disappointment, last year either. The spark of passion that had ignited when she'd thrown her arms about his neck had surprised her. Had surprised him. She hadn't meant for that to happen.

James himself had been unprepared for the deep stirrings within him. He'd thought he'd put his longing for Diana Worthing from his mind. But he had sure wanted her yesterday—against the wall, on the sand, anywhere. He still wanted her.

"There's nothing here," Jack repeated. He sounded uninterested.

James stepped back. He walked a slow circle around the cave and returned to the entrance. He looked up, scanned the low ceiling. He could reach up and touch it.

Nothing. No opening, no secrets.

"I am inclined to agree with you," he said to Jack. "But I don't like not knowing about a thing."

"Mmm."

"You all right?"

The young man's face was pale. "Too much sun, I think." He leaned against the wall again.

James left the cave. He stood on the sand and looked around him. To his left lay the path back through the rock, the way they'd come. To his right, the ledge ended abruptly at the edge of the cliff. Before him was the same cliff, its precipice dropping sharply into the sea.

Suddenly, he chuckled. Diana Worthing was clever, even more so than he'd first thought.

Jack was right. There was nothing here. There never had been. Diana, by kicking up such a fuss at his discovery of the caves, had focused his attention entirely on them. He'd wasted time wondering what she was hiding from him, when in fact, there was nothing there to hide. She had guided his attention to this place so that he would not find what she had really hidden, somewhere else entirely.

He'd pulled the same trick on her last year when he'd known she wanted to pry through his things. He'd left the locked trunk to tantalize her and put they key where she could find it. Once she'd rifled it and thought she'd discovered all his secrets, she would be satisfied. Not that his ploy had worked—she had found Paul's diary and read it anyway.

Her trick hadn't worked on him either, but he felt a strange joy. He nearly laughed.

He turned around to find Jack doubled over, holding his abdomen and breathing hoarsely.

"What's the matter?"

Jack pushed himself upright—very slowly. His face shone with perspiration. "My head. Hurts like fury."

"You remember anything?"

Jack hesitated. James's heart beat faster. *Tell me no, Lieutenant. I like you; I don't want to have to kill you.*

"It just aches. Too much sun."

His pupils were pinpricks, here in this shadow.

"I'd say you need to get back to the house," James said. "Have Jessup look after you."

Jack smiled ruefully. "I believe you are right. Each time I think I have recovered, the old noddle starts pounding again." He stopped. "And why, James, can I remember silly slang like *noddle*, but I cannot say my own name?" His lashes were moist.

"I'll help you back."

Jack pulled away. "No. I do not need a bloody nursemaid."

James fixed him with a look. A member of James's own crew would have quailed before that look. Ill sailors on the *Argonaut* were ordered to report to the surgeon whether they liked it or not. Any man who stayed above when he was ill and then dropped over was dismissed at the next port. James hadn't time for men who tried to brave it out, as Jack obviously was about to.

Jack gave him a belligerent look. Then, before James's gaze, he wilted.

"Sorry. I know you are trying to help. I'll go back to the house. But there's no need to accompany me. I feel better. I'll go straight to bed, I promise."

James acknowledged this with a faint nod.

Jack smiled. "Are you certain you are not a marine sergeant? I knew one could keep an entire rank of men in line just looking at them like that." His face whitened. "Oh God, James, I remembered that. But I cannot— Damn."

"Don't try," James said.

Jack balled his hands, closed his eyes. In a moment, he opened them, and pretended to be composed. The English and their damned sangfroid. "I will return to the house. While I rest I will think on my Royal Marines sergeant. Perhaps he will trigger some further memory." He tried a smile again. "I hope to God I was not in love with *him*. His stare could turn you green."

James forced a smile in return.

Jack at last ambled away toward the path. James watched him begin the climb. The lieutenant was shaky, but he gained the upper path without mishap.

James did not follow him. He really should, he thought, in case Jack expired along the way, but he sensed that Jack would only greet this offer with fury. Sometimes a man had to be allowed to be a fool.

Once Jack had disappeared from sight, James resumed his exploration. He followed the beach to its end, where it stopped abruptly at the cliff. He looked over the edge. He saw only black rocks tumbling into the sea.

He put his hand on the rock wall and leaned over as far as he dared. The cliff was sharp. Seagulls chased one another below.

He turned his head. To his right was a ledge. And that ledge held a crack in the rock.

The ledge would not be easy to reach. He would have to go two steps in nearly empty space, with only a slight protrusion of rock for his feet. He leaned around the corner, grabbed the rocks at head height, and hoisted himself onto the protrusion.

The wind shoved at him. It would dislodge him if he let it, and then, no more James Ardmore.

Someone had carved handholds, unnatural square cuts chiseled out all along the rock. He followed them, took the required two precarious steps, and dropped down to the ledge.

Succulents grew here in profusion. They disguised the edge of the cliff. Tiny blue blossoms rippled in the wind.

The crack in the rock was just large enough for a man's body. James squeezed himself through. His shoulders caught, but he tugged himself free and stood blinking in the darkness.

He found himself atop another ledge, this one under a roof of rock. Far below him, sunlight and sea streamed into a cavern. The waves hissed as they cut past the rocks.

The cavern contained a series of ledges above and below him. And on each he could just make out the shapes of crates.

A wooden ladder had been affixed to the rocks a few feet from him. It led to the very bottom of the cave. The sand there was damp, a patch that never quite dried. He imagined the high tide covered it.

He wished for rope, not really trusting the ladder. But it looked sturdy enough. Likely another of Jessup's duties was to make certain it stayed reinforced.

James swung himself onto the ladder and moved slowly downward. He reached the bottom, then climbed upon the lowest ledge he could find. Crates waited there, at least half a dozen of them. They were pressed back into a niche and covered with tarp.

James examined the crates and found one whose wood

was warped enough for him to pry its lid off with his hands. Inside, packed in dry straw, were dozens of small barrels. He smiled at the savory odor drifting from them. Not gunpowder. Brandy.

He replaced the lid. He turned around and found Diana standing below the ledge.

He had known she was there. He could sense the sweet stir in the air when she was near.

He said, "So you and dear Papa are smugglers."

Her face was streaked with dirt and sand. She wore a cloak hastily tied at her throat. Her hair straggled half loose from her braid. From under the cloak, she pulled out a pistol and pointed it at him.

He went still, his limbs instinctively tightening.

They eyed each other, he ready to spring, she with eyes as hard as any marine sergeant's.

"We are not smugglers. It is not smuggling."

James contemplated, out of the corner of his eye, the ledges and ledges of crates. "You're blockade runners, then. Whose side?"

"No sides. Or at least, whatever side is against Napoleon."

"I see. Commendable of you."

She did not move.

James said, "This is the secret you did not want me to see? Why did you think James Ardmore would care if you ran goods past Bonaparte's continental system? I engage in it myself when I have the time. The shippers in Gibraltar are making a fortune out of it, transferring banned goods to neutral ships and running them in."

"We do not do it for money." She bit off the word.

"No, you do it out of your fine patriotic spirit. After all, your papa is a legendary British admiral."

Her eyes flashed. "Why are you not afraid? I am point-ing a pistol at you."

"If you had wanted to kill me, you'd have done it already." He let his mouth twitch. "Why weren't you afraid of me last year?"

"I was afraid. You abducted me."

"No, you were spitting mad. Like you are now. You don't have to shoot me, Diana. I'm not going to tell anyone."

She regarded him, hard-eyed, for one more moment. Then, slowly, she lowered the pistol.

James's limbs relaxed—slightly. The problem with bravado was that it held no guarantee the other person would back down.

"My father trusts you," she said. "I have no idea why."

"Your father is right." He eased himself from the ledge. "But Lieutenant Jack might take it amiss. The Royal Navy frowns on slipping British goods to the con-tinent right now."

"He might not even remember who Bonaparte is."

But he remembered a sergeant of the Royal Marines. It was a beginning.

"I won't tell him if you won't," James said. "Cross my heart."

He made a slow *X* across his chest. Her gaze roved there. Her cloak, thrown back, revealed her cotton dress, and, like yesterday, he could see that she wore nothing under the bodice.

Foolish, foolish Diana. The dull brown cloth was thick enough that no color showed through the fabric, but the bodice hugged her delicious breasts. They tightened be-fore his gaze, becoming hard little points of arousal.

He reached out and brushed one with his finger.

She jumped as if he'd slapped her. The pistol came up. "Take off your coat," she said.

He stared at the pistol, then slowly let out his breath. She had not primed it. If she fired, it would likely not go off. No doubt she had been in a tearing hurry when Jack arrived above and told her what he was up to. No time to summon Papa, no time to prime the pistol, likely no time to load it either.

Her eyes narrowed. "I said, take it off."

He could easily take the gun from her. But it might be more enjoyable to oblige her.

James unfastened the two buttons that held his coat closed and shrugged it off over his shoulders.

As was his habit, he wore nothing beneath. He'd long ago learned that on board ship, one was soaked more often than not. He'd quickly grown tired of changing his shirts, so he just did without. Usually he did not wear the coat either, letting his torso bake in the sun. Most of the men did the same. Even Mr. Henderson, his dandy of a lieutenant, stripped down in the heat.

James had left all his shirts aboard the *Argonaut*, and on Haven, there wasn't a spare one that fit him.

Her lips parted, moistened with her breath, as she looked him over. "Unbutton your trousers," she said.

He got hard in two seconds flat.

"The tide's coming in," he said. "We'll be cut off from the ladder."

"We will be all right."

He slanted her a look. "You had better hope that pistol never gets into my hands."

"Unbutton them," she repeated.

"Yes, ma'am," he drawled.

Slowly and deliberately he unfastened each of the five gold buttons. He undid the last one. Holding her gaze with his, he slowly pulled his breeches open.

Chapter Seven

His erection, hard and happy to be free, tumbled out. Her eyes widened. Her chest rose and fell, and her cheeks burned red.

What did she expect he'd do? She'd pointed a pistol at him, for God's sake. He'd much rather bare his backside than take a pistol ball in his chest.

But then, he'd never stood bare before a fire-haired, wild-eyed woman like Diana Worthing. He'd never felt wanting like this in his life.

A wave crashed through the opening, then hissed and swirled about their feet. It tugged at her skirt, chilled his ankles.

"Darlin'," he said, his teeth closing. "That water is cold."

Diana could not even feel the water. Her heart was beating so hard she could barely breathe. The pistol handle was heavy in her sweating hand.

He stood before her, unselfconscious and nonchalant. He was breathtakingly beautiful.

His torso was bronzed, the deep tan of a man who spent his life in the sun. His wide shoulders were knotted with muscle, streaked with scars. A new scar, red and angry, creased his belly, the sword cut she had dressed.

His tan stopped at his waistband. Above that line, his skin was liquid brown. Below it, white. His breeches opened in a *V*, and from it, his arousal pointed long and hard.

She could not stop staring at it.

She dimly remembered her friends giggling to her about her husband, teasing her that a naval hero's organ must be as great as a mainmast. She could not for the life of her recall what Edward's had looked like. He'd always come to her in the dark; that is, when he'd bothered to find her bed chamber at all.

This was broad daylight. This was real. And terribly, terribly exciting.

She had wanted to look at him so much she hadn't realized what she'd done. The pistol was empty; he must know that. But he played along. It was her game, but he had taken over.

She swallowed the tremor in her throat. "Move your hands to the ledge."

He slowly lifted his bare arms, sinews sliding, and stretched them to each side of him.

Her heart skipped and bumped. He knew, he must know, her passion was consuming her. Any other man would stop her. Lieutenant Jack would.

She could not imagine playing this game with Lieutenant Jack. He was an ordinary Englishman. James Ardmore was something different.

He waited, his arms outstretched, his breeches sagging down his hips. She moistened her lips. She wanted to go to him, to lick him from the base of his arousal to his bronzed throat.

She would do it. He would let her. She would make him let her.

She took a step forward and another. Her hand shook so hard she had to lower the pistol before she dropped it. She leaned forward and up, her breath catching, and touched her tongue to the hollow of his throat.

He tasted like salt. His pulse beat beneath her tongue. She closed her eyes and breathed in the scent of him— warm, male. His erection touched her abdomen, probing gently.

He bent to her, and their lips met. He kissed her with slow passion, one that spoke of Southern nights and sweet magnolia.

There was possession in the kiss, yes, but so persuasive, that she barely understood she surrendered to him. His lips caressed, and his tongue took hers with gentle force.

The pistol was twisted, hard, from her grip. The movement broke their contact.

He came up with the pistol in his hand, leaving her wrist aching. He checked the trigger pan, his eyes neutral. "As I thought. Not loaded, is it?"

She shook her head, her heart pounding furiously,

"Never play with a weapon, Diana. It's dangerous." Before she could draw breath to answer, he caught her hand and wrapped it around his large, hot erection. "Now, that you can play with all you want."

She stared at it, stunned. It lay heavy in her shaking hand, as hard as the pistol. Dark and hard, it stood out from the circle of hair at the opening of his breeches, its tip pushing toward her, skin smooth. Her fingers barely closed all the way around it. She'd never touched a man's arousal before; Edward had always thrust his inside her without preliminary and withdrew all too soon. She'd never had the chance to look, touch, investigate the wonders of it.

She explored it gently, moving her fingers up the warm skin to the tip. A small bead of moisture lingered there. "What do I do?" she whispered.

James gripped her shoulder, his fingers gripping through her thin dress. "You're doing just fine, darlin'."

She ran her thumb across the tip, watching with fascination as his muscles bunched. Slowly, she stroked down to the hard, round base of him. Her throat was dry, and she could barely breathe.

His fingers threaded through her hair. He pulled her head back and kissed her hard on the mouth.

This was desire; this was real, not a game.

Another wave rushed into the cave. It soaked her to the knees with frigid water. She gasped. She lost her grip on his lovely arousal.

He stepped away from her, fully in control. "We need to finish elsewhere. Or wait out the tide on one of these ledges. I imagine you keep these crates snug and dry. But it seems like a cold way to spend a night."

Her knees shook. "There is another way up." She pointed past the opening, through which more water poured.

"Then we'd better hurry."

With swift movements, he buttoned his breeches, snatched up his coat and shrugged it on, pocketed the pistol. He was so casual, as though he were used to dressing and undressing in a cold cave.

Diana plunged through the icy water, now knee-deep, hoping the chill would lower the temperature in her veins. It did not. Her heart hammered, and she was very aware of him striding just a pace behind her.

On the other side of the cave, a series of rocks lifted against the black wall. A rough scramble would take them to the top. Jessup had hollowed out handholds, but only a very athletic person could climb this. She had no doubt that James Ardmore could do it without hesitation.

She scrambled up to the first rock. She was panting already, her fingers weak. She put her booted foot on the next rock, tried to pull herself up. She slipped.

He caught her with his large palm firmly on her backside. He boosted.

Lifted by his strength, she reached the second boulder as he rested on the first. Her thighs in form-hugging breeches, revealed by her lifted skirts, were at his eye level. He made no pretense of not looking his fill.

Quickly she grabbed the next rock and scrambled up. He boosted her again. They went on this way, she scrabbling to the next rock, he pushing her upward.

At last she reached the wide ledge at the top of the cavern, and the hole above. She'd climbed down this way, the quicker route from above when Lieutenant Jack had staggered back to the garden and made his heart-stopping announcement that James had gone on exploring.

But she'd reached the cave too late. He had already found the cache, was already examining it.

Her father had said James would understand. And he had, as far as James had guessed what the cache meant. He had not guessed everything, which was why she'd distracted him with her command to take off his coat. She'd not really believed he'd do it. Then the heady power she held over him had made her giddy. Would he bare himself for her?

She could make no pretense that she did not want him. She was no lady, was that not what her husband had always said?

But Edward had been a fool. Diana had flirted and teased, using the only power she'd had, but she had never gone beyond that, whatever Edward thought. Her coterie had danced attendance, had glared at each other jealously, had given her tokens they'd begged her to wear. They had wanted her. Hungered for her, they had whispered most inappropriately during ballroom dances.

But Diana had never returned the hunger. She had flirted to punish Edward, nothing more. She had locked away her desires, understanding their danger, and not wanting what they'd lead to.

And then she'd met James Ardmore. A man who overpowered any intention she had. She understood now that those other gentlemen, her husband included, had simply been easy to resist.

James pulled himself up beside her, ducking against the low ceiling. "Up?" he asked over the roar of the water below.

Mutely, she nodded. Before she could begin her climb, he wrapped his strong arms about her thighs and boosted her through the hole. She landed on the soft, sun-warmed grass outside. She rolled out of the way, coming to sit in the grass on the downward slope, her cloak all tangled around her. Impatiently, she untied the strings and pushed the garment away.

The hole to the caves was in the side of a rock. James slithered from it, scrambling through and landing on his back on the grass.

Diana got to her feet. The sun was warm, but she'd felt warmer in the caves, with his arms about her. Now they must make their way back to the house. She must damp down her wanting and take care of her daughter, her father, and Lieutenant Jack.

A strong hand closed about her ankle, tugged hard.

She lost her footing and tumbled down, to be caught in his arms and pulled full length on top of him.

"No you don't," he said. "You start a seduction, you finish it."

"Seduction?"

"Tellin' me to unbutton my trousers." His calloused hands cradled her loose hair. "Wicked woman."

"I was not certain you would do it."

"I had to. You were holdin' me at gunpoint."

Warm fingers found the buttons at the back of her bodice. The top one was already loosened. He unbuttoned the second, and the third, and the fourth.

"What are you doing?"

"What does it feel like I am doing?"

"James—"

His eyes were so warm. "I love it when you say my name. I like to watch your lips. Say it again."

"James."

More buttons loosened. His roughened fingertips drifted along her bare back.

"Say it again."

"Jam—"

When she reached the *m*, lips pressed together, he kissed her.

His lips were shaking, as though he held himself back. What would he do if he did not hold himself back? she wondered in lovely anticipation. She remembered his bruising grip on her shoulder in the cave. He had strength. He could do anything he wanted. The thought should frighten her.

It didn't. His fingers traced patterns on her bare back, dipped to the small of her spine. His touch slid beneath the waistband of her breeches, found the crease in her backside. She wriggled, letting herself feel pleasure.

When the kiss ended, she raised up on her elbows. Her loose bodice tumbled forward. She let it.

Sunshine touched her naked shoulders. She pushed her arms free of the sleeves and let the bodice crumple to her waist. His gaze, warm and green, slid to her breasts, watching, admiring.

He had not fastened his coat again. His chest, hard with muscle, lay bare to the sun. She laid down again on top of him, skin to skin.

For the first time since she'd known him, he smiled. It softened his severe face, and it promised untold pleasures. His eyes were half closed, hiding the sinful green. He wrapped his arms around her and pulled her close.

She tasted like sunshine and fine, rich rum. He could lie here and kiss her forever.

And why not? He wasn't going anywhere. Ian O'Malley had the *Argonaut*, and they had planned to part ways until James had finished what he wanted to finish. Right now, James could only play a waiting game. That meant he had time to lie here in the sun and kiss Diana Worthing.

His heart was beating in a strange, hard way. Diana was a woman worth kissing. She was worth touching. Worth having. Worth loving.

He did not fight the thought. A beautiful woman had told him a year or so ago that he would find someone. Out there, she'd said, looking at him with brown eyes lovely and large. He had not believed her.

And then he'd come up against Diana Worthing in that garden in Kent.

He eased her hair back from her face.

"Diana," he whispered, "Darlin'—"

She answered with a kiss like molten metal. She was

a fine, fine woman, even if she was English.

Best to get his fill of Diana Worthing before she started hating him. She pretended to hate him now, but she didn't really.

Her mouth was on fire. She knew how to kiss, the little devil. He let his fingers probe the crease in her backside. *Oh, love, we could burn down this whole island.*

A small shadow suddenly touched his face. He looked up into the blue-gray eyes of Diana's daughter.

Diana gasped. She jerked her bodice against her bared torso. "Isabeau."

Isabeau regarded her mother solemnly. The wind lifted her loosened hair.

She spun around. Her little dress swirled about her boy's breeches, mirrors of her mother's. She scampered away down the grass.

Diana thrust her arms into her sleeves. She scrambled to her feet.

James could not get up fast enough. Diana was already running by the time he gained his feet.

"Diana!"

She did not stop. She was running away, her bodice gaping in back.

James sprinted after her. There was a path at the bottom of the slope. It led around the rocks, curving toward the house. The tiny figure of Isabeau was already halfway along it.

James caught up with Diana, seized her shoulder. "Don't be stupid," he said in a harsh voice. "You go in like that, and you'll embarrass yourself."

She at least let him button the bodice. He even fastened the top button that had been undone in the first place.

She swung on him, her glorious eyes blazing. She balled her fists. "You—"

She spluttered. She could not finish. With a half scream between clenched teeth, she whirled around and ran down the path after her daughter.

By the time James reached the garden again, it was deserted. No sign of Isabeau, no sign of Diana, no sign of Lieutenant Jack.

The gate to the garden stood ajar. The wind creaked it.

Below the garden, the surf ran up to the beach. Wind tossed the wild trees, stirred the succulents on the rocks. Flowers bloomed blue and red. The house sat in the middle of this, wings running haphazardly, trees overhanging the roof. The open windows stirred Diana's lace curtains.

Haven. The name suited the place. Here one was far from the evils of the world, far from harm, safe. Or so it seemed.

Once, long ago, the Ardmore house on the Battery in Charleston had possessed that same air of serene safety. He had played in the garden with his brother and sister, and they'd quarreled and fought, made up, ran races, dared each other to climb the trellis. He and Paul had wrestled, while Honoria had stamped her feet and scolded them. She'd possessed a powerful kick to the shins, James remembered. He could scarcely imagine his stately sister kicking anyone now.

That house had echoed with laughter. Here in this place, he could remember his mother's clear voice, his father's booming answer. Coming across them kissing under the magnolia trees. Feeling superior at eleven years old because he would never do anything so foolish.

He remembered his mother starting up from his father's lap, blushing. His father smiling quietly, unem-

84

barrassed. His father had known what it was to be in love.

Now the house was nearly empty. His parents had died of typhoid when James had been fourteen. Paul was dead, too, and Honoria lived alone. She would be thirty-one now, unmarried, keeping up the house that was too silent. The last time James had visited home, four years before, the silence of it had driven him away. Honoria's loneliness had turned her bitter. She and James had quarreled long and hard, and he had gone.

Honoria would like it here, he thought suddenly. In this sanctuary. This haven.

She might even approve of Diana. Lady Worthing, the wife of a knighted naval hero, would be given high marks in Honoria's book.

Admiral Lockwood emerged from the library door and strolled into the garden. He saw James, gave him a nod, walked around the house on whatever errand he'd come out for.

Another plus for Honoria, James mused. Diana was also the daughter of another naval hero and a high-placed admiral. She had plenty of pedigree to satisfy even the genteel ladies of Charleston.

Isabeau followed her grandfather out of the house. James sobered. A deaf child would not be greeted with enthusiasm. She would have to be carefully introduced. In the weeks James had been here, he had come to nearly forget Isabeau was deaf, that there was anything "wrong" with her.

He could not understand everything she said with her hand signals, but he was learning. She said "Joo" for James, and "Maa" for her mother, and a gurgling noise that meant "grandfather."

And now she had caught James kissing her mother. In

a most compromising position. He could almost hear his sister's voice, "Really, James, what on earth were you thinking?"

The answer came easily. "I was thinking I liked kissing her."

Isabeau saw him. She made an abrupt turn, as smoothly as a ship with a practiced crew, and made directly for him. The wind lifted her fine, child's hair, bright red like her mother's.

She patted him on the forearm, the gesture she made when she had something to say. She began various signals with her hands, accompanied by a series of squeaks and muffled noises. James only recognized a few signs, the one for "mother," and the one for "there."

He shook his head. "I'm sorry, Isabeau. I don't understand you."

She started again. She got to the end of her lecture, waited, hands on hips.

Again James shook his head. "Sorry. I don't know what you're trying to say."

Isabeau rolled her eyes, an eight-year-old annoyed at grown-up ignorance. James would have to ask Diana to teach him more signs. Lieutenant Jack was learning rapidly.

Suddenly, Isabeau thrust her hands into James's. She dragged him out into the open space in front of the garden gate. She started to run in a little circle around him, still holding tight to his hands. She looked up at him, hoping he would understand *this* at least. She ran faster.

James caught on. Honoria had used to like this game when she was Isabeau's age. Honoria had also liked to slide down the banister of the sweeping staircase. He wondered dimly if she still did. He very much doubted it.

James turned in a fast circle. He dragged Isabeau off

her feet, holding her tight. Her legs flew out and she laughed out loud.

They whirled 'round and 'round. So long ago it had been when he, tall at fifteen, had twirled his little sister in their wide front hall on a rainy day. Her laughter had echoed to the elegant painted ceilings.

James saw the admiral stroll back their way. The man leaned on the gate and watched them.

James whirled Isabeau around a few more times, then tossed her up and gently landed her on her feet. He was panting, and the nearly healed cut was beginning to ache. "That's all I have, sweetheart."

Isabeau giggled. She walked away from James and the admiral, toward the beach. She exaggerated her staggers, playing dizzy.

The admiral watched her with calm eyes. "She was not born deaf," he said conversationally. "She was a normal little girl, very loud, as my tender ears remember. Diana was so proud of her. Showed her off everywhere. Her friends were embarrassed for her, obviously besotted with her own child." He smiled fondly. "Then, when Isabeau was two years old, she caught a fever. Diana had it too. It laid them both low for a long time. Diana recovered. Isabeau eventually got well, but the illness left her deaf. Her hearing faded little by little, until it was gone. She might still be able to hear a few things, very loud noises perhaps, but perhaps not." He paused. "Sir Edward blamed Diana."

James had already decided he didn't like Sir Edward. "Why?"

The admiral pushed himself from the gatepost. He strolled down the path Isabeau still staggered along. James fell into step with him.

"Edward wanted a boy, of course. Diana's joy over the

girl angered him. When Isabeau lost her hearing, Edward told Diana it was because of Diana's pride, her frivolousness. Punished by God, he said, and all her fault."

James said mildly, "I am sorry he's dead. I would enjoy killing him."

The admiral glanced at him sideways. He must be wondering if James were exaggerating. James was not.

"Edward was embarrassed by Isabeau. He wanted to put her in an asylum and never speak of her. I was surprised he thought Diana would capitulate. She argued with him day and night, even threatened him with divorce. In the end, he gave up, though not gracefully."

They walked companionably along the beach. The breakers slithered up the sand at their feet. Isabeau ran through them, holding her skirts high. Water splashed from her boots.

James could imagine Diana confronting her husband over a subject she felt so passionate about. He could picture her blue eyes blazing in rage, her flyaway hair snaking about her like Medusa's. Her barbs could cut, he hoped she'd flayed Sir Edward hard.

She must have been desperate to threaten him with divorce. In England, divorce ruined both parties. No doubt the legendary Sir Edward had been horrified to contemplate such a stain on his honor.

He was a fraud, Diana had sniffed.

"How did Sir Edward die?" he asked. "I hope it was messy and senseless."

The admiral glanced at him. "Messy, yes. He was torn apart by cannon fire. Died instantly. His ship was in a battle off Cadiz, two frigates against five French ships. Never should have happened. They buried him at sea."

"Was he really a hero? Or just lucky?"

"I do not know." The admiral sounded depressed. "He

was much decorated, and he is dead. Perhaps we should leave it at that. What about you? Are you simply lucky?"

James thought about the many times in his career that luck had been decidedly against him. "I make my own luck. And take any opportunity shoved at me."

Such as finding Admiral Lockwood's daughter alone in a garden at a house in Kent. A woman who knew the secrets of the island of Haven.

"I think happenstance guides us more than we like to think," the admiral said. He studied the sand at his feet.

James fell into thoughtful silence. He had never before in his life believed in remorse. Remorse never helped the living. Looking at the admiral now, he felt a twinge of it. He might destroy this man in his search for justice. Haven held the key, and he was very close to unlocking it. He thought of his dying brother, the blood caked around Paul's mouth as he'd extracted James's promise from him. What James had done fulfilling that promise had lifted him to the status of legend.

Remorse had no part in that. It would be damned inconvenient to start having remorse now.

"I'd have strapped Sir Edward Worthing to the front of a cannon, myself," he observed. "Made certain he felt that first shot."

"You are a man of violence, Ardmore."

"I'd not have lasted this long if I weren't. And an English admiral is not exactly the most peaceful of men."

He shook his head. "Battle is different."

"Different from hunting men down and making them beg for mercy? The men I have killed deserved it for what they did. The men I humiliated equally deserved it."

"Perhaps they did. But do you have to enjoy it so much?"

"I'm afraid I do, Admiral. There is much romance spun about pirates and privateers, but in truth, most of them are simply murderous and violent. Few of the legends in circulating libraries in London mention pirates who slice open a woman from throat to crotch because she won't capitulate. That is why I am violent."

They walked a few minutes in silence. Isabeau capered in the waves, singing tunelessly.

The admiral said, "It must have come as a bit of a shock to be rescued by an English admiral and his family."

James shrugged. "There are diamonds in every dung heap."

"You flatter me. You will forgive me for observing, Captain Ardmore, that you are not the kind of man I wish my daughter to fall in love with."

James hesitated half a step, then walked on. "She is not in love with me."

"Isabeau told me she found you kissing her. Diana did not deny it, and she was certainly embarrassed enough for it to be true."

"That does not mean she is in love with me."

James had fantasized earlier about taking Diana home with him, showing her Charleston, and the house his father had built. The slow warmth of Southern nights. The other side of James Ardmore. Pleasant fantasies did not always come true.

"I do not want to watch her heart break," the admiral said.

If any heart breaks, it will be mine, Admiral.

"She won't break her heart over me. She does not trust me at all; I'm certain she doesn't like me. I'll leave here, and she can fall in love with Lieutenant Jack."

The admiral was silent. Clouds on the horizon had

jumbled together. The sun bleached the tops of thunderheads a painful white. Their flat undersides were black.

"What do you know about him?" the admiral asked. "Lieutenant Jack?"

"What I told you when I arrived. Nothing. I never learned his name. He did not exactly stop and introduce himself."

"Yet you rescued him. Why?"

James watched the thunderheads and Isabeau dancing for a moment. She stooped and picked up a shell.

"He loosened the chains binding me when the storm hit," James said. "So that I might have a chance to save myself. When I saw him floating by, I thought I would repay the favor."

"It was good of you."

James shrugged. "Jewels on the dung heap, like I said. How is he, by the way?"

"He had a screaming headache, but refused to admit it until he fell over. Jessup had to carry him upstairs. He's in bed with the shutters drawn and a cloth over his eyes."

James put his hands behind his back. "I wish I did know more about him."

"So you could help him? Or to know what kind of threat he might be?"

"I like him. When it is time for me to leave, he might remember who I am and think it his duty to stop me. I do not want to battle him."

"Because he could stop you?"

"Because he would lose. I don't want to have to kill him."

The admiral stared at him for a heartbeat. "I will help ensure it does not come to that."

"Kind of you."

"You are a complicated man, Ardmore."

"So many have told me. Except my sister. She thinks I'm simple. Do everything James's way, she says, and he is sweet-tempered. Not that she ever followed her own advice. She has a determination that would make any French admiral flee straight back to Le Havre."

The admiral laughed appropriately.

James wondered why he kept thinking about Honoria. Their last parting had not been amicable. She had told him, in fact, to go to the devil and not come back until he was dead.

Well, she might just get her wish.

Admiral Lockwood liked him. And he liked the admiral. He wished he didn't. If Lockwood didn't want to cooperate with James, James would have to force him. Maybe he could do it gently. Diana would probably shoot him, regardless.

"That storm will likely hit," the admiral said, gesturing to the clouds. "Weaker ones blow off. We'll have to help Jessup batten down the hatches. I believe Lieutenant Jack is down for the night."

He turned back, holding out his hand for Isabeau. She whirled once more in the wind, scampered back, and seized both their hands.

James felt her little fingers close around his. He looked down. Isabeau grinned up at him. James thought again of the day he'd found his mother and father spooning in the garden. Silly parents, he'd thought. But at the same time, he'd felt warm and happy. He had sensed the difference between love and vulgar display.

Perhaps Isabeau did, too.

"Tell me, Admiral," he said as they walked back to the garden. "What is in those crates under your island?"

Chapter Eight

The storm broke just as Diana put Isabeau to bed. A flare of lightning lit Isabeau's room like brightest fire, and the clap of thunder that followed drowned out Isabeau's squeal.

Diana delighted in the fierce storms, and at the same time they terrified her. London rarely had lightning works like those that attacked unprotected Haven. Winds moaned in the eaves and the chimneys. The entire house creaked, sounding as though any moment it would blow into the sea. Trees scraped the roof and across the windows, tearing at the shingles and glass.

Isabeau shared Diana's joy and fright. She'd stare at the windows with round eyes, and when the lightning glared, she dove headfirst into the pillows. A few seconds of hiding, and then she'd creep out again and watch the window.

Diana felt the soaring thrill in the storm as well as the terror. It was much like kissing James Ardmore.

To Diana's horror, Isabeau had relayed the tale of finding Diana and James kissing to her father. Isabeau had found the whole thing enormously funny. Her father had given Diana a sharp, worried look, and she'd nearly died of mortification.

Fortunately, Jessup had come in to say that poor Lieutenant Jack was in a bad way, and Diana had hurried to minister to him. She had given Jack some chamomile and had soothed his brow with a damp cloth. That seemed to have helped. She hoped the thunder would not keep him awake.

Another lightning bolt struck close. Isabeau squealed and hid her head. The crack of thunder sent Diana down after her.

Voices gathered in the hall. James Ardmore's rumbling baritone. "Is everything all right?"

Her father chuckling. "Isabeau is afraid of lightning. Diana is afraid of thunder. They will weather it."

James's warm voice joined her father's. "Good night, Admiral."

"Good night, Captain."

Go away, gentlemen, Diana thought crossly. *Let us ladies have our little fright in peace.*

Doors closed. Silence prevailed.

The thunder roared on for another hour. Isabeau wore herself out bouncing in and out of the covers, and finally she settled down, her cheek pillowed on her arm. Diana sank down next to her, exhausted.

Lightning flickered. Diana counted, one, two, three, four, five. The thunder, less powerful now, rumbled, more than a mile away. Drifting farther.

She heard Isabeau's bedroom door softly open. She lay motionless, listening. The door closed more softly still. Footsteps, slow and quiet, crossed the floor, stopped beside the bed.

She lay still and breathed his scent, the warm smell of

soap and musk. He had stripped down to sponge himself off after their adventure in the cave and before supper. She knew this because his door had been ajar, and she'd glanced in. She'd seen the flash of tall body, tanned muscle, taut backside, paler than the rest of his skin, and then he'd moved out of sight.

That vision had stayed with her throughout supper and was with her now. Should a woman want a man so much? Should the image of him remain in her mind so long? Should she want to reverse time, to enter the room where he bathed himself? He would embrace her, all wet and soapy, and she'd get all wet, and then he'd kiss her.

She wanted it with all her might.

The mattress listed. James climbed onto the bed, stretching his full length against her back. A strong arm came around her waist, warm through her thin nightdress. He settled himself, holding her against his chest.

She felt the smooth velvet of the dressing gown her father had lent him, a bare, strong foot brushing hers. He reached down and slid the covers up over himself, her, Isabeau.

Isabeau turned and looked at him sleepily. She smiled, patted his hand, and settled back down. Her breathing evened and quieted.

Diana lay back against his warmth, letting his strength seep into her. He did not caress her, but his palm rested on her stomach and heat spread from there. She felt his lips in her hair, his breath at her temple.

They lay like that for a long time, while Isabeau drifted to sleep. Despite her tiredness, Diana was wide awake, eyes open. The lightning flickered, far away and quiet.

At last, James unwound his arm from her waist. He rose from the bed, so smoothly and quietly that he barely disturbed the mattress. He reached for her hand and tugged her to join him.

Diana climbed out of the bed less gracefully than James had. Isabeau did not wake. Tired out from the storm, she slept on, even when Diana smoothed the covers over her and pressed a kiss to the girl's forehead.

James led Diana to the door, and together they left the room.

The house was dark, but the clouds had cleared and silver moonlight poured through the unshuttered windows on the landing. James pressed her back into the wall, resting his large hands on each side of her. Her lips formed a question, but before sound could emerge, he kissed her.

She loved kissing him. He opened her mouth, caressed her tongue with his. No teasing this time, no playing at seduction, just a long, warm, loving kiss.

He softly untied the ribbon that closed her nightdress at the throat and slid his hand inside the placket. His palm was rough against her skin.

This was what she needed. Kisses for the sake of kissing. No disappointed, swallowed passion, no suppressed emotion. Just James and his strength. In the morning, she would worry about herself and her father and Isabeau and the turmoil in her mind. Tonight, she would enjoy this.

He kissed as though he liked kissing her. He trailed his lips down her throat, and she leaned her head back against the wall and emitted a little sigh. In her younger days, she had wanted her husband to do what James did now. Edward, the first time she had confessed her attraction to him, had sneered. She had spent two agonizing months while Edward was at sea, wondering what she had done wrong.

When Edward returned, her longing swamped her once more, and once more, he sneered. Being eighteen, she had thought it her fault that he did not want her. Her mother-in-law had told her repeatedly that marriage aged a fresh young lady like her almost overnight.

She threaded her fingers through James's hair and pushed unhappy memories away. This, she thought, warming deliciously, was what it was like to be with a man who desired you as much as you desired him.

She did not explain that Isabeau had liked finding James kissing her mother. She had asked Diana when they would marry. Diana wondered if such information would make James flee the house, jump into the gig and head out to sea.

She felt his erection against her abdomen. He never made any attempt to hide his desire. He had no reason to tame his passion, probably never had in his life.

She tried to harden her heart against him. This was casual to him. He saw a female he desired and he kissed her, nothing more.

It didn't work. His kisses washed fire through her; his hands on her waist excited her with their strength.

He raised his head, easing his lips from hers. Leisurely, like he had all night. He traced her cheek. "James," she whispered.

He put his finger to her lips. He leaned down and kissed her again. Then he took her elbow and led her to her room at the head of the stairs.

He opened the door and steered her inside. The fire burned low and no candles were lit. He closed the door.

She stopped in the middle of the carpet, a lump rising in her throat. He came to her in silence. He began kissing her again, holding her arms. She firmly and deliberately stepped away. "No, James."

He gave her a puzzled look. She pulled the placket of her gown together, looked everywhere but at him. Her heart thumped and throbbed, and the fires he'd lighted in her still burned bright.

His green eyes went cool. Whenever she had denied Edward, and after Isabeau's birth she always had tried to, he'd gone tight with rage. James looked—neutral. As though he could take her or leave her alone.

"What's the matter?" He kept his voice low.

"Nothing is the matter."

He frowned. "I know when a woman is on fire for a man. You still are. Now, what is it?"

She tried to give him a freezing glance. "Is not morality reason enough?"

"Not for you."

Her mouth dropped open. "How dare you."

"Spare me, Diana. You shoved a pistol in my face and told me to bare my backside. That's a fine example of morals."

"That was a game."

Anger flared briefly in his eyes, but then the coolness returned. He mastered himself easily. "You can get yourself into a lot of trouble playing games like that."

"I know that. I already have."

He came to her, cupped her shoulders. "You weren't playing games. You wanted me and you wanted what we were leading up to. Now that I'm offering it, you back down. I want to know why."

His touch was so warm. She wanted it forever. Her voice shook. "If you stay a moment longer, I will have to scream. Then you can explain to my father what you are doing here."

His eyes narrowed. "I think he'd have a pretty good idea what we were doing. In fact, why don't you call him? I could tell him a few things about you."

She summoned a haughty glare. "Do not be absurd."

"It won't work, Diana." He turned away. She heard the click of the key in the lock, and her heart turned over. He came back, key in hand. "You're trying to anger me, and yourself, but for what reason, I don't know. We both have been dying for each other. We might as well get on with it before we burn up inside."

She barely heard him. She stared at the key in a wash of fear. Not for what he would do with her on the bed because that would be glorious. Her fear was for what would come after. For what must come after. She thought of Isabeau tucked in bed, unable to hear the thunder that had shaken the house. She could never do it again. Never, never.

His gaze turned puzzled. "Diana, what is it?"

"I cannot. Please do not ask me why."

He stood looking at her for a long time. "I think I deserve to know why."

She clenched her hands. "It is entirely inappropriate—"

He tossed the key to the table, finally losing his temper. "Don't start bellyaching on about morals. You don't give a damn about morals. You're afraid of something. Me?"

"Do not flatter yourself. I have never been afraid of you."

"Other women have told me that. A few I threw overboard. Mostly they learned respect."

"And I certainly do not want to hear about your other women. I know I am only one in a long line of mistresses—"

"Then you don't know a damn thing." He came a step closer.

He really was a large man. And tall. And very strong. His eyes held no remorse and no warmth.

He lifted her before she could so much as scream. Despite his strength, his arms were gentle. He carried her across the room and dumped her facedown on the bed.

"What are you doing?" she gasped.

"I'm going to spank you."

Outrage brought back strength. She sat up hurriedly. "No, indeed, you are not."

"Why not? It might be fun. But I've just thought of something better."

She caught up her pillow, readying it as a weapon. "I already told you no."

His gaze lingered on the nightgown as though he could see through it. "Not that. You don't want me, so I'll swallow my pride and say it's your loss. Not that I really believe you."

He would not insist. Sudden, acute disappointment touched her. Then anger because she should have felt relieved. Why the devil did she *never* feel what she was supposed to?

James sat down on the bed next to her. His warm thigh touched hers. He smoothed her hair and pressed a kiss to it. "I am going to show you pleasure, Diana. Pleasure alone. Do you want that?"

She tried to shake her head no. It came out as a rigid nod. Yes.

He leaned back against the headboard, and untied his dressing gown. He lay there long, and well-muscled, his chest shadowed with dark hair. His eyes were liquid green in the darkness. He held out his hand. "Come here."

He took her stunned assessment for hesitation. "I

promise you," he said softly, "we won't do anything you don't want."

She gave up. She took his hand and moved to him. She settled on his inviting lap, not minding a bit when he wrapped his warm arms around her.

It felt right to be here, sitting back against him. Holding his strong hands felt like holding a lifeline.

"I am just a man, Diana," he breathed into her hair. "I can't help wanting you."

"You're a legend," she corrected. "Like my husband."

"I am flesh and bone. Like you."

His warm breath touched her neck. He laced her fingers through the back of his hand. "Now, Diana," he said softly. "You show me how you want me to touch you."

Her heart slammed against her ribcage. Silly Diana, to think that he could destroy her only by actually coupling with her. No, he would take her down one finger's breadth at a time until she belonged to him entirely. He was determined to melt her into one, smoldering heap.

She had no choice. Before she could think about what she did, she slid his hand under her breast and held it there. She closed her eyes, letting go, and leaned back into his embrace.

James buried his nose in the soft crinkles of her hair, loving the smell of it. Diana had washed her hair today after their encounter in the caves. He knew because he'd seen Mrs. Pringle carry basins of water upstairs into Diana's room. He had lingered in the doorway of his own chamber, imagining Diana lying with her bodice pushed down and her head back over a basin, while Mrs. Pringle poured ewers of water over her hair. Lavender-scented water.

The feel of her through the cotton nightdress was unbearably good. The curve of her breasts, the points that rose under his touch, the softness of her belly, the outline of her thigh. His lips touched the embroidered collar that rested modestly at the nape of her neck.

He did not know what she was afraid of. Not him. Not even desire. She feared something else that she kept tucked away from everyone, even her beloved father and daughter.

No, she liked desire. She knew what she wanted. Under the loosened nightdress, she guided him to her breasts, her belly, her fingers and his twined like ropes.

She drew one leg up to her chest. He smoothed the firm muscles of her calf to the warm fold behind her knee. He lingered there, their thumbs dipping together to stroke the soft skin.

To her thigh now, muscled from climbing and sailing her father's boat. From there her hip, so firmly placed against him. Up to her belly again, inside the nightdress, warmth and comfort there.

The fabric dragged up with their movements, exposing her long legs, legs that by day filled out her man's breeches with fine suggestion. They were as lovely as he'd imagined.

She turned her head and sought his mouth. Their lips played for a time, while their hands together stroked her bare skin.

She tugged downward, pressed the heel of his hand to the fold between her bent leg and her lowered one. He met slippery heat. Oh yes. Her thoughts must be traveling along some fine lines.

Sparks, he'd told her. Raining on a man until he crumbled to ash. The great James Ardmore was about to burn up.

He dipped his fingers into her waiting fire. She stirred,

laid her head back against his shoulder, eyes closed. He stroked her sweet opening, and her fingers followed his.

"James," she murmured.

She was starving. Her father and daughter loved her, but they could not fulfill every part of her. She was starving, just like he was.

"It's my pleasure, pleasuring you," he said. "A gentleman always obliges."

She was not listening. She had focused, eyes closed, on inner fire.

"Always obliges," he whispered again, and kissed the fiery line of her hair. "Do you know how beautiful you are? When I woke up on the beach I was delighted to see you again. I decided I wanted to stay here a good long time." He kissed her behind her ear. "I'll bet every man says that."

He dipped his first two fingers inside her. She was tight, and yet, so giving. Her chest lifted with her breath. Her just-washed hair bathed him in the scent of lavender.

"You smell good, darlin'," he murmured.

Her eyes grew heavy, her face, flushed. Their joined hands moved over the wiry hair that was even redder than that on her head. Their fingers touched, skimmed, teased, and James's desire grew tighter.

He wanted so much to take her in a wild frenzy, but he was also enjoying this quiet pleasuring. Her cheek was soft against his, her moist breath brushing his mouth. His erection pressed nicely between her buttocks, fitting against the soft niche where it so longed to go.

Her hair drifted across his skin, soft and cool and filled with her scent. This was pleasure, pure and simple. He'd not felt this in a long, long time.

The fire cracked, embers smoldering like the heat in

James's veins. She looked up at him, eyes shining and languid.

"You see, love?" he said softly. "I am flesh and bone. Just like you."

He kissed her temple. "I want to tell you some things, Diana, while I have your attention. I wasn't lying when I said we could be good together. I still want that, no matter what happens, understand?" Heat snaked through him. "I want that tall, lovely body you don't bother hiding from me. I want to taste you and make love to you and hear you laugh. I want to see your eyes get all sparkling when you're mad at me."

Her breath came more quickly, her desires spinning faster now.

"I'm going to break you of your habit of being a tease, Diana. I'm not leaving this island until I do."

She made another lovely noise of pleasure. He knew she could not hear him, not really.

"You give and pull away, give and pull away. Before I go, I want you to take me by the hand and show me some long, slow loving. No teasing, no flirting. Just some good, sweet loving because you want it."

Her eyes flew open, and her inner fire took over. She came sweetly, making soft feminine noises, her hand clamping to his like a vise. Her inner muscles squeezed, hurting his fingers, and yet he would not withdraw them for the world.

Her buttocks rubbed on him most dangerously, but he would honor her request. Or rather, her imperious command that hid stark fear. Before he left this island, he'd figure out what she was so afraid of. He'd banish that fear. Because if he didn't, if he was forced to leave before he could have her, he truly would ignite. All that would be left of James Ardmore would be a pile of ash. Diana Worthing would laugh.

She wasn't laughing now. Her face twisted in pleasure, and she whispered his name with low, happy desire.

"That's my girl," he murmured, and they shared a kiss that made the earlier thunderstorm seem like a weak summer shower.

Later alone in his chamber, James watched lightning flickering on the edge of the horizon. The wind had blown the storm away, and the disk of a moon filled the sky with silver light.

He donned his breeches and boots, pulled on his long coat. The feel of Diana and her scent had not left him.

The moonlight pleased him. He would have plenty of light in which to sail around the island and to the huge cave where Diana's father had stashed his smuggled goods. Brandy, nails, rope, innocuous things, the admiral had told him. *Not quite, Admiral.*

No one stirred in the house. He'd left Diana asleep. He'd kissed her forehead and tucked the sheets in around her and departed the room as quietly as he could. She'd not awakened.

James left his chamber and closed the door silently behind him. Just as silently, he made his way down the stairs, avoiding the creaking stair, four from the bottom. He had tasks to accomplish. He could not simply walk away from them because he'd found a woman he wanted to dally with.

The house was utterly silent as James left it. Not a light shone in the windows. The gate clicked when he opened it, squeaked.

He followed the path, clear in the moonlight, down to the beach and around to the cove where the one-masted ship was moored. It bobbed next to a little dock, ropes tying it firmly to the posts. He stepped aboard and cast off.

Here was the test of his recovery. He lifted the oars, slid them into the water, and began to row.

Chapter Nine

James's wound pulled. It hurt, but nothing dire happened. His muscles had knit enough that he could at least row a boat.

Once out of sight of the house, he stashed the oars and raised the sail. Plenty of fresh wind should make his journey fairly simple as long as he avoided rocks. He tied the ropes off firmly, then steered with one hand on the rudder and moved the sail with the other. Not the easiest way to go, but better than nothing.

He searched for the cave opening for an hour and a half. The crack in the rock eluded him, and he ground his teeth. He would lose the moonlight, and he wanted to be back in his bed well before the sun came up.

The island hid its secrets well. Just as James was about to give up and return another night, he noted a gull, white against the black sky, fly past what looked like solid rock, then disappear.

He turned the boat sharply and made for the side of the cliff, never taking his eyes from the spot where the gull had vanished. His vigilance rewarded him. As he drew closer, he saw that one rock protruded slightly in front of another, and between these lay the sliver of an opening.

He dropped the sail and found the oars. He piloted the boat carefully, avoiding the swirls of foam that spoke of rocks beneath. A wave lifted him gently and deposited him inside the cave, scraping the boat against the tiny beach on which he and Diana had stood earlier that day.

He spent a moment remembering the heady rush of what they'd done in this cave. Then he lashed the oars to the bottom of the boat and struck flint and steel to light the candle in the lantern. A breeze rushed down at him from the top of the cave. He looked up at the natural shelves of rock and the many crates resting on them.

The innocuous brandy had rested in barrels on the lower levels, easy to find. More interesting things were probably awaiting him higher. He lifted the lantern to the highest ledge he could reach and climbed up.

Diana had shown him the way earlier today, and he followed it now, climbing ever higher, using the lantern to light his path. He paused on a ledge halfway to the top. Below, the boat rocked, straining its tether on the rocks. Waves sloshed into the cave on cold wind and spray.

James pulled out the pry bar he'd brought from the boat, fitted it under the lid of one crate, and pulled. Screeching, nails gave way. He yanked the wood free, then lifted the lantern and looked inside.

At least twenty muskets, neatly laid side by side, filled the crate. James let out his breath. He was not very surprised.

He opened another crate. More muskets. Methodically, he went through every box on that level. All were muskets. On the next, he found bullets, boxes and boxes of them. On the next, crates full of the little pouches of gunpowder infantrymen would rip open and pour down the barrel of their guns before loading the bullet.

He moved to another level. More crates, more weapons, but these were of French manufacture. James rubbed his upper lip. Another stash of muskets proved to be Prussian.

The admiral was a fool. He'd hoped, since meeting the man, that he'd been wrong.

Last year, when he'd pinpointed Haven as the place he needed to find, he'd assumed the admiral who owned it would be corrupted through and through and as nasty as the man he hunted. This end game should have been easy.

Now, everything was complicated. He liked Admiral Lockwood. The man had every quality James admired, courage and integrity and respectfulness. And then there was Diana.

He kicked a crate. Why had he supposed it would be simple? He should have taken one look at her and run the other way. Or he should have abducted her permanently and locked her up somewhere while he got on with his vendetta. She was making this the hardest thing he'd ever done.

No, what he really should have done was taken her in that tavern in Kent and been done with her. On the table, next to the remains of the soup. Should have turned her skirt up and plunged right in. . . .

She burned with passion—a man could be blind and know that. She sizzled every time he touched her. And yet, he'd not mistaken that flare of unreasonable fear when he'd silently proposed they finish what they'd started.

He snarled, burning with frustration. He shoved one

of the admiral's secret crates to the edge of the rock shelf and toppled it over. It crashed to the bottom of the cave with a satisfactory shatter, breaking open in the water.

He sent the next one down and the next. He moved from ledge to ledge, tossing down crates. Some broke open, others stuck fast in the sand or floated before sinking, water covering them partway.

"Stop!"

Diana's voice soared above the hollow sound of the waves. James looked up. She crouched a few ledges above him, in shirt and breeches and stout boots. Her hair hung in a single braid, and she glared at him over the barrel of her pistol.

He took a step away from the circle of lantern light. "Darlin', you have an uncomfortable fascination with firearms."

"It's loaded this time."

"I'm sure it is." He hooked his foot around the lantern, shoved it from the ledge. The tiny spark of candle floated a few feet, then extinguished, plunging the cave into blackness. The lantern clattered to the crates and rocks below. "I'd not move if I were you," he said companionably. "You might fall in the dark."

"So might you." She sounded as though she would enjoy that.

"What are they for?" he asked. "All these firearms and all the gunpowder, which is now soaking wet?"

Her voice was tight with anger. "For British troops, of course. For their relief on the Peninsula. We are fighting a war with Napoleon, you know."

"Is that what he told you?"

"Why should he lie? These will go to Gibraltar, to be taken north through French lines to British forces."

He smiled in the dark. "The French have pretty much

abandoned southern Spain, did you know that? Your General Wellesley is giving them a good run toward the north. Not long from now, he'll take France itself, I'd bet. He does not need this little stash of British, French, and Prussian weapons."

"French? What are you talking about?"

"This is not a stockpile, Diana. This is plunder."

She laughed once. "What are you accusing my father of now?"

"Pirate activities. I hunt pirates. I know what plunder looks like."

"I was correct before. You are conceited. My father is not a pirate."

"No." He kept his words soft. "I would not have thought so, either. But pirates made this, and I have the feeling pirates will return for it."

As he spoke, he very slowly and carefully lowered himself down to the next ledge. He had to move at a snail's crawl in the dark, but that was fine because he'd make no noise.

"My father is not a pirate," she repeated stubbornly.

"Why did he come out to this island? Such a long way from home?"

"This is his home. He tired of the city, and he'd retired."

James moved farther down the cave. "He was a hero. Lauded for his actions at Trafalgar. He was a damned good sailor. He could be high up in the Admiralty, running the war from the luxury of Whitehall. But he chose to retreat a hundred miles from England. An abrupt decision was it?"

She was silent. He dropped to the bottom of the cave, his boots sloshing in the water. Luminous moonlight flowed through the cave, lighting the rocking boat, shining on the metal edge of the lantern.

He retrieved the lantern, set it gently in the boat. He'd rather do this with light, but then Diana could aim.

He lifted the first crate by touch and heaved it into the boat. Broken crates and muskets littered the floor of the cave. He scooped them up one by one and tossed them into the boat. This would take several trips.

Diana spoke again, her voice shaking. "My father is no traitor."

"I didn't say traitor. I said pirate."

"Why the devil should my father become a pirate?"

"I don't know. Men turn pirate for any number of reasons." He untied the boat. "I intend to ask him."

Silence reigned above. James tossed the ropes into the boat. Now came the tricky part. When he rowed into the moonlight, she would see him and she could shoot. He untied the oars.

He heard the clatter of rock on rock, heard her grunt and gasp as she hurt herself on the ledges. She was climbing down. In the pitch dark with a loaded pistol.

"Stay still, for God's sake, Diana."

"I will not let you make a fool of him."

He leapt from the boat.

She had already begun her descent. He heard rock strike rock, a grunt as her foot slipped. He hastened to her, but she had been climbing through these caves for years. Probably she'd scrambled up and down in the dark as a little girl, helping her father hide his stashes of weapons.

He caught her as she came off the last ledge. One twist to her hand, and the weapon fell with a quiet splash into the water at their feet.

She flailed against him, getting in a few good jabs. He

tightened his grip, dragged her to the boat. Sorry, sweetheart, he thought. He really did feel regret. There was that remorse again.

He lifted her over the gunwale. Her shriek rang above the roiling water. "What are you doing?"

He pulled her to face him, kissed her hard on the mouth. The kiss went on, her neck bending under his assault. She fought back with her own mouth, trying to gain mastery of the kiss, trying to defeat him at his own game.

He ended the battle by pushing her to the bottom of the boat. She was strong, but he was stronger.

She told him exactly what she thought of him. He hadn't heard curses so colorful since leaving the *Argonaut*. She could give Ian O'Malley lessons.

He snatched up the ropes that had bound the oars. Memories of her bedchamber rushed back at him. She'd writhed against him so sweet and hot. Too bad she'd hate him now.

He pushed both her hands around the mast and lashed the rope about her wrists. Not tight enough to hurt her, but tight enough to make her stay put. He contemplated securing her feet, but decided against it. She could kick all she wanted. By the time he loaded the crates, there wouldn't be much room for her to move.

He lifted himself rapidly away and leapt from the boat. She shouted after him, not in the least subdued.

She never would be subdued. He'd found a hellcat, and the trouble with hellcats was there was no safe way to let them go.

He piled the crates and loose guns in the boat as fast as he could, packing them around her. The waves came faster, swirling around his boots. Diana at last fell silent, saving her breath, no doubt, for later.

Only about half the stash would fit. James knew how to balance loads, and he managed this one, giving himself room to climb into the boat and take up the oars.

He pushed off, leapt to the top of the crates at the last minute, and made his way to the bench. Diana lay directly behind him, her feet stretched toward the stern. He took up the oars, bending his back to get the boat out of the cave.

Diana was quiet as they moved out into the sea. Moonlight spilled over the boat and the water, giving the foam a strange luminescence.

She would be cold. The wind had a bite to it, sweeping in from the spent storm and down from the rocks of the island. James shipped the oars, slid his coat from his back and laid it over her. He could keep warm with his labors.

Did she thank him for this kindness? No. She snarled several more insults about him, his habits, his heritage.

Once they were about a mile from the island, where Lieutenant Jack had told him the deep water began, he again shipped the oars. Climbing back over crates, he loosened the anchor and dropped it over the side. He followed that with the first crate. It broke open as he dropped it, and all the guns inside fell to the bottom of the deep blue sea.

"What are you doing?" Diana shouted.

"What I'm best at," James answered. "Confounding pirates."

"Confounding my father. You have no idea what you are doing."

"I have some idea. Keep your head down. I don't want to hit you."

He tossed over crate after crate, the guns that had fallen loose, the smattering of bullets. His muscles worked, sweat accumulating faster than the sharp wind could dry it.

He tossed in the last crate and turned the boat for shore.

Diana ducked her head as the mast's boom swung over her. The sail crackled as it filled with wind. Diana hung on to the mast, hot with fury. The bonds he'd tied were loose enough not to hurt her, but sturdy enough so that she could not get free.

They reached the cave. He filled the boat a second time, and a second time sailed them out to the deep water. Crate after crate went into the sea. James's breathing was hard, and he grunted with effort as he pitched her father's cache into the waiting waves.

She called him every colorful name she knew. She'd grown up with naval men and therefore knew quite a few. To think she had softened to him when he had agreed not to take their fierce flirtation to its logical conclusion. Sir Edward would have raged and either forced her or bathed her in scorn so cutting she bled. James had simply drawn her into his arms and told her to choose her pleasure.

She hadn't even known it could feel like that. He had played her like a skilled musician might play a fine instrument. He'd known exactly how to coax her passion from her and exactly how to soothe it. Of course he did.

Her father ought to have put him in chains as soon as he'd landed. But unless she and her father and Lieutenant Jack and Jessup surrounded James and locked him in the root cellar until June, they could do nothing. Her father was far too compassionate.

Diana's compassion had long since run out.

James made a third run, flung a final armload of weapons into the sea. Then he turned the boat and headed, not to the cave, but to the sandy cove where they usually moored the boat.

Diana lay still, tired of struggling. He tied up the boat on the little landing, furled the sail, stowed the oars, doing everything right to put the boat away.

Not until he was finished did James come for Diana. He slide a knife blade expertly under the ropes, and in one slice had them open. He lifted her under her arms, his grip tight enough so that she could not turn around and kick him. He dragged her from the boat, dumped her on the beach.

As soon as her feet touched the sand, she tore herself from him. "You pox-rotted liar. You seduced me. You thought I would let you rob my father after you made up to me."

"Scream a little louder, Diana," James drawled, calmly sheathing his knife. "I think a few peasants in France didn't hear you."

"I want them to hear me. I want my father to hear exactly what you have done to him. He will arrest you. He will—"

"He'll likely be happy I didn't shovel the whole lot into the sea." He caught Diana's arms. "Listen to me. What he is doing is dangerous. If you let me, I can put that right. I've been wanting to put it right for years."

She jerked away. "What are you talking about?"

"He didn't get these goods here by himself. He had help. I intend to ask him whose help, and then I'm going to hunt down the pirate he names. Simple as that."

"Simple? And then what will you do to my father?"

"What do you want me to do to him?"

"Nothing. I want you to leave him alone."

His face hardened. "I can't do that, darlin'."

"Stop calling me that. Why should he answer to you?"

His eyes flickered, cold as Arctic ice. "Pirates are violent murderers, Diana. If they're threatening him, I'll get him free; if he's collaborating, I'll stop him. No matter what."

"Or you could leave my father alone. Why does a cache of used bits threaten you?"

Moonlight made his gaze, if anything, still remote. "Because I think I know which pirate made that cache. I've suspected for a long time. That's the reason why I wanted to know so much about Haven. I want this pirate, and I'll do anything to get him."

Awful realization suddenly flooded her. "Dear God. My husband, of all people, was right. You did see me at Admiral Burgess's house in Kent. You did kidnap me on purpose."

He nodded, the infuriating man. "That's right. I was there to rescue Kinnaird, but when I spied the daughter of Admiral Lockwood, I saw a good opportunity. I'd have snatched you out of your own bedroom if you hadn't walked right in to Ian O'Malley and made my task easy."

Her heart beat swiftly, sickeningly. "So all along you— I played right into your hands, damn you!"

"I wouldn't say you played into my hands. You wouldn't tell me a blessed thing. Even kissing you didn't soften you up. I didn't particularly want the entire British fleet chasing me, so all I could do was throw you back."

She stared at him for a stunned moment, and then she launched herself at him. "You—" She pummeled his chest. "You *used* me. I let you—" She stopped, forcing away the memory of the hot tightness inside her, of his hands stroking and teasing, of his lips, so warm and gentle. "You are the worst blackguard I have ever known. And I am a bloody fool!"

His large hands closed over hers, stilling them easily. "You're a beautiful lady. Exasperating too."

"Stop trying to flatter me. I'm done with your flattery." She wrenched herself from his grasp. "I will tell my father all you have done tonight. Will you try to stop me?"

"No," he said mildly, his eyes cool "In fact, I'll go with you. We'll tell him together."

She hoped her glare made his insides churn with fury, just like hers did, but his cold eyes betrayed nothing. "Very well," she said, trying to sound frosty and failing miserably.

She turned from him and marched toward the house. She heard him follow, his tread soft, not speaking. The fact that he refused to argue back infuriated her most of all.

Chapter Ten

James was very aware of Diana glaring at him across the room, even though he avoided looking at her. They were in her father's study, windows overlooking the sea, the one in which her father had interrogated him the other night.

Diana sat bolt upright on a chair near the fire. Her father leaned against his desk, dignified even in a dressing gown, and watched James.

James himself could not sit down. His legs just wouldn't bend. But he didn't feel as though standing gave him an advantage. Diana could kill him with her glance no matter what position he was in. The venom in her voice when she'd shouted at him still grated across his nerves.

Go ahead and hate me, Diana. I'm used to it.

Diana had roused her father as soon as she'd reached the house. The admiral had come out of his room, alarmed, and yet, at the same time, calm, as though he'd been expecting this. It had been his suggestion that they convene in his study.

"Well, James," he said quietly. "What do you want me to say?"

"I want you to tell me the name of the pirate who has you working for him."

His eyes hardened. For an instant, James saw where Diana came by her wonderful scorn. Many a lieutenant must have quavered under the admiral's glare.

"I work for no one," he said.

"So you plunder ships and steal booty by yourself, do you?" James was in no mood to be gentle. "In that little gig with your daughter and granddaughter working the tiller?"

"Leave this affair alone," the admiral answered in a cold voice. "It hardly concerns you."

"It does concern me. I am a pirate hunter. Do you have a name to give me? Or do you want me to tell you one?"

"For the sake of my daughter, please leave it alone."

James grew silent. Diana, arms folded, still glared, but her expression betrayed uncertainty. She had truly believed that her father was storing arms for the British army in Spain.

James was realizing that if he hadn't been so abrupt and stupid, he might have found an ally in Diana. She knew nothing of this beyond what her father had told her, and she did not like what she was learning. When he'd abducted her last year, he ought to have told her the truth. James had intended to frighten her into answering questions and then let her go. That plan had gone awry faster than a greased pig at a county fair. He'd made the mistake of thinking her an empty-headed officer's wife, basking in the backwash of her husband's fame. He'd been quickly disabused of that notion.

She'd infuriated him, and he'd wanted to subdue her. After that, he'd just wanted her. James Ardmore, a man famous for his cool ruthlessness, had let his emotions run high. They'd ended up kissing like it was a battle between them. He'd even begged her to come with him on his voyages. He must have been severely crazed to do that.

If he'd simply told Diana instead of getting into that food-throwing argument with her, she might have understood. She had read Paul's diary, seen what James kept locked in the trunk in his cabin. He'd been furious with her about that too.

Paul's very last entry had been a broken-hearted, half-crazed address to his dead wife. James hated that diary, but he'd never been able to throw it away. There was too much of Paul in it, and he did not want to lose even that piece of his brother.

James had found Diana with the diary in his cabin—which she had ransacked to annoy him. Her silk gown had been water-stained and torn, the bodice revealing one very kissable shoulder. She'd looked up at him from his bunk, eyes wet, and whispered, "Who was she?"

He'd snatched the diary from her, locked it away, then dragged her from the cabin and taken her back to shore.

The admiral sighed. He looked very old. "I cannot help you, James. I ask you as one gentleman to another to let things be."

James halted his restless pacing. Diana watched him, daring him to make a move. Even abducting her hadn't made her as mad as she was now.

"I really want to get some sleep tonight," James said, his patience at an end. "So I'll say a name, and you tell me if it's right."

"Very well," the admiral said. "In the interest of sleep."

James folded his arms. He did not want to do this. But

the memory of Paul drove him. After his brother's wife had been raped and killed, Paul never had been quite sane again. James had not been there for him. James owed him.

"Black Jack Mallory," he said.

The admiral's face did not move. But the slightest flicker of eyes told James he was right.

"Did I hear my name?"

In the half-open door stood Lieutenant Jack. He wore breeches and shirt and boots.

Diana's eyes widened, as though she believed the innocent lieutenant to be the pirate in question.

"Come in," the admiral said tiredly. "James is speaking of another Jack."

"If my true name is even Jack." The lieutenant closed the door. "Would you mind telling me what you are discussing? It sounds important."

The admiral said nothing. He looked defeated. Diana, on the other hand, sprang to her feet. "You may leave off bullying my father," she said to James.

"What's going on?" Jack insisted. He stood in the middle of the carpet, folded his arms. "Ardmore, explain yourself." He looked primed to call James out if he didn't like his answers. Damned Englishmen.

"Admiral Lockwood is working with, whether against his will or not, a gentleman by name of Black Jack Mallory," James explained. "Mallory is a pirate. I've been hunting him a while, but he's eluded me. I suspected he used an island in this area for a base. It took me a long time to find it. I didn't realize how close I'd gotten until I was shipwrecked on it."

"Why didn't you simply inquire at the Admiralty?" Jack asked, puzzled. "They'd know about Haven, would they not? Presumably they'd want to be informed about pirate activities involving it."

James gave him an ironic look. "Because the Admiralty is a little reluctant to give me information."

"Why should they be?"

"Because he is James Ardmore," Diana said in ringing tones. "Wanted by the British Admiralty for numerous crimes against the navy. He is a legend, or a notorious criminal, depending on who tells the tale."

Jack said, "I see."

The room went quiet. The fire popped once, and the wind, still fresh from the storm, sang in the chimney.

The lieutenant looked James up and down with no recognition in his eyes. He turned to the admiral, then Diana. "Do you all mind explaining why you did not tell me he was a criminal? Why he is allowed to roam freely here, alone with me, or Isabeau, or Diana?"

"Because"—the admiral sighed—"I trusted him."

Jack looked at James and said conversationally, "Tell me why were you on the frigate with me."

He sounded quiet yet stern, just like a damned aristocrat. Probably he was one. They all spoke with an air of authority, the certainty that they were right. They were in charge, and everyone else had better capitulate. Even James's old rival Grayson Finley, a pirate turned viscount, had that annoying, masterful manner.

"I was a prisoner," James replied. "Your captain caught me helping out some American smugglers. Your ship was heading for Gibraltar to take me to the garrison there."

Jack watched him quietly. "Is this why you refused to tell me the name of my ship? And my own name?"

His eyes held fury. James's information might have triggered some of his memories, if he'd bothered to tell him. James withholding it was like a betrayal, even greater than the revelation that James was a criminal in the eyes of the English.

"The ship was the *Constantine*. That help?"

Jack waited a moment, then shook his head. "I do not remember it. What about my own name?" He looked at James without heat.

"I don't know," James said. "I swear that. You never came off the quarterdeck until the storm, and I never heard the captain address you by name. Your captain was called Christianson, but I don't know anything else."

Jack stared at him a moment longer, then looked away.

"I'm sorry," James said. The words hurt his throat. He so rarely apologized to anyone. Hadn't, in fact, in about a decade.

The admiral broke in. "Perhaps, Diana, you should go to bed."

James hid a snort. The man could not possibly believe his daughter would bow her head and scuttle away.

"I want to hear this, Father," she answered. "Is James right about this Mallory person?"

The admiral studied the carpet. "He is right." He raised his silver head and directed a glance of fury, worthy of Diana herself, at James. "I hardly wished to be exposed in front of my daughter. Could you not have spoken of this to me when we were in private yesterday?"

"I wasn't certain yesterday. And Diana was adamant that you should face me. She wanted to prove me wrong, you see."

Diana's eyes flashed. "Do not dare blame this on me, James Ardmore."

"I'm not blaming you; I'm blaming me. I ought to have left you tied up in the boat. Or locked in your room from the start. I had no idea you'd try to climb down the caves in the pitch dark."

The admiral looked momentarily pained, as though he had long tried to dissuade his daughter from risky endeavors—without success, of course.

"Be that as it may," Lieutenant Jack interrupted, "we all know now." His face was set, hard, but cool. Damn, he had to be an aristocrat. They all had that look of supreme self-confidence, even in the face of stupid odds. "Who is Black Jack Mallory?"

"A violent criminal," James said. "He's an Englishman, who started off as a privateer against French and American ships, and he was sanctioned by the English government. As the admiral knows, the English have always been happy to blockade American ships, something I take high objection to."

The admiral looked annoyed, Diana furious, Jack patiently waiting for information. James went on, "Privateers are encouraged to plunder in the name of British sovereignty. But some of them, like Black Jack, find they like plundering a little too much. So Black Jack decided to go off on his own. The English are after him now, as well as America and France and any other country you care to name." He turned to the admiral. "I find it unbelievable you let him anywhere near your daughter."

The admiral's face was suffused with anger. Lieutenant Jack broke in. "I imagine the admiral did not *let* him do anything."

Diana put her hand to her lips. "Oh, Father. Did he threaten you? You ought to have told me."

"Stop!" the admiral snapped. "If you will let me speak, I will tell you." He calmed himself, drew a breath. "Mallory never threatened me. I helped him willingly."

"Willingly?" James asked in surprise. "The man is a murderer."

"Not any longer, James. He came to me in desperation, and I helped him. I owed him a favor."

James's anger tasted like burned copper. "He rapes and murders women. For the enjoyment of it. Remember when I mentioned a pirate who slit a woman open from throat to crotch because she did not cooperate? Well, I was talking about Black Jack Mallory."

The admiral whitened. "I'll thank you not speak of such things in front of my daughter."

"She has a perfect right to know what company her father keeps."

Diana was staring at him. Not in anger or in anguish, but with a slightly puzzled expression, as though she were fitting pieces together.

"He is no longer who he was, James," the admiral said, tight-lipped. "He saved my life during a battle off the coast of France. We'd lost two ships off the line, and my frigate was the last against most of the French fleet. And then Black Jack Mallory came sailing up. He joined in the fray, and when I was lost overboard, he pulled me out. He told me he was patriotic enough not to want to see the French get the better of brave English vessels. He helped us and the crew of the other two ships get away. When he came to me a few years ago, ill and wretched, I could not turn him away."

"He played upon your sense of honor."

"If you like. I knew what he was. I'm not a fool. He needed help. I gave it to him to repay what he had done for me."

James's anger burned fresh. "By letting him use your island to store his plunder? I found it all, despite the best efforts of you and your daughter."

"Much of it is old," the admiral said. "He used this island before as a bolt hole. Haven belongs to my family, but after Diana married and until I retired, it stood deserted for several years. He has toyed with the idea from time to time that he will turn merchant and sell the things, but he knows no one would deal with him."

Diana said nothing. She only stared at her father, mouth closed. Most unusual for her.

"When is he due to return?" Lieutenant Jack asked.

The admiral did not answer.

James folded his arms. "He can tell you he's reformed all he wants, Admiral, but that does not erase his crimes."

The admiral's eyes were the same color as Diana's and held the same clear intelligence. "I know," he said.

"When Black Jack comes back, he'll find me here. And then I'll decide what I want to do."

"You cannot confront him," the admiral said.

"I can and I will."

Diana gave a harsh laugh. "This from a man who insisted to me that he was not a legend. So you believe you can single-handedly stand against this formidable pirate?"

"I know Black Jack, and I know his habits," James said doggedly. "I've hunted him for a long time."

"And you found Haven," Diana said angrily. "Do not tell me, James Ardmore, that you planned to wreck in that frigate and wash up on our shore."

"No. That was luck." He glanced at the admiral. "I just thought I'd make the most of it."

Diana's glare could have ignited varnish. "You lied. You have lied from beginning to end."

"So did you, Diana. You and your father."

Diana had the grace to look ashamed. Another silence

fell. Outside, the last vestiges of the wind sent a tree limb scraping against the glass.

After a time, Diana said lightly, "I believe Lieutenant Jack is the only honest one among us."

Jack regarded her quietly. "Only because I don't remember enough to lie about. But we have a more immediate problem. Your pirate will be coming back to find that James has destroyed half his plunder. What are we going to do about it?"

James shot him a grateful glance. "I like a man who can keep to the point. I will meet Black Jack Mallory when he comes. With or without your help, Admiral."

"Have you given me a choice?" the admiral said testily.

"Yes." He gave him a cold smile. "You can take Diana and Isabeau and sail far from here. He will know I forced you away and that you did not betray him."

The admiral glared at him like his daughter. James studied each in turn. They were all on their feet, angry at each other and at him. Good. Anger made a man—or woman—stronger than did sorrow. Sorrow would come later.

He knew that when he lay in bed alone, knowing Diana truly hated him, sorrow would come pretty hard.

The next day, Diana lifted a teacake from the plate beside her and hurled it at James's head.

He caught the cake in midair. His eyes remained cool. "What was that for?"

"Just keeping in practice," she answered, lips tight. "Where is my father?"

James took a bite of the cake. "With Lieutenant Jack and Jessup. They are making repairs to the boat."

"Why are you not with them?"

"Because they don't like me much today. And I wanted to talk to you."

He came toward her. She didn't want him to. He was too tall, and his presence edged everything and everyone else out of the room. Including her.

"If you are going to ask me to forgive you," she said waspishly, "know that I will not. Do not bother."

"I wasn't going to."

"Good," she said. She peered up at him. "Why not?"

"Because I haven't done anything I want your forgiveness for."

Hot words tumbled to her lips. Before she could speak, he hauled her to her feet. "Come out and walk with me."

She tried to resist, but he simply pulled her along.

In the garden, Isabeau looked up from where she helped Mrs. Pringle pick spring beans for supper. She jumped up and signed hopefully, "Walk?"

Diana held out her hand. "Come along, Isabeau," she said brightly. "May I borrow her, Mrs. Pringle?"

Mrs. Pringle flashed white teeth in her tanned face. "She's been a good help today."

Diana's heart beat faster as Isabeau clasped her hand and danced a little at her mother's side. *What a coward I am.* She remembered what James said to her the day he'd found the dry caves. "Don't hide behind her. She doesn't deserve that."

Isabeau liked James very much. She'd told Diana so. Mrs. Pringle liked him too. Whenever Diana got flustered about James, Mrs. Pringle would just smile.

Isabeau wanted to climb the steep path behind the house to the highest place on the island, a flat space of overgrown rock from which the entire island could be observed. James did not release Diana's hand until the three of them stood atop the summit. Isabeau climbed onto a black boulder and peered out to sea. James joined her, pulling a spyglass from his pocket and lifting it to his eye.

The day was fine and clear, the breeze, clean. The storm had long since dispersed. White puffs of cloud floated in the sky, and the air was as warm as in early summer. The sea was blue, and Diana could see frolicking dolphins in the distance.

James stood silhouetted with his spyglass against the brilliant sky. The sight of his tall, hard body, coat unbuttoned, pulled her. She remembered the feel of his muscled chest against her back while his large, scarred hands pleasured her. That feeling would not go away.

Her emotions were mixed, confused. She was angry, but not at James. Well, not entirely at James. She was annoyed that he'd not only lied to her, but had so easily succeeded at seducing her. But her father came in for a fair share of the anger in her heart.

"He ought to have told me," she said before she could stop herself.

James lowered the glass and looked at her. He had power in his strong body. Having it at her back, with his arms around her, had been heavenly.

"Fathers like to protect their daughters," he said. "They also don't want to look shameful."

"Perhaps, but I do not like the way you bullied him. Why could you not leave well enough alone? He would not even speak to me this morning."

His eyes went cool. "If I'd left well enough alone, your father would continue to be Mallory's slave. Mallory might claim he's reformed, but I know him. He'll probably murder your father when he's done using him. You are not stupid, Diana. You know it could happen."

"Yes," she said dully.

"With Mallory, it is a certainty. He's done much worse."

Isabeau tugged on James's coat. He looked down at the little girl, and once again, she saw a transformation. The hardened pirate hunter changed into a man who, unused to children, was surprised and pleased that one seemed to like him.

The little wretch simply wanted her grandfather's spyglass. James handed it to her with grave reverence. She put it to her eye in a practiced way and turned to focus on the far horizon.

"I ran away to Haven to find peace," Diana said. "Instead, I found you. Or you found us. I believe God brought you here as a fine joke."

He seemed impervious to her glare. "If he hadn't brought me, I'd have found my own way."

"Humph. All the legends about you have gone to your head, James Ardmore. You think you can do anything."

"Not anything." He came far too close, his body an arm's length away. "Just what I'm best at."

She frowned at him. "Plaguing the life out of me?"

"I enjoy it." His look turned warm. "I believe you enjoy it too."

His unnerving gaze saw right through her. It made her remember his hands on her in the dark of her bedchamber. He knew it did. "You are a conceited, foul-hearted, bas—"

His brows climbed. "In front of your daughter? I'm betting she can read her mama's lips." He gave her his rare smile. "And what fine lips they are."

His smile made his eyes so warm. To others he gave his cool assessment, but Diana caught glimpses of the man inside. Or perhaps he let her see on purpose to unnerve her.

131

She darted a hasty glance at Isabeau. The little girl was still staring out to sea through the glass, humming a tune in her throat.

James said, "You have beautiful lips, Diana."

"I know," she answered, her temper rising. "I've had poems written about them. And an ode to my eyebrows."

Chapter Eleven

He stopped. For a moment, she thought he would laugh, but he merely stared at her with his green, green eyes. "I could imagine far better things to write an ode to than your eyebrows. For instance . . ." He brushed his palm over her bosom, cupping her breast fleetingly before letting his hand drop.

She swallowed. "The poetry was not very good."

"Then I can understand why you ran off out here. I would too, if I kept hearing bad poetry about my eyebrows." His amusement faded. "They didn't appreciate you, Diana." He brushed her cheek. "I appreciate everything about you. I hope to make you understand that."

His touch drew fire. He was tall and strong and every time he touched her, she felt strong too. She wanted to hate him for exposing her father, for bringing forth that worried light in her father's eyes.

But Diana had seen what James Ardmore kept in his trunk in his cabin, she had read the diary that had belonged to his brother, she had seen his face when he'd come in and found her reading it. She believed she knew why he'd tracked Black Jack Mallory to Haven. She believed she knew why he'd been helping the smugglers who had been sailing near Haven, even why he'd given himself up to the English frigate without a struggle. There'd been a chance that the frigate would sail near or even call at Haven, and then he could make his escape. . . .

He was here not because of her father, or because of her, or because of Haven. He was here because of Black Jack Mallory. He was hunting, just as a man in India might hunt a tiger or a man in the Americas might track a bear. He was hunting, and Haven was his hunter's blind.

What she and James had shared last night, after the storm and before he'd gone to the caves, had changed. She was hopelessly smitten with him, but she understood now that he'd never completely lose himself to her. He was too complex a man, and too many things drove him.

He never once asked her why she had been so frightened when he'd offered to take her to bed. He had watched her speculatively, but never broached her privacy to ask. She did not know how to tell him that if he wanted to play as they had on her bed, she would not mind. She would learn all his games, as long as she was in no danger of conceiving again. She'd made a brutal mess of her first go at motherhood. God knew what she'd do the second time.

He cut into her silence. "I intend to show you how much I appreciate you. Last night was just a taste." His green eyes held heat.

His words, and his bloody arrogance, both excited her and fueled her temper. "I have felt desire," she said. "I was married."

"To the cold-hearted Edward Worthing. He never gave

you what you wanted. If he had, you wouldn't be such a firecracker."

"We are back to only you being able to fulfill my needs."

He brushed his thumb across her lower lip. "It's true. I think I'll have to pleasure you again and again and again before your fire is quenched. I hope that takes a long, long time."

Diana hoped so too. Last night, even through her fury at him and her father, she'd dreamed of the drowsy pleasure of James's hands on her body. The dreams had nearly driven her mad, and she'd awoken sweating and tangled in the sheets. A tight twist of them had pressed hard to the hotness between her legs.

She unconsciously leaned toward him. Her tongue darted out to taste the tip of his fingers.

His eyes darkened, and he leaned to her, his coffee-scented breath brushing her skin.

"No," she murmured. "Isabeau."

"Is watching the water and isn't interested in fools of adults."

That was probably true. She turned her head and met his lips. He smiled into the kiss, then cradled her head in his palm and drew her to him.

He explored her mouth, every corner of it, with warm, slow strokes. She smoothed his hair, warm and rough under her fingers. He had charmed her all the way through her frivolous heart. She was a fool, but right now foolishness was making her happier than she had been in a long, long time.

Conscious of Isabeau, who truly was far more interested in what lay on the horizon than James Ardmore kissing her mother, Diana eased away.

He smoothed her hair, his breath warm on her temple.

"A lady told me, not long ago, that out on the waves somewhere I'd find the woman of my dreams. I thought she was being dramatic because she likes that. But she was right."

Diana looked at him, surprised, and half pleased. "What lady was that?"

"Her name was Alexandra Alastair. Until she married, that is. Now she's Viscountess Stoke, God help her."

The name sounded familiar. Diana frowned, and then her eyes widened. Alexandra Alastair had been the granddaughter of a duke and daughter of a wealthy gentleman of Kent. After being widowed, Mrs. Alastair had married again, this time to the mysterious Viscount Stoke.

Sir Edward had been invited to the wedding, but he had been to sea at the time, and Diana had not wanted to attend alone, which would only have fueled gossip. Alexandra Alastair and the viscount were rather above her in social rank and she had not known them personally. However, she had read with interest the articles describing their rather peculiar wedding at St. George's, Hanover Square.

She looked at James curiously. "How on earth did you know Mrs. Alastair?"

His look became enigmatic. "It's a long story. The viscount she married was a grinning idiot called Grayson Finley. Once upon a time, he was my partner and friend. Then we became great rivals, and finally, enemies."

She thought a moment. "I remember hearing rumors that the viscount had been a pirate. I hadn't believed them." She peered at him. "I do not know why I am surprised that you know him. I should not be surprised by anything you do."

"He was a pirate," James affirmed. "One of the best.

I used to hunt him. Caught him a few times, but he always managed to slip from the noose."

"Are you still hunting him?" she asked cautiously.

"I gave it up. For the sake of his lovely wife."

Diana breathed a little faster. "But he truly was a pirate?"

"Probably still is. He still sails around in that ship of his, though he claims he's only keeping it for his daughter."

Diana recalled now the tittering gossip about the daughter the viscount had brought home with him. Half foreign they said, from some South Sea island. She remembered high-bred ladies making very rude speculations about the girl's origins, and felt a dart of sympathy for her. Mayfair was intolerant of any person who was different, as she had cruelly learned when Isabeau had lost her hearing.

Diana's curiosity was thoroughly aroused, but their gossip was cut short by Isabeau, who turned and tugged on James's coat again. She squealed and signed, then pointed to the water.

"What is she saying?" James asked, even as his alert gaze went to the horizon.

"The sign means 'ship,' " Diana said, her limbs tightening.

James took the glass from Isabeau, climbed up beside her, and peered through it. Diana's heart beat faster. James had thoroughly distracted her, damn him, from the pirates and her father and their danger. She fumed at herself for letting him.

"What do you see?" she asked sharply.

"It's way off," he replied, the glass trained on one seemingly empty spot.

She had her hand out for the spyglass even before he lowered it. "Let me see."

He handed it to her, looking amused. She raised the glass, fiddled with it until she trained it on the tiny dot James and Isabeau had spotted. She stared at the tiny ship until she thought her eye would pop out.

James gently pried the glass from her hand. "Don't hurt yourself." He handed the spyglass back to Isabeau, who eagerly sought the ship again. She, at least, thought it only a fun game.

"We'll watch him," he said. "Don't worry. We'll see him a long time before he makes shore."

"And then what? You'll challenge him to a duel?"

"I do have a plan, Diana. I'm not going to let him have this island or harm your father."

"Do you?" She folded her arms. "What is it then?"

Again, his gaze became unreadable, his thoughts closing to her. "I am not going to tell you. The nature of a plan is not to follow it too closely. And not to anticipate. I have many contingencies based on what Mallory says or what he does or who is with him."

"You mean, you're going to make it up as you go along."

The corners of his mouth twitched. "A little bit."

"You could at least tell me a the basis of the plan. So I will be ready for it."

He slid his arm about her waist. Trying to distract her again, and doing a fine job. She rested her head on his shoulder, her body simply doing it without her permission.

"Your part in the plan will be simple. You and Isabeau will be hiding in the house, and you will not come out until everything is finished."

"Oh, thank you very much. So you wish me to wait

wringing my hands not knowing whether Mallory has murdered you and my father until he drags me out of hiding?"

"I know it's hard." He eased his hand down her back. "But I can't take the chance that Mallory won't try to use you or Isabeau to get around me or your father. He would do whatever it took, and he would not care about hurting either of you."

His gaze had gone remote, his voice, as cold as it had been when she'd first encountered James Ardmore the pirate hunter. "And if anything happened to you—"

He broke off. His voice had been quiet, but suddenly the mask dissolved, and Diana saw in the depths of his eyes a pain so raw and old that she barely understood it. This man hurt, and he hurt all the time. He hid it, she suddenly realized, behind his coldness and sardonic humor and the flares of passion he sometimes let her see.

She wanted to reach for him, to go to him, but the cold rose again, shutting her out. He turned on his heel and walked away, the chill wind stirring his hair and the tails of his coat.

For a week, the ship hovered on the horizon, coming no nearer to Haven, yet not drifting away. During that week, James remained remote and elusive. He and Lieutenant Jack and her father often closeted themselves in her father's study. Planning their strategy, she assumed, although she often heard the clink of the brandy decanter and smelled thick cheroot smoke. Male rituals, she'd think, rolling her eyes, designed mostly to exclude females.

Diana busied herself helping Mrs. Pringle and Jessup keep house, and hunting for the small mirror Mrs. Pringle had kept hanging in the kitchen. The mirror had gone mysteriously missing. Isabeau loudly protested her innocence. It never turned up.

On the afternoon of the sixth day, James descended from the island's summit to tell them that the ship had turned and was heading straight for Haven. Diana experienced a moment of watery, unthinking panic.

Her father, Lieutenant Jack, and Jessup made ready to follow James's orders. The admiral wore a haunted expression, but Jack seemed to have been swayed to James's side. The two of them loaded pistols with looks of grim anticipation. The admiral would not speak to any of them, but he had insisted on accompanying them to meet the ship.

James surveyed them with eyes like ice. He had resumed the role of the pirate hunter, damned if he'd let anyone stand in his way. His cool arrogance made her furious.

"If you get yourself killed, I will never forgive you," Diana snapped at him.

"Then I'll stay alive," he returned calmly. "The last thing I want is you scolding me for eternity."

She glared, and he returned the look unblinkingly. Then he turned away and was gone.

"Men!" Diana exclaimed as she watched them stride away. She dashed the tears from her eyes and swung back to Mrs. Pringle and Isabeau, who stood behind her. "Pox on the lot of them. They run off to face the danger and leave us to pick up the pieces." Isabeau watched her, puzzled, but Diana could see that Mrs. Pringle, scowling at the retreating backs, firmly agreed with her.

James felt only tightening fury as he, the admiral, and Lieutenant Jack made their way down to the boat. They were to row around to the caves while Jessup would descend later after sending James's signal.

His anger rose until his vision was red around the edges, and he had to stop, panting, halfway to the cave. He had to remain calm, play out the scene with the icy coolness that made James Ardmore famous. But he was perilously close to igniting. He'd hunted Black Jack Mallory for years, and to at last have the chance to get his hands on the man's neck made James almost sick with eagerness. The admiral would have to understand. This was James's fight.

The water and sand outside the cave were bright, but inside was nearly black, and that was where he and Lieutenant Jack and the admiral waited.

He glanced at the lieutenant now, and Jack nodded back, his face grim. James had offered to let Jack stay out of it, but the Englishman had refused. James knew that partly the lieutenant felt useless, and indeed, twice more that week, had been laid low with headaches that had left him weak and sick. But the man had a natural gift for strategy, and he and James had worked out several scenarios for dealing with Mallory.

James had made certain that the admiral had not gotten a clear view of the approaching ship. He wondered what the admiral would do the moment James revealed he knew the truth. Shoot James? He'd have to explain to Diana, and James didn't envy any man that.

Rock clicked on rock. All three men looked up, but it was only Jessup, descending through the rocky caves. Right on time.

The man reached ground and trudged to the other three. "Did what you asked," he said in his scraping voice.

"Good," James answered. His fury filled his lungs,

making breathing hurt. He stepped forward, brought up his pistol, and put it against Jessup's forehead.

Jessup looked at the pistol for a startled moment, and then his face drained of color. "Damn," he said.

Chapter Twelve

Lieutenant Jack, to his credit, did not even flinch. The admiral flushed, but his eyes remained defiant. "This man is under my protection, James."

Silence fell in the cave, broken only by the hollow boom of the waves and a gull crying as it swept past the entrance.

James's pistol never moved. Finger tight on the trigger, he kept it against Black Jack Mallory's forehead. The man met his eyes, quieted.

"You know, I really liked you, Admiral," James said slowly. "I'd never seen Black Jack face to face, so it took me a while to catch on. If you'd have told me, I could have saved us a whole lot of trouble."

Admiral Lockwood's eyes held sorrow. "I cannot let you kill him."

"Why not?" Lieutenant Jack asked. "From all Ardmore has said, he is a killer himself."

"A brutal killer," James said grimly. "I don't think I can forgive you for letting this man near your daughter. She thinks he's your friend and such a help to you.

You've left her alone with him. That has me mighty riled."

"He *is* a friend. And a help."

Anger burned through James like lava through trees on a South Sea island. "He is a pirate who would think nothing of cutting your pretty daughter to ribbons."

Black Jack didn't move. "That was a long time ago. I'm not a pirate anymore."

"Well now, I'm sure the women and children you murdered will rest easier knowing that."

James took a second pistol from its holster. He cocked it. Black Jack watched him.

"James," Admiral Lockwood said, his voice stern.

The affable man who'd called himself Jessup looked haggard and exhausted. His dark blue eyes were ringed with shadows.

"You need to go back to the house, Admiral," James cut in. "While Black Jack and I have a conversation."

"Let it go, James."

"Now, I can't do that."

Admiral Lockwood also looked tired. "I made a promise. He came to me for help, and I honored his plea. What's more, he has become a friend. He could have killed or betrayed me many times, and he chose not to. He has told me what he was and of his remorse for what he has done. That was the past. Let him live in the present."

Remorse. That word again. James Ardmore felt no remorse. Black Jack Mallory should feel a lifetime of it.

His finger shook on the trigger. "What happened is this, Admiral. His crew threw him off his ship. That's what pirates do when they want a new captain—they hold an election. It's real democratic. They elect a new captain, and that captain gets to say what happens to the old one. Sometimes they kill him, but most of the time they just toss him off and say good-bye." For the entire exchange, he'd held his gaze steadily on Mallory. "The *Argonaut* caught up with your ship about a year ago. My crew enjoyed themselves, but old Black Jack was gone. So I decided to go hunting on my own."

The admiral's face whitened. "Regardless of what happened, he nearly died. I found him, half-starved and ill. I nursed him back to health and told him he could live here and help me. He has done just that. He has become a loyal companion and a friend."

Hatred nursed for a dozen years ate through James's veins. He shook with it. He was almost sick with it.

"Friend, is he? Mallory and his pack destroyed my brother's life. Did you know that? They were a fine, happy family, my brother with his beautiful wife and two pretty daughters. And then Black Jack Mallory came along. Do you feel remorse about that? Murdering a woman and her two daughters just for fun? My brother turned into a madman. Even I could never match his drive for vengeance, and mine is pretty good."

Mallory returned his look quietly. "Maybe I did that. I was drunk most of the time. I know I did some pretty bad things."

James barked a laugh. "Does the fact that you can't remember mean you don't have to pay for what you did?"

"No," Mallory whispered.

"James," said Admiral Lockwood.

"Admiral, I'd be obliged if you'd shut up."

"You will not allow me to plead for a man's life?"

"Any other man, yes. Not this one."

Water swirled at their feet, cold as ice. From above, James thought he heard a soft noise. Diana. He knew she was up there somewhere, listening. She would never stay tamely in the house just because he'd ordered her to. She'd have followed Mallory to the opening far above, stayed there when he descended.

"Lieutenant," he said. "Take the admiral back to the house."

"I think I should stay," Lieutenant Jack said. "His ship is on its way in any case."

"That's not his ship," James answered. "It's one of mine. The captain owes me some favors. I asked him to stop by in case I needed help."

Lieutenant Jack looked at him, his mild brown eyes now filled with hard anger. "So you lied to us all this time, did you?

"If you're waiting for an apology, I'm not giving you one."

Jack lowered his pistol. "I had made up my mind that you had honor."

"I don't give a damn about honor."

"That's why I'm staying."

James's precarious temper splintered. He brought up his second pistol and shot the pirate Mallory through the fleshy part of the arm. Black Jack cried out, clamped his hand to the spreading scarlet stain.

The admiral took a step forward. James thrust his other pistol against Black Jack's throat. "Stay away."

"James—"

In an abrupt move, James dropped his spent pistol, twisted Lieutenant Jack's from his grip. He brought both up. "See, I'm about to become very violent. If you stay, I just might have to shoot you too."

Lieutenant Jack stared at him, white to the lips. A deep anger stirred in his eyes, one that James had not seen there before.

"James!"

The word echoed from above, clear and feminine. It trembled through the cavern, then was lost on the next crash of the sea.

"Diana knows," James said, "why I became a pirate hunter. Do any of you?"

"No," Mallory answered, his voice filled with pain.

"I made a promise to my brother. Do you know why *he* became a pirate hunter?"

Mallory breathed shallowly. "No."

"Because of you." James had left Paul's diary far away on the *Argonaut,* but he did not need it. He could recite every word of it by heart. *"They cut her,"* he began, reciting the words his brother had written so long ago. *"Because she would not do what they said. She did everything to spare my daughters, but they took them all the same. Just babies, with dark curls and their grandmother's green eyes. I lie awake sometimes thinking how terrified they must have been, my girls and my lady, who'd known only gentleness. I go to church and hear about forgiveness, but there is no forgiveness in my heart. When I find this man, whoever he may be, he will know what wrath means."*

The words resounded through the watery caves, each one slinging back toward them. He imagined Diana, clinging to the rocks above, watching him with her heart in her beautiful eyes. She had read the words too, had felt the pain in them.

"Paul never knew the identity of the man who'd murdered his wife," he went on. "When he died, he made me promise I'd continue the search. I hunted all over the world until I found Black Jack Mallory. You ran for a long time," James said. "But I still found you."

Mallory's face was still. "I didn't know. I don't remember."

"But I remember. And Paul remembers. And I'm sure his wife remembers."

A thin skin of water rushed at their feet. The gull ducked past the entrance again, its scream echoing through the high caves.

Mallory swallowed, his face gray. "Go ahead and kill me."

The admiral waited, tense. James sensed Diana holding her breath, high above. He could feel her blue-gray gaze waiting in the darkness.

He could pull the trigger, and Black Jack Mallory would die. The man who had killed Paul's wife and destroyed the Ardmore family.

Diana's father had given Black Jack Mallory parole on this island. This Haven. Likewise the admiral had given Lieutenant Jack a place to heal. He had given James parole as well.

James did not believe in remorse. James Ardmore pursued his course, no matter what the personal cost.

He remembered how, on the first day he'd awakened here, Diana had said something about calling Jessup to change his bandages. That meant that Black Jack Mallory had helped Diana and her father nurse him back to life. The man had helped nurse Lieutenant Jack as well.

"Why the hell," he asked Mallory, "didn't you try to kill me right away? You must have known who I was."

"You were hurt and needed help." Mallory replied, face straight. Blood seeped from his arm, staining the water at their feet.

So much blood. James firmed his shaking finger. He lifted the pistol from Mallory's throat and fired straight out of the cave.

Sound exploded and reverberated up and down the caves. High above, he thought he heard Diana gasp.

He flung the spent pistol into the water and strode from the cave. The bright light outside pounded into his head and nearly made him sick. The waves tossed the boat that waited for him in the sunshine. He climbed into it and rowed away, alone.

Diana lay flat on her back in bed, staring unseeing at the ceiling when she heard James return at last. It was well past midnight, and all the others had gone to bed, including her father and Mallory. Mrs. Pringle had dressed Mallory's arm, her face grim, and they'd given him laudanum for his pain.

At dusk, James still had not returned. She could not spy him from the island's summit, though she knew the island held places hidden from view. She had found on the summit, tucked under scrub, the kitchen mirror, which James had obviously used to signal the ship. Not a pirate ship, her father had explained, but a French frigate. That ship had faded over the horizon at sunset, and Diana spent the following dark hours wondering if James was on it.

She had heard every word of his exchange with her father and the man she'd known as Jessup. She'd burned with anger at her father for hiding Black Jack Mallory's identity all this time. She was furious, and yet, the man was still the Jessup who collected shells with her and Isabeau, fished with her father for their supper, and had helped her save James's life.

She had watched James fire his pistol out to sea, walk out of the caves. He had chosen, and she knew what that decision had cost him.

She'd gone to her room after putting Isabeau to bed.

Mrs. Pringle had insisted Diana change into her night-dress and be tucked in, and Diana had obliged her. After Mrs. Pringle had gone, Diana rose again and spent the next few hours at her window in the dark, watching the path from the cove.

Tiredness had sent her to at least lie on the bed, but she'd not slept, her ears straining for any little sound of his return.

She heard it now, the creak of the garden gate, his firm footfalls on the path, the soft scrape of the door as it opened.

She lay still, heart hammering. Should she go to him or leave him be? Rail at him for frightening her half to death? Or lie here in the dark wondering what he would do?

Her heart told her to run to him, but her heart had been wrong before. Most of the time, in fact.

She wondered if the others lay awake listening as well, or if they had succumbed to their exhaustion. Only Isabeau had seemed immune—everyone was safe, so why was no one happy?

Boards creaked as James reached the landing; his soft footsteps sounded as he entered his room at the head of the stairs. For a while, all was silent.

She heard the sound of splashing water. It made a tinny sloshing noise in his basin. Mrs. Pringle every night left water and a sponge in everyone's room, so they could wash themselves before retiring or upon rising as they pleased. Saved her the trouble of hauling water upstairs in the morning when she needed to begin breakfast.

Diana imagined him soaking the great sponge, then letting the water flow over his naked body, washing the sand and sweat and dirt from his skin. He would wash from himself the frustration of the day, wetting his skin, his hair dark with water.

She listened to the crash of water in the bowl as he wrung out the sponge, the trickling sound as he skimmed the sponge over his body, the slosh as he dropped the sponge back into the water.

It went on for some time. *Crash, trickle, splash. Crash, trickle, splash.* He would stop soon, dry himself off with the rather threadbare towels, lay himself on the bed, try to sleep.

Minutes went by. The moon moved to beam straight into her window, and she knew it also beamed straight into his. *Crash, trickle, splash.* Steady, monotonous, unhurried, unceasing.

Diana rose from the bed. Her feet found slippers, but she was too agitated to fumble for her dressing gown. She shuffled across the room and out, then across the landing to James's narrow bedchamber. She pushed open the door as the water crashed into the basin again.

He stood with his back to her. Moonlight glistened on his wet shoulders, the shadow of his spine as it dipped to his narrow waist, the pale firmness of his buttocks. Shadows played on his muscular legs and on the sinews of his arm.

Water covered the floor. More rained to it as he stroked the sponge from wrist to shoulder. His long hair lay flat and wet against his head and neck, the ends dripping rivulets down his back. He did not turn his head, did not acknowledge her as she stepped into the room and closed the door behind her.

She eased her slippers from her feet and walked barefoot across the sodden floor to him. The basin rested on a stand Mrs. Pringle had brought up. The small rug in front of it was soaked. He dredged the sponge back in the basin as she stepped in front of him and closed her hand over it.

He lifted his eyes, his lashes spiky with water. What she saw in his gaze gave her a qualm. His eyes were blank, dark pools devoid of emotion. He looked at her, and through her. He made no move to take the sponge from her, but simply let her hold it beneath the water of the basin.

"James," she breathed. "Let me."

He dropped his hand to his side. Water rained from his fingertips, pattering softly on the floor.

She squeezed out the sponge, her hands shaking. He stood silently, watching her. She wiped the water over his throat, down the muscles of his chest to his tight abdomen. The bandage was long since gone, and a long pinkish streak creased his skin from his side nearly to his groin. She eased the sponge across it, then drew it back up to his shoulders.

He simply watched her. She filled the sponge again and moved to his back. She smoothed water across his shoulder blades, all the way down his spine, over his buttocks. He never moved. She circled him again, this time washing his arms, each from shoulder to fingertips, taking her time.

She sponged off his sides, circling the sponge over his waist. She moved it up to his throat, massaging slowly, as he closed his eyes.

Her nightdress was wet by now, and perspiration curled the wisps of hair about her forehead. She squeezed out the sponge again, then, her heart beating faster, she sank to her knees to wash his thighs.

He was not unmoved by what she did. His erection was already long and hard. His beautiful, smooth organ she'd seen at the cave when she'd commanded him to bare himself.

Pretending to ignore it, she slid the sponge down his thigh and over his muscular calf. Her nightdress soaked up the water from the floor, wetting her knees. She moved the sponge to his other leg, washing it slowly.

There, she was finished. She could rise now. Except she could not take her eyes from him. His erection was firm and stiff, the balls beneath it tight. Curls of hair coiled with water surrounded it.

She studied his shaft for a long time, watching moon shadows play across it. His pulse beat there, rhythmic and hard. She drew a breath, leaned forward, and licked the tip of it.

He tasted wet and velvety, and the ridge between the tip and the rest felt smooth to her tongue. She licked down, tasting him all the way to his balls.

His body went rigid. "Damn, Diana. I'm not dead yet."

He gripped her elbows and hauled her to her feet. His eyes were alight, flaring with desire and anger.

She dropped the sponge into the water. "There," she said shakily. "Finished."

His muscular arms slid around her back and ground her to him. "I will say when we're finished."

The kiss was brutal. He meant to punish her. She hadn't left him in peace to wash his skin raw. She'd come to him and awakened him, and he was angry.

She realized that even in the public house in Kent, when he'd snarled at her, his kiss had held playfulness, even a tenderness. All tenderness was gone from him now. This was a cruel man, this pirate hunter, who answered to no rules but his own.

He furrowed her hair, fingers twisting, pulling her head back until her neck ached. His wet body was hard against hers, soaking the front of her nightdress and her skin beneath.

He explored her in long, hard strokes of his tongue. His fingers bruised her back, his grip tightening until she could scarcely breathe. "Tell me you love me, Diana," he said fiercely, lips brushing hers. "Tell me that."

"I love you, James," she gasped.

He wrenched away from her. She fell against the high mattress of the bed, breathing hard. He pressed his balled hands to his chest. "There is nothing here to love."

She shook her head. "It's true. I love you, James."

"Stop," he snarled.

"You told me to say it. Do you think I *want* to love you?"

"You know nothing about love. You loved that idiot Edward Worthing."

"I thought I did. I discovered my mistake."

"What you feel now is a mistake." He could sneer better than Edward ever could. James Ardmore could have given Edward lessons.

"I learned what love is. Isabeau taught me that. She showed me the difference between love and infatuation."

"Really? Suppose you tell me what it is."

She steadied her voice. "Infatuation means you want the other person to pay attention to you, that you will do anything for their attention. Love means that you will change the entire world, even if it costs you your life, to make it better for that other person." She lifted her chin. "That is how I feel about Isabeau. And it is how I feel about you."

His chest rose and fell. "Don't you dare try to change life for me. I like my life just fine."

She laughed, softening it so the sound would not carry. "You do not."

"Don't you dare do anything for me."

Her throat ached with unshed tears. "You do not have to love me back, it is all right." She laughed again, harshly. "No, it is not all right. It hurts like fire, but what am I to do? I cannot force you to love me."

"You can try."

She blinked. "What?"

His scowl was fearsome. "If you love me so much, let me have you."

Her heart beat faster. Her old fear streaked through her, but it faded just as suddenly. This was different. This was need. "Why would that help?"

"You came in here to make me want you. Well, you did it, just like you knew you would. Why don't you finish it? Make my world better, Diana. Then you'll learn about love."

She balled her fists, the heat of desire fanning itself into anger. "Why do you do this? Every time I soften to you, you make me lose my temper."

"I don't want you to soften to me. I can take your tantrums and you throwing dinner at me better than I can take you looking me in the eye and telling me how you really feel."

She wanted to lift the basin of water and dump it over his head. "I am so sorry I have upset you. Are you telling me I'm not *allowed* to love you?"

He snarled, "Love has done nothing but cut me open."

Her gaze strayed to the healing scar on his side, but she knew what he meant. It had cut her to the bone as well. "Love is supposed to heal us," she whispered.

"I don't want to talk about healing. Stop crying."

The tears she'd held in spilled from her eyes. "I do not have to obey every word you say."

"Damn stubborn woman. I want you, Diana. I'm burning with it. Whenever you get mad at me, it just fires my blood. If you don't want me to take you, get out of this room."

She wiped the tears from her cheeks, but more just poured down. "Perhaps I do not want to go."

"Then you'd better get on the bed if you want to land somewhere soft."

He stood rigid, his erection hard, his muscles tense. Diana quietly unbuttoned her nightdress and slid it off over her head.

Chapter Thirteen

James hadn't thought his heart could beat any faster, but it did. It throbbed and pounded until he could barely hear the soft swish of the nightdress as it landed on the floor.

Moonlight touched her long, slim limbs, the thick braid of hair falling over her shoulder, her curved hips, probably a little wider than she liked them. Breasts round and taut. Fists clenched like his, her exquisite face set in stubborn lines. Tears glistened on her cheeks.

"Get on the bed," he repeated. He was amazed his voice was so calm. "Or it will be the floor, and it's wet."

For a moment, she did not move. He took a step toward her. She turned and scrambled up to the top of the mattress, her red braid swinging.

God, she made him want to swear and shout and laugh all at the same time. Standing there bleating about how he didn't love her. Was she blind or stupid?

No, just confused. Like he was.

He never remembered how he got himself up on the bed, but he was beside her sinking into the lumpy mattress that he'd slept on now for more than a month.

When Diana Worthing had first thrown a hunk of bread at him, he'd imagined taking her in some creative, seductive way that would last all night long and well into the morning. But coherent thought had long since left his head, and he could only react with desire. He had once reflected that Diana stirred ancient mating desires in males, and those desires sure stirred now.

Lying down with her seemed far too tame. He dragged her to her knees. She leaned against his arm, her lips parting, eyes half closed in passion.

Fire, yes, she had it. He wondered how he'd been so polite to her so far, so restrained. She wouldn't have called it restrained, but she didn't know him, did she?

Then again, she knew him better than anyone had in his life.

He wanted her with a primal urge he'd not felt in years and years. He'd grown cynical about women, learning to satisfy his appetites on the parade of ladies who threw themselves at him, while closing the door on any of his feelings. He'd learned to completely separate the act of lovemaking from emotion.

Diana had broken down his door. He shouldn't have let her, but it was too late now.

Emotions poured through him, rage and hate and anguish and heartbreak. She knew what he had done and why, and why it had almost killed him.

Her skin was as wet as his, her face damp, her hair curling and slipping from its braid. He caught her tears on his tongue, the salty taste driving his frenzy tighter. He loved the taste and the scent of this woman. She wrapped her arms around his neck and kissed his lips.

His madness would not let him be slow. Slow would come later. He slid her knees apart. His throbbing arousal stood straight up, the focus of the madness inside him.

She gasped. He saw the fear rise in her eyes, felt the tensing of her muscles.

He needed her. His body screamed for her. His hands shook as he held her back. "Why?" he said viciously. "Tell me why."

Her answer came rapidly. "I do not want to have another child."

He stopped. Her eyes were wide, blue-gray shadowed by pain. "Is that all?"

"Yes," she whispered.

He would have laughed, except it would have hurt. "Then you're in luck, my fine Diana. You will never conceive with my seed."

She said a surprised, "Oh," and then he was tired of waiting.

She fit neatly on top of him. She was so slick and hot that he went right inside, no barriers.

"You're tight," he whispered into her skin. "I like you being tight."

She closed her eyes, her nails sinking into his back. He licked the moisture from beneath her breasts, chasing a droplet with his tongue.

She squeezed him, and he kissed her skin and took her nipple between his teeth. She threaded her fingers through his wet hair. He wanted to be in, in, in, farther and farther. She drove him wild. He felt like a cocoon enclosed him and he was striving to batter it apart and break free. He was almost there, almost there. *Diana, what did you do to me, you demon witch of a woman?*

"James," she whispered, and then her voice broke as she started to come. "I love you."

Oh, damn you. He didn't know he'd said the words out loud until he heard the echo. She opened her eyes. The blue-gray darkened with passion and also with hurt.

159

He cupped her hips, pulled her hard on him. "Eat me alive, why don't you?"

He rose, lifting her, and then he dumped her onto her back and forced her into the mattress. He was still in her, and everything was hot and dripping, his skin still wet from his bath, hers from him and her sweat. He drove himself in, fiercely finishing what he'd begun.

This coming was like none he'd ever experienced. A wave of pure exultation poured over him. He could live forever or die right here, he scarcely cared. He did not notice the lumps in the bed, the cold breeze from the window, or the rain of droplets from his hair to his skin. He did not notice the narrow room, the moonlight on the spilled water, the confines of the tumbled bed.

He felt only her, her braid about his throat, and the burning of his lungs. Only her, and she was the only person in his world, always had been and always would be.

He had no idea what he shouted, but his throat was hoarse with it, and he was shaking all over, and she was crying.

He collapsed on her, still inside. He kissed her eyelids and her wet cheeks, and murmured a few broken, soothing sounds, before sleep hit him like a pile of boulders.

Sometime in the night, he must have dismounted her, because when James woke again, he was lying on his side, breathing the fragrance of her hair. Diana's fine backside fit right against him.

They were both naked, piled haphazardly on top of the bed. One of his arms draped heavily over her, the other thrust beneath the pillow to cradle his head. Diana was asleep.

As gently as he could, so not to wake her, James

reached for the crumpled coverlet and pulled it over them both. Her heavy, even breathing did not break.

She was exhausted, poor woman. She'd had a hell of a day. James settled back down beside her, letting his limbs go slack. He'd had a hell of a day too, but it did not seem important anymore. He felt as though someone had scrubbed him inside and out.

He'd made a choice, and he hated himself for it. If he had made the other choice, Diana would have hated him. He'd have been gone by now, partway to France on the frigate, and she would have hated him. Instead, she was here against him, her face eased in sleep.

His half-awake mind dimly remembered how Grayson Finley, a pirate who'd roamed most of the world with his John Thomas out of his trousers, had told him, his eyes serious, that what he felt for Alexandra Alastair was different. James hadn't believed him. He'd known that the lovely Mrs. Alastair was an extraordinary woman, but he'd dismissed Finley's declaration as aggrandized.

He had not understood. As James lay wrapped in Diana's loosened hair, he knew what Finley had felt. Diana had found the empty places inside him. Not only found them, but forced them open. It was brutal, and it hurt. He lay still, letting it hurt.

He'd pursued vengeance for so many years—against his enemies, against Finley, against those who'd robbed him and his brother of happiness, against those who'd robbed his brother of his life. Now he felt fragile. In his father's stables, he'd seen newborn foals staggering on spindly legs, shaking and uncertain. They'd stared at the world with amazed eyes and tottered weakly.

He knew now what they felt. When he'd washed up on Haven's shore, he'd been too weak to move. An enemy could have killed him as easy as anything. Instead,

Diana had found him. She'd snarled at him in exasperation, then had taken him home, and she and his enemy had healed him.

He lay quietly, getting used to his newfound fragility. Occasionally, he touched her hair or her skin, just to enjoy the feel of it. The air trickling through the half-open window was getting very cold, but he couldn't be bothered to get up and close the shutter. Diana was warm. Good enough for him.

This is different, Grayson had said. A clumsy explanation. But anyone who'd not experienced it would not understand that the words were perfectly adequate.

Once, years ago, James had fallen in love. Or thought he had. Diana had summed up the difference. Infatuation was not love.

Sara had been the Polynesian woman over whom James and Finley had fought their first battle. James had found her first, and then she'd moved from him to Finley when James's back had been turned. He'd thought himself in love with the woman. In a brief two months, Sara had given James the sexual experiences of a lifetime. There didn't seem much the woman did not know—she'd certainly known more than the twenty-two-year-old James.

Infatuation. It had made him furious and frustrated. He remembered returning to Tahiti after a fortnight away, sauntering to the tavern that he and Finley had liked best. In the dim interior, he'd seen Finley, his blond hair bright in the gloom of the place. His muscular arm had rested firmly around Sara's waist, and as James stood on the threshold, Finley had turned his head and given Sara a deep, long lover's kiss.

James had tried to kill him. His former best friend had

protested, his blue eyes wide, that he hadn't known. He'd thought James done with her. Honest.

In the hot tropical night, with sweat and an out-of-reach insect crawling down his spine, James had believed him. Sara often lied to meet her own ends. But Finley had only given him that ingenuous blue stare. Said he was sorry. He'd never once offered to give Sara back.

What was more, Finley, for a joke, had married her.

Five men had had to separate them. Then and there, James had quit himself of Grayson Finley. He'd walked away. Ian O'Malley and a dozen others from the crew he and Finley had shared had followed James.

Looking back, he knew that he and Finley would have broken anyway. Sara had just been the final straw. They'd been too different. Grayson an Englishman, James who'd despised Englishmen; Grayson a laughing prankster, James holding his emotions close to his chest; Grayson who'd fled a miserable life for the sea at age twelve, James who'd come from a close family, finished most of a fine education and still had a home to return to.

Here in the quiet of Haven, with Diana breathing softly beneath his arm, it all seemed far away and insignificant. Grayson Finley had turned into Viscount Stoke, married, and was the father of four at last count. And James Ardmore had fallen in love.

Tomorrow, he'd have to decide what to do about it. Tonight, he wanted to make love to Diana again. He leaned over and kissed her lips. Damn, but she tasted good.

She stirred. A few more kisses, and she opened her eyes. "James," she murmured.

"Hey, love."

She half smiled, but did not move. "I must go back to my room."

He licked her earlobe. "What for?"

"What would my father say?"

"He already knows, Diana. We made plenty of noise. They heard us all the way in Portsmouth."

"*You* made plenty of noise," she retorted with a hint of her usual fire.

"You were pretty far gone." He glanced at the ceiling. "I think you shook off some of the plaster."

"I did no such thing." She looked at him again, and then her hands flew to her scarlet cheeks. "Oh dear heavens."

He chuckled. He kissed her hands and her flushed face. "You were enjoying yourself."

"You *seduced* me. That is what I'll tell them. Stop kissing me, confound you."

He did not stop. "Now, what I recall is you coming in here without an invitation and washing me all over. And me telling you to leave. And then you"—he brushed the tip of her nose—"throwing off your nightgown and standing right in front of me bare naked. I don't recall any seduction. At least not on my part."

She gave him a mock-severe look. "You showed no regard for my virtue."

"Nope."

"Or my status as a lady."

"True."

"You did not behave as a gentleman should."

He let himself smile. "If I'd been a gentleman and pushed you out the door, you'd have been mad as hell."

"Very possibly."

"So what could I do but take you down?"

She traced his cheek. "We might have had tea."

"You would have thrown it at me."

"I do not always throw food at you, James."

"Only when you're angry. And that's most of the time."

She smoothed her thumb across his lower lip. "I am not angry now."

"Sure sounds like you're angry."

"No. I am just pretending." She laced one finger through his hair.

"You pretending and not pretending sound a lot the same."

She gave him a little smile. "You will have to be careful which is which."

"How about if I just kiss you no matter what?"

Her smile widened. "I do not mind." She stopped him as he bent to her. "Except when I am truly angry."

He snorted. "You'll just have to get used to it whether you're angry or not."

He kissed her, hungrily and deeply, then traced her lips with his tongue. "I'd like to show you a few things."

"Mmmm?" she said drowsily. "What things?"

His erection, which had been steadily rising, tightened. "I think you'll enjoy them."

"I am not certain. Perhaps I should return to my chamber."

He rolled full length on her. "I don't think you should."

She pressed feather-light kisses to his chin. "I should run away and be afraid. You've abducted me once already."

"Are you afraid?" he asked, very softly.

She looked up at him shyly. "No."

"Good. That's good."

She glanced at him from under her lashes. "What did you wish to show me?"

His heart beat hard and fast. "Many things," he breathed. "Many, many things."

And so he began.

James knew amazing things. Diana had always thought of herself as sensuous, knowing more about desire than she ought to. She realized, at the end of another several hours, that she'd only stood by the road of desire, a road that led to places she never could have imagined.

Her voice was hoarse and broken, her limbs sore. Her wrists burned where James had held them fast against the bed. His warm weight covered her now, his body as damp as it had been when she'd washed him, hours ago.

He was still inside her, hot from lovemaking. The core of her being was tired and content. He lay quietly, smoothing her hair under his palm.

She touched a line of bruises across his neck. "I hurt you."

He smiled, wider and warmer than she'd ever seen. "You're a demon."

"You liked it." She was surprised.

"I sure did."

She did not even remember bruising him, but she could fit her stretch of fingertips precisely over the marks. She blushed.

James had taken her in pure need, and she hadn't minded giving herself to him one bit. But somewhere during the third or fourth time, things had changed. He could have eased his heart, finished, and sent her away. Their lovemaking had changed into something more personal. He had begun giving back what he'd taken.

Giving back tenfold. He'd shown her pleasure she'd never known was possible. She felt as though all her life she'd been peering through a wavy-glassed window, not really seeing what pleasure was, and now the panes had not only been broken, but she'd been dragged inside the house. He'd introduced her to pleasure clearly and cleanly. She would never be the same, and that was fine with her.

He moved to lay behind her, threading his fingers through her hair. "Tell me why you were so afraid before," he said softly. "Why you're so afraid you'd conceive."

She stilled. "I would have thought the answer obvious."

"Not to me."

She pretended to grow stern. "A woman bearing a child out of wedlock is a horrible scandal."

"Not good enough, Diana. You and your father and a good lawyer could rope me into marriage simple enough. It's not that." He kissed her hair. "So why don't you tell me the truth."

She lay still a long time, trying to slow her breathing. "Because of Isabeau," she said at length.

"Because she's deaf?" She sensed him frown. "You're not making sense. She wasn't born deaf."

"It makes perfect sense. I should not have another child. That is all. May we change the subject?"

He raised up on his elbow. His warm hair brushed her shoulder. "You're thinking Isabeau's deafness is your fault? It's not. She got sick."

She flopped onto her back. "Yes, it is my fault. She fell ill because I did. I insisted on spending every moment with her and taking her with me wherever I went. I could not leave her in her nursery where she belonged. I caught a fever, and then she caught it too. I made her

167

ill, and she suffered for it. What kind of mother does that make me?"

He stared at her, eyes glittering in the darkness. "Are you telling me you're carrying guilt for that? Fevers are tricky. She could have caught it locked in her nursery with smudges burning outside the door day and night."

"You may be right, but how can I know that?" She stared at the bowed ceiling, eyes dry. "I was so proud of her. I showed her off everywhere, to everyone. Look, look what I've done. I created a beautiful child. Well, God punished me for my vanity. It was stupid, stupid."

"Flog yourself all you like, Diana. It still doesn't make it your fault."

She folded her arms over her bare chest, glared at him. "Well, if you think that explanation is feeble, hear the rest. When we discovered Isabeau was deaf, I was horrified. Not only for her sake, but for mine. I was terrified of her. I didn't know what to do. When Edward first suggested putting her in an asylum, I wanted to." She pressed the heel of her hand to her eyes. "I wanted to, James. If I locked her away, I would not have to face my own shame and my fear. I could just let her go, never see her again." She wanted to cry, but the tears would not come now. "What does that make me? I was willing to lock away an innocent child. My Isabeau, the daughter I loved so much."

He laid his warm hand across her belly, where she'd so proudly carried Isabeau all those months. "That explains why you're so protective of her." He kissed the line of hair at her temple. "I'm surprised she turned out so normal with you trying to smother her."

She bathed him in a glare. "I should have known better than to expect sympathy from you, James Ardmore."

"I have every sympathy for you, darlin'. You've gone

through a world of hurtin'." His fingers traced her navel, warm on her flesh. "But you have to let the hurtin' go. I should know."

She glanced at him, tense. "Why? Because of today?"

"Because I wasn't there when my brother died. If I had been, I could have stopped it. What do you think that feels like?" He gave a grim laugh. "I always prided myself on not feeling remorse. But I feel it all the time."

His green eyes were so empty, as they had been when she'd come in tonight and found him washing himself. He went on, his voice bleak. "At least Isabeau forgives you. Paul never will. Neither will my sister. One of the many reasons we don't get on."

"That's not fair of her."

He shrugged. "She feels guilty too. After Paul's wife was killed, Honoria spurred him on to find the killer. She tasted vengeance, even if she couldn't have a direct hand in it herself. We're a vengeful family."

He fell silent, lips closed, finished with the subject. He traced creases on her abdomen and would not look at her. She did not pursue it. Too soon.

She asked instead, "Why did you tell me I would never conceive with you?"

He looked pained. "I don't really want to talk about that. A man doesn't like to admit his seed is no good."

"But how do you know?"

He slanted her an ironic look. "Let's just say I have cause to know."

"Meaning that your mistresses have never produced children."

"Something like that."

She considered. "Well, perhaps they simply could not have children. Many women cannot, you know."

"Not that many."

She thought about that a moment. She half sat up. "Good Lord, James."

"And no, I'm not going to tell you how many."

She drew herself up. "Do you think I am vulgar enough to want to know?"

"You're damned curious, even if you won't say it out loud." He kissed her before she could keep spluttering. "Turn over."

"What?"

"Turn over. I want to show you something else."

She glanced quickly at the window, which had already lightened. "I don't want you to show me anything else. It is almost morning."

"It's not morning, yet."

"James—"

"What's the matter? You too tired?"

She ran her tongue across her swollen lower lip. "Not really."

"Then turn over."

She fumed. But she rolled onto her stomach, her veins tingling with anticipation. She pushed the twisted sheets about, trying to find a comfortable place to lay. Not that it mattered. Without even a warning, James clasped her hips, pulled them firmly toward him, and entered her in one long stroke.

Her eyes widened, and the gasp pried from her lungs turned into a moan. She'd thought she'd felt pleasure that night. Now she knew what it was *really* like. The flittering thought that perhaps he'd show her still more later danced just out of reach, exciting her beyond comprehension.

For now, coherent thoughts were mere shadows. James was in her, large and hard and hot. She bunched the sheets in her fists, stuffed a fold into her mouth to stifle her screams. The hot friction of him made her writhe and cry out, his hands on her buttocks were heavy.

He said, "Still love me, darlin'?"

She was never certain what answer she yelled, but he seemed satisfied. He laughed softly, and then he was pressing her down into the bed, his chest on her back, whispering her name, kissing her hair.

She slowly, slowly returned from the far-flung place of pleasure. She felt again the rumpled sheets beneath her, the damp pillows, the dawn breeze on her sweating skin. He was heavy, but not uncomfortable. In fact, she loved lying beneath him. He was so strong, and so beautiful, she wanted to snuggle in next to him for the rest of her life.

He withdrew himself, spent, and lay half on and half off her, his lips playing feather-light kisses over her skin.

"Are we going to sleep now?" she whispered.

She felt a puff of breath on her back, though his laugh was too soft to hear. "Yes, Diana. I'll let you sleep."

" 'nk you."

She was already falling into the warm arms of slumber, and barely heard his answer. "You're welcome, darlin'."

Thick slices of bread with plenty of goat's cheese. Oranges still bright from the trees in the garden. Early berries made into jam. Dried cuts of pork fried like bacon. Rich coffee fresh brewed and sweetened with sugar and rum. James piled everything he could reach on his plate and ate his way through it while sunshine poured through the breakfast room window and the admiral pretended to read a newspaper six months out of date.

They needed to talk over many things, but James had been too hungry to address the questions right away. He hadn't been this hungry in a long time. Then again, he hadn't made love all night with a woman like Diana in his life. The barrier between physical love and emotion had tumbled like a ruined wall. He'd never known how draining and how wonderful experiencing pleasure in his heart and in his loins all at the same time could be.

He finished the pork slices and helped himself to more. A jar of mint jelly sat next to the platter. He slathered it on, then reached for another slice of bread.

"Mrs. Pringle is a fine cook," he remarked.

The admiral let the top of his paper fold down and peered at James over it. "That ship."

James swallowed his bread and began separating his orange slices. "What about it?"

"Very convenient that it turned up just when you wanted it."

"Very convenient," James agreed.

Admiral Lockwood set down his paper. "How long had you been planning this little adventure?"

"Years."

"You make conveniences work for you, is that what you mean?"

"I try to." He lined up his orange sections into a neat, bright row. "You also keep your secrets, Admiral."

"What will you do now?"

"Go. Staying here with Mallory is not a good idea. I spared him for your sake, but that doesn't mean I might not lose my temper and try again."

"That won't matter." The admiral looked grim. James threw him a questioning look. "Mallory is dead. He drank most of a bottle of laudanum this morning."

Chapter Fourteen

James paused with an orange slice halfway to his mouth. He put it down. "Hell."

"The story you told was terrible, James. I know in my heart that Mallory reformed, but you were right too. That does not erase his crimes. He hurt you through and through." The admiral looked at him a moment. "He told me last night he would go. This is for the best, I suppose. He was able to do the honorable thing."

James bent his face to his hand. He tried to decide what he felt, but he didn't know. Anger and relief and fury at the resolution ripped from him swirled through his mind. He raised his head. "I can't pretend I'm sorry."

"I feared you would be angry that he robbed you of any chance of vengeance."

"I made my decision yesterday in the caves. I spared him for you, and for Diana."

"I thank you for that. You let him make his peace his own way."

"Don't make me a hero. I was a hair's breadth from shooting him. If he hadn't done this, I might be tempted

173

to shoot him again. Nothing's that simple."

"I know."

They shared a look. James didn't know if the admiral was angry, relieved, or remorseful. The admiral lifted his paper again, took on a neutral expression. One thing James disliked about the English was the way they put a brave face on for everything, chin up, don't fuss—even important things like life and death and love.

"We will give him a burial at sea this afternoon. I would like you to attend."

James's lips tightened. "Best I don't."

"Very well, then. You have not answered my question about that ship, by the by."

Well, James could play along too. "It was a French frigate. I asked the captain to stroll around these waters, but to lay back until he saw a signal from me."

"Why did he not land? A French captain might think it a fine thing to find an island, however tiny, belonging to an Englishman. We are at war, you know."

James carefully slathered soft cheese onto his toast. "I told him that if I needed him to land, I'd signal again. If not, to stay away."

"And you have not signaled him?"

"No."

"You could have easily left with him yesterday."

"I know. But I have one more thing I want to do before I go."

The admiral tensed. "Which is?"

He spent some time spreading the white cheese into the exact corners of his bread. "Ask for your blessing. I want to marry Diana."

The room got very quiet. James laid down his toast without taking a bite. The admiral stared at him with blue-gray eyes that were mirrors of his daughter's.

"You want to marry Diana." He gazed at James for another long moment. "Why?"

James felt faint surprise. He had expected the admiral to say something like "you'd damn well better marry her." The man must have known that James spent all night furrowing her.

He answered carefully, "Because she's a beautiful woman and I'm in love with her."

The admiral blinked once, but the stony glare softened a little. "She had a very unhappy first marriage, you know. I blame myself. I never should have approved it. But Edward Worthing's captain spoke highly of him."

James looked up. "You mean he was a man with a fine career ahead of him."

"That is exactly what his captain told me. Why I thought his fine career would make him kind to Diana, I do not know."

"You heard what a father wanted to hear. You did not know Edward Worthing."

The admiral inclined his head. "But I should have. For that matter, all I know of you is the stories of your heroic deeds. How you seem to appear every time a ship is under attack by brigands, how you save the day, and sail off without reward. It's the stuff of ballads."

"I don't write the ballads. Some say the *Argonaut* is a ghost ship, but we're real enough."

"I cannot say you are an honest man," the admiral said. "Far from it. You lie to serve your own ends however honorable they might be. But I've observed you. You've been kind to Isabeau, you saved Lieutenant Jack's life, and you do not take Diana's temper tantrums as a slight to yourself."

"I like Diana's temper tantrums. She's pretty with her eyes all fiery."

"She looks just like her mother," the admiral said, and suddenly his eyes teared. He looked away swiftly. James picked up another orange slice and slid it into his mouth.

The door opened, and Diana walked into the room. James's gaze flew to her as though pulled by chains. The admiral also looked up, fixed his eyes upon her. Diana turned beet red.

She'd combed her hair and tightly braided it, but little curls stood out around her forehead. Her plain gown was clean and uncreased, and the ruffles of a chemise lined the rather high décolletage. James had left marks all along the tops of her breasts. She slid into her place at the foot of the table with pretended casualness.

"We were just talking about you, darlin'."

Her hand trembled as she reached for the bread. "Oh? Can you not find a more worthy topic?" She yanked two slices of toast to her plate, plonked cheese on top of it, then snatched up jam and pork and mint jelly and oranges as hungrily as James had.

The admiral watched her, his eyes softening. James closed his mouth. The man loved his daughter, and he'd already lost her once to the idiot Sir Edward. He would find it difficult to let her go a second time.

"Where would you live?" he asked James.

Diana froze in midbite. James pretended to ignore her. "Charleston," he said. "And here. No reason to abandon Haven, is there?"

"Except that you are an outlaw," the admiral reminded him.

"Only in England. And I might be persuaded to curb some of my more extreme anti-English tendencies."

"For how long? England is on the brink of war with America."

James shrugged. "We will see."

"And there is Isabeau to consider."

"I have considered her. She is a fine and lovely child. Like her mama."

Diana snatched up her knife. Her face had gone redder still. "May I ask you gentlemen just what you are discussing?"

James countered, "Where is Isabeau this morning?"

"She is dressing. She and I went out for an early bathe in the ocean."

James's desires, which he'd been sure he'd sated last night, snapped to life. The orange that hovered at his lips stayed there. He imagined her stripping off her dress and breeches, wading out into the waves, letting the water tumble over her naked body. Damn. He was sorry he'd missed that.

"Maybe she'd like to take a walk later," he said, tightening his muscles. "With us."

Diana shot him a severe look as she spread cheese on her bread. "I am certain I will be busy all day. Mrs. Pringle needs my help."

"Diana," her father began.

He was interrupted by Mrs. Pringle, who walked in to lay down another platter of toasted bread. "Good morning, my lady. You are all hungry this morning."

Diana was now as red as her hair. She said quickly, "Where is Lieutenant Jack? He should have been down by now."

Mrs. Pringle lifted the empty bread plate. "He said he was feeling poorly when I took him some coffee. His head again. I told him to lie quietly. That always helps."

She left the room, sending James a knowing look. As soon as the door closed, Diana jumped from her chair and snatched a plate from the sideboard. "I'll just take breakfast up to him."

"Diana," the admiral said quietly. "Sit down. I would like to talk to you."

Diana tossed bread and fruit and meat into a jumble on the plate. "While Lieutenant Jack starves? That would be rather rude. Carry on discussing without me. You obviously did so before."

She fled, plate in hand, and slammed the door behind her.

Both men looked at each other, brows raised. After a long moment of silence, broken only by the sound of the sea beyond the open window, the admiral said, "Tell me of your home in Charleston."

James studied the closed door. "It is a fine house. Built by my father's father. Looks right out into the harbor. My sister has had the keeping of it for a long while, so you can be certain everything in it is perfect."

"Would you have room for a visiting English admiral? One retired and finished with his work?"

"To be certain. The house has ten bedchambers. I'm sure we'll find one to your liking. Honoria would be tickled to play hostess to someone as lofty as an admiral, and I wouldn't mind repaying your hospitality."

The admiral sighed. "I am tired, James. It has been a long war. I thought I would find sanctuary here, and then—"

"Then I came along," James finished. "To ruin your peace and steal your daughter."

"I want only to see her happy. She has lived through much distress. Edward made things as difficult as he could for her."

James started to reply that he would make her happy if she'd let him, when Diana entered the room again, still bearing the full plate. "Father," she said, her voice subdued. "Something is wrong. I cannot wake Lieutenant Jack."

They left the room and took the stairs quickly. Diana was concerned enough that James's conversation with her father ceased worrying her for the moment. James had looked as though he thought Black Jack Mallory had done something to the lieutenant before departing his life. That was ridiculous. Mrs. Pringle had found Mallory dead in his bed early this morning, before she had spoken to the lieutenant.

When Mrs. Pringle had told her the news about Mallory, Diana had felt a twinge of relief, which had in turn made her feel awful. She hadn't known the man they called Jessup as well as her father had, but he had been a loyal man and a friend to Isabeau. But Diana too had experienced rage when she'd learned he'd caused the death of Paul Ardmore's wife. Perhaps Mallory's death could release some of that terrible hurt in James; perhaps he would be able to heal.

Mrs. Pringle had tended to Mallory's body while Diana had taken Isabeau out to bathe so she would not see. Isabeau had cried when she'd learned her friend had gone.

Isabeau stood at the top of the landing now, peering anxiously down as Diana led James and her father upstairs. She turned and pattered down the hall before them, her tight braid swinging.

Jack had the small chamber at the rear of the house, one that butted up against the cliff behind it. A small slit of window gave a view of the beach below the garden. The chamber had been unused before their unexpected visitors, and contained as little as James's—a bedstead, small corner cupboard, and a washstand. Lieutenant Jack lay on the bed, utterly still.

At first Diana had thought him sound asleep. He looked peaceful enough except that his face was dead white.

James crossed to him. He put his hand on Jack's still chest. So had Diana when she'd grown alarmed that he wasn't waking.

"He's breathing." James clasped his shoulder and shook him. "Jack. Come on, wake up."

Jack's head lolled on the pillow, his golden hair dark against his white face. James lifted one of Jack's eyelids, let it drop. He frowned at the admiral. "He does not look good."

Her father moved to the bed while Diana bit her lip. "That wound he had was nasty. I fear it never healed, was beyond our help. Or it's opened up again, inside."

"What can we do?" Diana asked. She moved to the foot of the bed. Poor Lieutenant Jack. He'd never been well, and they'd dragged him all over the island in their adventures. She'd been so distracted by worrying about James that she had not paid much attention to the English lieutenant. He still had not regained his memories. He was always determinedly cheerful about it, but she'd seen the haunted look in his eyes.

Guilt pricking her, she waited for her father's answer.

James had turned Jack's head, examined the place over his ear where the original wound had been. He probed it gently, his face grim. "He needs a surgeon."

"In short supply on Haven," her father answered, equally grim.

Mrs. Pringle pushed into the room behind Diana, looking alarmed. "I knew he looked queer. I spoke to him right after you and Isabeau went down, my lady."

"Did his head hurt?" James asked her.

"He said it hurt something fierce."

James laid his hand on Jack's forehead. "His wound is hot, but his face is cold. Ever do any trepanning, Admiral?"

"I've seen it done once, at a distance. The surgeon was competent. I have no idea what he did."

Diana clasped her hands. "What is trepanning?"

James had gone cold and remote again. "You drill holes in the head, through the skull. It relieves the pressure, or lets out the humors; I really don't know. Seems to work, though."

"Can you do such a thing?" her father asked.

"I always employed a surgeon who knew what he was doing."

"As did I."

The two ships' captains looked at one another. "We could attempt it, I suppose," her father said.

"We'd likely kill him. I wouldn't know where to begin." He looked at the admiral. "But you have a boat."

His lined face cleared. "Your French frigate."

"Perhaps. If I could catch them. Or I can make for Plymouth. One hundred miles, is it? I'd likely find a ship of some kind between here and there. More, probably."

"English ships, happy to capture you," her father said, looking stubborn. "I ought to go."

James said, "I can sail that craft faster and farther than you can. And Diana will need you here."

"I am too old, in other words?" the admiral snapped.

James's face hardened. "If you like. This is not about pride, this is about Jack's life."

Her father deflated. Diana clenched her fists. "If you gentlemen will actually let someone else speak, I think you are both mad."

James's gaze was heavy lidded. "I'm sure I know what *you* think. But there isn't a better idea."

"I could go. I can navigate that boat as well as any officer. I often do when we sail it."

"No!" James and the admiral said at the same time.

She ground her teeth. "I am an excellent sailor, taught by the best." She shot her father a glance. "And I am not wanted by the British navy."

James raked her with a cool gaze. "Sure about that?" While Diana drew a breath for a furious answer, he went on. "I'm sure a crew would be delighted to come across you alone in that little boat, all fire-haired and in distress. Besides what would happen to Isabeau if you wrecked and sank like a stone?"

She stilled, blood heating her face. James was right. Harm to herself meant harm to Isabeau. Also James's sarcastic comments about a crew finding her alone chilled her. She was Admiral Lockwood's daughter, but not all ships roaming the waters were English.

"Are you saying," she began, her throat tight, "that *you* ought to go because it matters to no one else if you die?"

James looked at her for a moment. "I think that is what I'm saying, yes."

"You're a bloody, arrogant fool, James Ardmore."

"So you keep telling me."

He straightened from the bed and moved to the door. Without pausing, he went out. They stood still, watching after him, then Diana realized what he was doing.

She pushed past her father and Mrs. Pringle, and fled the room. She heard Isabeau come behind her, heard her father start after Isabeau and pull her back.

She hurried down the stairs and out the front door that James left open behind him. He was not leaving so the rest of them could debate what to do. He was not tact-

NAME: _____

ADDRESS: _____

_____

_____

TELEPHONE: _____

E-MAIL: _____

_____ I want to pay by credit card.

__ Visa   __ MasterCard   __ Discover

Account Number: _____

Expiration date: _____

SIGNATURE: _____

Send this form, along with $2.00 shipping and handling for your FREE books, to:

Historical Romance Book Club
20 Academy Street
Norwalk, CT 06850-4032

Or fax (must include credit card information!) to: **610.995.9274.**
You can also sign up on the Web at <u>www.dorchesterpub.com</u>.

Offer open to residents of the U.S. and Canada only. Canadian residents, please call 1.800.481.9191 for pricing information.

fully giving them time to come to a final conclusion. He was going to the cove to launch the boat.

He could move swiftly and decisively when he wanted to. She'd seen that at the caves when he'd thrown away the stock of weapons. By the time she reached the gate to the beach, he'd already stopped at the well and filled two skins. She picked up her skirts and dashed after the striding figure. She knew he heard her calling, but he did not turn around.

She pounded down the beach and to the cove. He had already untied the boat by the time she gained it. She grabbed the gunwale and held on, panting. "James!"

He just kept coiling ropes and throwing them to the bottom of the boat. "I am coming with you," she declared.

He turned and looked her up and down. She expected him to drawl something sarcastic, or even to lift her over his shoulder, carry her somewhere, and tie her up—because that was something he *would* do. His green eyes were cold, unyielding.

He tossed another untied rope into the boat. "All right. Come on."

She'd opened her mouth to argue. It hung there, open for a moment while she wondered if she'd heard right. He gave her a level look, then turned his back and pushed the boat into the water.

She got herself over the gunwale and onto a seat just as the first wave caught the prow. James continued to untie and coil ropes, as though he did not notice her.

"Wait," she cried, standing up. "They will not know I've gone. I must tell them."

He continued to tie off ropes.

"James!"

He looked at her. Without changing expression, he laid

down the last rope and climbed back to her. He crouched down, shoved her skirts up to her hips, and reached for the waistband of her breeches.

"What are you doing?"

"Untying your britches." He tugged the drawstring loose, ignoring her attempts to stop him. He ruthlessly dragged the breeches down over her backside and off. Rising, he balled the garment in his hands and flung it as hard as he could at the retreating shore.

The breeches landed with a splat on the wet sand. The constant breeze ruffled them.

"James!"

"They'll likely figure out that you went with me when they find them." He watched her steadily, his eyes hard as glass.

Diana gaped at him. His countenance was blank. She could not tell whether he was teasing or triumphant or angry. The shore receded behind them, the breeches a forlorn lump in the sand.

She closed her mouth and glared. "Oh, for heaven's sake."

Without another word, he moved back to the mast and began hoisting the sail.

Her father kept an astrolabe and compass and chart stowed carefully under the bench with the tiller. As James worked the sail, he barked an order to steer the boat north northeast.

She knew he tested her boast that she could navigate as well as any lieutenant. She raised the astrolabe to the horizon, sighted along it, checked the reading, checked the compass, checked the chart, and adjusted the tiller.

James raised the sail and positioned it to catch the wind. The small craft rocked, out of the cove now and rushing into the swells. James tied off the sail and made his way to the stern. The wind caught his hair, which had grown still longer during his stay on Haven, the sun burnishing the black until it shone.

James took the astrolabe, checked its reading and then looked at how she'd positioned the tiller. Diana looked back at him, one brow raised. "You see? As good as any lieutenant."

James did not answer. He seated himself on the bench before her and held the sail's ropes, ready to wind or tie off, whichever way the wind shifted.

She watched his muscular back play beneath the coat. "Did you not believe that a mere woman would be any use on a boat?"

He slanted her an odd look and finally deigned to speak. "I've had women on my crew. Only one now. Her husband taught her to sail, and she's damn good. One of my best."

"What happened to her husband?"

He shrugged. "I think she killed him. He was a privateer and beat her black and blue for the fun of it. I never asked her straight out."

She digested this in tight silence. "If I had gone with you when you asked me," she ventured, "would you have expected me to join your crew?"

He threw a look over his shoulder. "No. But if I'd found out you could navigate, I'd have put you on the quarterdeck with Henderson."

She imagined that life—by day marking charts and taking readings, looking after Isabeau as the little girl scampered all over the ship. At night, lying in his arms, gazing out the window as the stars went by.

"James."

He tied off the rope, rose, and unwound another one.

185

She asked, "Have you had many women on your crew?"

"Probably about ten. Over the years."

"Were any your lovers?"

He did not answer right away. "Why do you want to know that?"

"I simply want to."

The wind blew his hair across his eyes. He raked it free. "Two of them."

"Will you tell me about them?"

"No."

She watched him across the wave-tossed boat. His gaze remained impenetrable.

She gave a cool shrug. "No matter."

He looked away and shifted the sail. She shivered. The sea wind was sharp, though the sun shone mightily. She'd have a sunburn in no time.

To stop herself thinking about what he'd just said, she opened the cabinet beneath the seat where she'd found the astrolabe. She yanked out a fisherman's knitted pull-over and pulled it over her head, trying to put her arms through the sleeves and hang on to the bouncing tiller at the same time.

She got tangled in the garment. Her head jammed against the shoulder and she flailed her arm, trying to punch through the sleeve.

A strong hand pulled her head free. He sat down next to her, holding the sleeve steady so she could thrust her hand through it. She wriggled around until the pullover sat right, then drew a deep breath. The garment cut the wind somewhat, and warmed her chest and back.

James wrapped his arm about her and pulled her close. "I'm glad you came with me," he said into her hair.

His arm was warm and strong behind her back. "I

heard you argue fiercely against it," she answered.

"I argued against you going alone, which would have been idiotic. But two can manage the boat better than one. I'd say we can average about five knots, if the weather holds, and we'll be in Plymouth by dawn."

"You going alone would have been idiotic too. What happens when you land and start asking for a surgeon in that accent of yours? You'll give yourself away as soon as you open your mouth."

"I know people in Cornwall who are willing to help me. Just like I did in Kent last year." He gave her the ghost of a smile. "For certain services rendered."

His face, clean-shaven, still smelled of soap, and his green eyes warmed her. "Services? Did you expel pirates for them?"

"Let's just say we share a dislike of prowling English frigates."

"Smugglers, you mean?" She gave a resigned sigh. "I ought to have known. Your world is upside down from mine, James Ardmore."

"Those smugglers are fine people compared to your respectable captain husband."

She silently agreed. If his friends could help Lieutenant Jack, she would overlook a little smuggling. She knew that for the poor families living along the coast, smuggling was sometimes the only way they could put bread in their bellies. Of course James Ardmore would seem a hero to such people.

She adjusted the tiller as the wind shifted. James wound up another rope. He sat back again, cradling her against his chest. She felt his heart beating against her back, slow and steady. He must have made voyages like this hundreds of times, dashing across open water on some mission or other, foiling pirates or harassing British frigates.

He rested his broad hand across her abdomen, warm through the pullover. If their purpose were not so dire and the danger not so great, she would love this. Sailing alone with him under the late spring sun, cradled in his arms. Facing whatever adventure they encountered together would be heaven.

It was illusory, this feeling. Likely when they made Plymouth and found a surgeon for Jack, James would simply send her back and rejoin his own ship. His mission of finishing off Black Jack Mallory was done. He had no reason to stay on Haven.

"James," she mused. "Why did you come to Haven by yourself?"

He kissed her hair. "I was shipwrecked, remember? I didn't have much choice."

"But why did the *Argonaut* not try to rescue you? Are your men so callous as to leave you stranded on an English admiral's island? They should be combing the waters looking for you. Your Irish lieutenant seemed competent enough to find you."

He waited a moment before he answered. "The *Argonaut* has something else to do."

"But you could have gone with them, whatever they are doing to the English navy that you do not want me to know about, and then hunted Black Jack Mallory. Why did you want to do it alone?"

She waited for him to snarl at her or simply not answer. But he said in low tones. "It was something I had to do."

"But you let him go."

His hand tightened, his fingers going white. "Yes. Now it's over."

He spoke in a monotone, emotionless. Diana turned in his arms and looked up at him. His gaze bore the same blankness that she'd seen when last night he'd washed himself over and over. A stark look, a vast emptiness.

She grew angry, because that would keep her from hurting for him. "How can you say that, as though it does not matter?"

Green anger flickered in his eyes. "Because it does not matter. Would killing him have brought Paul's wife back to life again? Restore my brother's life and happiness? I can never do that. No matter how many pirates I hunt down, I can never make it better for him."

The bleak conviction in his voice made her heart pound. "You were trying to avenge her," she said.

"Revenge is an empty waste of time. I knew that. I have known that for a long time. But I had to pursue it. I had no choice."

She remembered her own petty vengeances against the husband she knew would never love her. She had encouraged her suitors and behaved scandalously, all to punish Edward Worthing for disliking her. But all her theatrics had not brought him to her, had not made him care for her as she'd hoped a husband would care for a wife.

"There is a choice," she said softly. "We both chose revenge."

He frowned down at her, his dark brows formidable. Diana reached up and brushed his face with her fingertips. She smoothed her palm across his cheek and leaned her forehead into it.

He did not speak or change expression. When he next rose to fix the sail, he did not return to sit with her, but remained on the middle bench, staring moodily out to sea.

Chapter Fifteen

They pulled the boat onto a strand near Plymouth in the early hours of the morning. Diana was asleep on her feet. She stumbled behind James as he half led, half dragged her across the shingle and to welcome yellow lights.

She wanted nothing more than to fall upon a bed and sleep, and she hoped James's friends, or whomever he was speaking to, would let them into those tantalizing, warm rooms and allow her to sleep. But no, they were walking father up the strand, and the person James had spoken to was leading them, babbling in an almost unintelligible accent.

Then they were in a dark village, and then a public house, with more yellow lights and a plump woman missing most of her teeth. She led them up a narrow, enclosed staircase. Diana had to hold on to the walls to keep from tumbling back down. But James was behind her, James had her hand, she would not fall.

A room, a parlor with firelight and a table and a large, fat bed with curtains.

Diana could not remember why she was here, or even

where she was. Her mind raced to events of the year before—had any time passed since then? Perhaps she had dreamed the intervening year, and she was still in the cozy parlor, quarreling so desperately with James Ardmore, wanting him to go on kissing and kissing her.

James lifted her and laid her on the bed. There should be soup on the floor, she remembered, but perhaps someone had cleaned it up.

James pulled off her boots, smoothed a coverlet over her. He began to turn away.

She lifted sleepy arms to him. He hesitated. "You want me to stay?" he asked in that low, liquid accent she so loved.

She could only nod, too tired to speak. He sighed, looking almost displeased. "All right."

He stripped off his clothes. She drifted in and out of sleep as she watched, and then there he was, naked and beautiful, the firelight touching every one of his muscles and glistening on the unshaven bristles on his jaw.

He climbed under the covers with her, slid his warm body next to hers. He laid one arm over her abdomen and cradled her against him. She murmured, happy, and snuggled down into sleep.

James watched her sleep. Her canny questions on the boat that morning had unnerved him. She'd always seen right into his heart, even last year when he'd abducted her and made her furious. Best for him to leave her, find a lady who did not know him at all, sate himself physically, and forget all about Diana Worthing.

Not likely.

The night was quiet. The village lay about a mile from shore, too far to hear the familiar roar and hiss of breakers on the beach. He had sent word to a friend in the village, Augustus Tolliver, a fancy name for a man who mended fishnets. Augustus had a second occupation, of course, as did most people on this coast, one way or another. Augustus had sent messages off to Plymouth for a surgeon, who would no doubt arrive after breakfast in the morning.

James had been tempted to ask for news of the *Argonaut*, but he only trusted Augustus Tolliver and his wife so far. The man would do anything for a handful of coins, and James did not want to let it be known that he'd become separated from his crew. He'd begin discreet inquiries tomorrow. He'd missed his scheduled rendezvous with the *Argonaut* by weeks, but O'Malley and Henderson would linger in the area for a while.

James's eyes drifted closed, but he did not want to sleep. He needed to stay alert for Tolliver's return message, and he was never easy when he landed in England. He'd wanted to decline Diana's invitation because he did want to stay awake and watchful. It would be best if he could find the *Argonaut* and get Diana safely on board. He could dispatch the surgeon to help Lieutenant Jack, and then James would have Diana to himself.

He could teach her how he really felt about her. He amused himself thinking of ways he could convince her. What they'd done the night before had been only the beginning. He wanted to teach her and teach her until he had gone through all the things he knew, and then they'd learn a few more things together. He'd read books. . . .

When his imagination gave out, he simply thought about her sweet-smelling hair, the honey between her thighs, the way her voice broke in the depths of passion. She had so much passion. Last night he'd only touched the surface. He wanted to dip down and find every bit of passion in her and bring it forth.

He did not mean to sleep. That was the danger in surrendering himself to blissful thoughts of Diana. He was not even aware that he'd drifted off until he swam back out of slumber to fire-hot kisses warming his skin.

The thoughts that had sent him into the dreamless void had made him rock hard. Sleep had not softened him. He kept his eyes closed, enjoying the play of her lips on his body. Her hair brushed his chest and arms, her kisses moved across his breastbone.

He furrowed her hair. "Morning, Diana."

She started, lifted her head. "I did not mean to wake you."

He snaked out an arm, pulled her to him. "You planned to ravish me while I was asleep?"

"Perhaps."

"I'm sorry I woke up, then. Might have given me some pleasant dreams."

"You did not look like your dreams were particularly pleasant. You were frowning most fearsomely."

He smoothed her hair. "I don't remember. I suppose I'm worried about staying here." He glanced at the window, which was just going gray.

"We could have slept under a hedgerow," Diana suggested. She laid her head on his shoulder and traced the muscle at the hollow of his throat. "Like outlaws."

"That would have been wet and uncomfortable. And you wouldn't have started kissing me."

Her hand roved to his chest. "Do you like me kissing you, then?"

"Yes."

She trailed kisses where her fingers had been, and then she pressed a kiss to his navel.

James made a noise of satisfaction. "That's dangerous."

"You have always said I was a dangerous woman."

She licked the pale skin below his navel, which his breeches usually covered. Her long hair brushed his erection, which was begging for her if she'd only look.

His hands curled to fists. He remembered when he'd woken up in bed on Haven with his side bandaged and her smoothing his sheets. He'd mused then that this woman stirred a raw and primal passion in a man. She'd stirred it then, and she stirred it now. It was fire in his veins.

He held his breath. She continued kissing, down, down. Her breath brushed the very tip of his wide-awake erection. He jumped like she'd thrown hot soup on him.

She raised her head. "I do not really know how to pleasure you," she whispered.

She was blushing. His sweet, wild woman was stammering, and shy.

"You're doing just fine," he said, his voice cracking. "You do whatever you like. I'm sure it will be to my great pleasure."

"You will tease me. You always do."

"I assure you, not at the moment."

She smiled, a little triumphantly. "You truly want me."

"I thought that was obvious."

She looked shy again. "I mean that I desire you, and you desire me back. Things do not always work that way."

His heart pounded furiously, his blood molten. "Then we are fortunate."

Her hair brushed him again, silken and warm, like light fingers. He was going to explode.

Her look turned reproachful. "I am pouring my heart out to you, James. You could at least look interested."

"What the hell are you talking about?" His entire attention was focused on her, only her. Her voice, her lips, her tongue, her scent. He'd turned into a raving beast.

"You are speaking very calmly about our mutual desires. Rather as though I'd pointed out an interesting cloud on the horizon."

She had to be crazy. "I am trying to be gentlemanly. You're killing me, Diana."

"Why? What have I done?"

"Do you want me to stop being polite and gentlemanly?"

"If you let out what you truly think, yes."

His limbs quivered. "Be sure. You might not like it."

"Why should I not like it?"

"Ah, well. Too late."

He seized her shoulders and thrust her down into the bed. The straw mattress crackled as they both landed heavily, he on top of her. He had one glimpse of her wide eyes, and then he was kissing her with such fury he thought the mattress would tumble straight through the bed.

Too late, love. He tore at the hooks fastening her bodice. They gave way reluctantly, with much rending of fabric. His mouth fell upon her bosom. She wrapped her arms about him, fingers in his hair.

He thrust her skirt upward, glad he'd thought to get rid of the interfering breeches. Even in the half light, he could see the fiery red hair at her thighs, already glistening with moisture.

"You want to taste my desire?" he whispered. She murmured something, but he'd not really expected an answer. "Shouldn't wish for things, darlin'. Might not like what you get."

The night before had been nothing. Wildness flushed through his veins the like of which he'd not felt for years. He'd not let himself go in a long, long time.

He pressed her thighs apart and lowered his mouth to her. She gasped aloud as his tongue entered her. She tasted like the sweetest wine. He did not bother to be gentle. His fingers pressed her flesh hard, thumbs stroking her to life while he caught her on his tongue.

She writhed on the bed, clutching the sheets. Her fingers again found his hair. She was not gentle either.

He drank her, pushing himself deeper into her. He felt her climax begin, the frantic pulsing around his tongue. She arched to him, breathing in deep gasps.

He lifted himself away from her, then repositioned himself and slid his erection smoothly inside her. Her arms came around him, pulling him to her, and their mouths found each other. He thrust once, twice, and then they came together.

"Diana."

Her face twisted, eyes shut tight. Then she opened her eyes, which were dark blue and drunk with passion. "James," she said, her voice wavering. "I love you so much. I hate loving you, but I love you so much."

Tears slid down her cheeks. He spilled his seed deep inside her, then he collapsed onto her, and kissed away the tears.

"Marry me, Diana."

Diana jumped about a foot, but she kept her back to him. She was dressing and pretending not to notice him.

After their frenzied lovemaking had wound to silence, Diana had fallen into a dreamless slumber. When she'd awoken, she'd been alone and the sun had been high.

She jumped from the bed, her disheveled dress sliding to the floor. She'd taken it off, shaken it out, and slid it back over her head. One of her garters had torn. She'd tied it on over her worsted stockings, but she needed to

197

mend it. Not only that but James had torn off half the placket of her dress. He'd left bruises on her upper arms and her thighs. She imagined he had bruises on his arms as well and scratches all over his back.

When she'd heard him walk in, calm as you please, she'd found she could not look at him.

"I brought some bread," he'd said. "Not much breakfast but better than nothing."

She absorbed herself in hooking together what remained of the placket. "I must ask the landlord for a needle and thread. I cannot think what people would say if I walked outside like this. You might have been a little less, er, enthusiastic."

Amusement filled his voice. "I remember you demanding I stop being a gentleman."

"Yes, but did you *have* to rip my bodice?"

"Damn your bodice, Diana. Marry me."

She sucked in a sharp breath. It was all so unreal— being here so far away from her father and Isabeau, Lieutenant Jack dying and waiting for them to bring help, Jessup dead, the long and tiring voyage, the brutish passion of their lovemaking. He could not really have just asked her to marry him. Or, rather, ordered her to marry him.

"You have not had enough sleep," she said without turning around. "You are raving."

"No, I'm not. I admit I'm insane to want you as my wife, because you are the most irritating woman I've ever met, but that's not stopping me for some reason."

Her heart thumped hard. "Leave off, James."

"You don't have any choice, Diana. Sleeping with me these past two night isn't exactly what a genteel lady of the upper classes should do, is it? What will your papa think?"

She swung around. He stood near the fire, which flickered low, with his arms folded, his feet slightly apart. His voice had been light, but his eyes were still.

"I was already ruined," she said. "Even before I met you. I was a most scandalous lady. My father knew that."

"You were ruined in the eyes of the world. That's different from ruin in the eyes of your father or your daughter."

She knew this in her heart. She had been anxious not to let James go alone, fearing both for his life and for the possibility that she'd never see him again. He was James Ardmore. Why should he risk his life to save an English lieutenant he barely knew? He might simply take the boat and depart, never to return.

She understood now that he'd had no intention of deserting them. He'd known exactly where to go to find help for Lieutenant Jack. She felt a bit ashamed for doubting him. Her father might even understand why she'd impulsively followed James, but when she returned, she would have to face him, knowing he knew she'd become James's lover. She wondered if she could bear the disappointment in his eyes.

He said, "Let me do the gentlemanly thing for once in my life."

Her throat worked. "What is it you are offering? Your name so that I can live in peace with my father? While you run away hunting pirates or badgering English frigates? While I live out my life on Haven?"

"If you like," he said quietly.

Her temper broke. "Well, I do *not* like! If I marry you, I want you near so I can shout at you and nag you and kiss you whenever I wish. I want Isabeau to play with you and teach you her signs. I want you to be friends with my father and smoke those awful cheroots with him and swap stories. I do not want to marry your name, James Ardmore. I do not love your *name*."

Tears spilled from her eyes again, for the third time in as many days. She was tired of crying. She'd never cried until she'd met the blasted man.

He did not look sympathetic. "You know what happened to my brother's family. I will never risk that."

"Well, you ought to have thought of that before you started ravishing me, hadn't you? Am I safe once everyone knows I've become Mrs. Ardmore? No doubt the Admiralty would love to interrogate me to discover where you were. Not that I'd ever know."

"You would live in Charleston. The Ardmore name is respected there. You'd be welcomed."

"So I must abandon my father now, must I?"

He brought both fists down on the rickety table. Crockery danced, and the bread quivered on the plate. "Damn you, Diana, you are the most infuriating woman I've ever met. I shouldn't have abducted you, I should have run the other way!"

She clenched her fists. "I will not be left behind, James. I am tired of being left behind."

"I've no doubt you'll do exactly what you please. I tried to leave you behind yesterday, and look what happened."

"You were bloody stupid to try to go alone. Besides, you seemed happy to see me. You never tried to toss me overboard."

His eyes glowed green. "I would dearly love to toss you overboard. You'd make such a satisfying splash."

"You bloody heroes are all the same. I am tired of heroes. Tired of applauding their deeds while I am left alone. I am so damned tired of being alone."

"So am I."

She barely heard him. "I want a dull man, one who stays home and talks to me and does not do anything in the *least* exciting."

"The hell you do. The only reason you like me is because I am dangerous. Because I abducted you. You didn't want me to be a dull gentleman earlier this morning. Begged me not to be, as I recall."

Her fury surged. "You arrogant—" She snatched up half the loaf of bread.

"Diana, don't you dare throw that at me. You'll pay worse than you ever thought."

She drew back her arm and took in a breath, ready to tell him how much she hated how he made her feel, when they heard footsteps on the stairs.

Not just footsteps. The ringing sound of many, booted feet.

Diana dropped the bread loaf. It spun away across the dirty floor. James was already moving. The room had only one window, and it was high up in the wall, above the bed. James grabbed her, shoved her toward it.

"Get through," he said in a rush. "Go to Plymouth. Find someone who knows your father."

He boosted her upward. "What about the friend you talked to last night?"

"Looks like he betrayed me. Grab the sill. You can climb down, I've seen you climb."

Diana reached for the shutter. Too late. The door burst open. Seven English marines in bright red uniforms ran in, and pointed seven muskets straight at James.

Chapter Sixteen

Diana slid back down the wall, the rough surface gouging her fingers. James acted swiftly. He unsheathed his knife, dragged her around in front of him, and touched the cold point of the blade to her throat.

"Gentlemen," he said in his most drawn-out drawl. "This lady is the daughter of Admiral Lockwood. I don't think you'd want to have to explain to him why she's dead."

A blue uniformed man walked in and stood between the marines, who hadn't moved. She recognized him. He was Francis Carter, a captain much admired by Edward Worthing. Edward had regarded Captain Carter as a mentor and a very dear friend.

"Let her go, Ardmore," the captain said. His voice was very cold.

"There's too many muskets pointed at me for that."

His hot breath touched Diana's ear. She remained utterly still.

Carter's gaze flicked up and down her, taking in the torn placket, her disheveled hair. "I see you've already

203

helped yourself to her. One more thing you will pay for."

"Why don't you let me take her back to her papa. Less messy all around, eh, Captain?"

Diana had no need to feign terror. Fear poured through her. James could not keep hold of her forever, and as soon as he let her go, those muskets would fire. Seven of them. So many shots for one man.

"Let her go," the captain repeated.

"Easier on me if I don't."

Carter's mouth hardened. "If you believe I would not let my marines shoot her to get at you, you are mistaken." He gave Diana a cool look. "It would be most regrettable, of course."

James went silent. Diana saw in Carter's eyes that he would do just as he said. He'd let his men shoot, and then she and James would die together. Romantic, perhaps, but not really what she wanted.

A few more heartbeats passed, and then James removed the knife from her throat. He pushed her away hard enough that she stumbled out of the path of the guns. She saw the marines' fingers tighten on triggers.

"No!" She flung herself between James and those terrible, round openings, her arms outstretched.

"Damn it, Diana, get out of the way."

"I have come from my father," Diana babbled at Carter. "We need a surgeon, on Haven. A man is dying there. Please."

Carter's eyes narrowed. He looked her up and down again, while she watched him, desperate. His gazed flicked behind her. She saw him assess and understand the situation. "Drop the knife, Ardmore. Or my marines open fire, and she dies."

Another heartbeat of silence, then a steely clatter on the floor. Diana's limbs were watery with fear. She was surprised she didn't wet herself right there in front of them.

Carter held out a hand. "Come with me, Lady Worthing." He gave a curt nod to his marines. "Take him."

"No!" Diana cried.

But the seven marines shoved Diana rudely aside, and she could only watch in helpless fury as they converged on James.

James was getting used to being chained to the deck of a frigate. The manacles that confined his wrists and ankles and the chain that bound him to the rail were little different from the bonds used by the last man who'd had held him captive. British captains had no imagination.

They'd stripped him of his coat and boots, taken his knife and everything in his pockets. James had let them. The marines had given him the opportunity to get away no less than three times, but James had not taken them. He knew Carter would use Diana to make him behave, and he did not like to think about what he'd do to her if James escaped. Carter knew damn well who she was, but the look in his eyes when he viewed her held no respect.

Diana, the stubborn woman, was still arguing with Carter. "We must return to Haven. A man's life depends upon it." Her eyes glittered with temper, and her beautiful face was flushed.

Whether Carter believed her was open to question. He let her tell the entire story, about how Lieutenant Jack had been washed up on Haven's shore, saved by James, and had remained unwell, though he'd tried to bear up, until he'd fallen gravely ill, hence her errand. The captain listened, but made no move to hoist sail and make a run for Haven.

Diana talked until her voice went hoarse. Carter did not respond.

She followed him across the deck, feet stamping in her hard-soled boots. Carter stopped before James, looked him over in a pleased way.

Impervious, Diana went on at him as though she were a royal princess and Carter a disobedient servant. "Captain Ardmore risked his life to help the lieutenant. Twice. There is no need to hold him captive."

"Yes, I heard of the wreck of the *Constantine*," Carter said smoothly. "Strange, is it not, how Ardmore got away when so many other lives were lost? Like as not he caused the wreck in the first place. Saving the lieutenant was either an arbitrary impulse, or the man was a fellow conspirator."

"How can you think—?" Diana began hotly.

James drawled, "No, thank him, Diana. He's giving me divine powers now. I must have caused that storm, wrecked a whole frigate, and got away, all the while chained to the deck rail."

Carter gave him a wintry smile. "You try to provoke me, sir. I will not be provoked."

The empty cold in his eyes bothered James. Easier to conquer a man who was volatile and readily driven to anger.

Diana was trying again. "Captain, you knew my husband. He spoke highly of you. In fact, he always tried to emulate you. I know you had a hand in his career. Could you not, for his sake, at least return me to Haven?"

Carter swung around. Diana took one uncertain step back. "I knew your husband well," Carter purred. "Very, very well. We were the closest of friends. That means he told me all about *you*. He thought he'd married a hero's daughter, and all he got was a wife with a devilish temper and no better than a whore."

Diana's face went sheet white. Incandescent rage flashed through James. If his irons could heat as hot as his anger, they'd melt away. *That was a mistake, Captain. A bad mistake.*

"Begging your pardon, Captain."

A young man stood at Diana's elbow. He was not more than twenty, and his brownish hair was thin and slumped on his head. He wore lieutenant's insignia and uniform, but he could not have held the post long.

The captain regarded him with poorly concealed annoyance. Diana, on the other hand, turned to him in surprised recognition. "Mr. Pembroke!"

He gave her a polite nod, but there was nothing shy about him. "My lady. Captain, my father is well acquainted with Admiral Lockwood. Indeed, our families were ever close."

"Fine news, Lieutenant," Carter said sarcastically. "What of it?"

"I believe the admiral would be displeased if we held his daughter. And most grateful if we returned her home safely."

Carter looked at him in dislike. "Admiral Lockwood is retired."

"That may be, sir, but he is still highly thought of among other admirals, including my own father, who would be distressed at a slight on his daughter. Also, of the lieutenants listed on the *Constantine*, one was Richard Delacroix, brother to the Duke of Carlisle. His body has not been found. If this ill lieutenant is he, you could garner much by saving his life."

Carter's expression turned thoughtful. James watched the young man with interest. A lieutenant with intelligence, connections, and arrogance. He should go far in the Royal Navy.

Carter flushed, but his icy calm won. "I believe a short excursion to Haven will do no harm. After I am finished with Ardmore."

"Aye, Captain."

"And, Lieutenant," Carter went on, enjoyment in his eyes, "since you are so solicitous of Lady Worthing, you will have care of her during the voyage. She will take your cabin, and you will busy yourself bringing her tea and hot water and whatever she requires. Understood?"

Pembroke's eyes glinted with humor. If Carter expected to cow his young lieutenant with the assignment of playing lady's maid, he'd miscalculated. "Understood, Captain." The young man saluted. "If you will come this way, my lady."

Diana looked back at James. Her lips parted, her throat worked.

Close your mouth, Diana, James thought silently. *Spend the voyage in the lieutenant's comfortable cabin, not locked in the hold. Good girl.*

As though she heard him, Diana turned abruptly away, and followed Lieutenant Pembroke.

She had the finest backside on the seven seas. His throat ached. He knew what he had to do, and he knew their paths would have to diverge. For now. Diana, Lady Worthing, was far too precious to let go. He'd find her again if only to finish that argument about her marrying him. There wasn't a place in the world where she could hide from him. He'd found her twice. He'd find her again.

"Diana," he called.

She turned. The wind caught her hair, burnished with sunshine.

He crossed his manacled fists, raised them to his chest, then opened them. Isabeau's sign. *I love you.*

Diana stared at him for one long moment. Then she lowered her gaze, turned away, and followed the lieutenant below.

"What will he do with Captain Ardmore?"

Diana paced Lieutenant Pembroke's tiny cabin. The fact that he had a cabin to himself spoke of his status. Either he'd moved swiftly up the ladder, or Carter was wary of offending Pembroke's father, who was high in the Admiralty. If Carter were anything like Diana's husband, then the latter was true.

Pembroke had brought her tea in a cracked mug and a soft loaf of bread. She'd drunk thirstily, but could not make herself eat.

The young man, who she'd last seen as a gangly sixteen-year-old just before he'd gone off to be a midshipman, leaned easily on the doorframe. "He will be taken to London to be arrested and tried."

Diana's panic had hardly lessened. She'd been pleased to find an ally in Julian Pembroke, but though he'd intervened for her, he'd done nothing for James.

"Can you not persuade Captain Carter to let him go? Or at least deliver him to my father at Haven?"

Pembroke spread his hands. "James Ardmore is an outlaw. My father is not adverse to the hanging of criminals."

"But he is a good man. He hunts pirates who destroy ships and murder crews. He has saved many lives. He is not a legend because he is a criminal."

Pembroke took on a patient look. "He has sunk seven English frigates and captured several East India men. A few years ago, he had a hand in kidnapping the French king, and then he shot a French spy before the Admiralty could question her. He boarded a slaver and released all the slaves, who then took over the ship and turned pirate. I know all the legends, Lady Worthing."

"My own father believes in him," Diana said angrily.

"Then perhaps he can help, if he acts quickly." Pembroke sighed. "James Ardmore once flogged a captain called Langford. Langford was disgraced and his career finished. Captain Carter is Langford's cousin."

Diana stood up fast. Her teacup fell to the floor and smashed in a dozen fragments. "No," she breathed. "Oh, no."

"So I am afraid," Pembroke finished, "that Captain Carter has no sympathy for James Ardmore. No sympathy whatsoever."

"*Mr.* Ardmore," Carter said pleasantly. "What do you know of revenge?"

James bathed Carter in a cool stare. His cheek scraped the rough wood of the mast to which two sailors busily bound him. "Quite a lot, actually," he said, playing out his accent to its fullest drawl.

Carter did not appear to hear him. "I beg your pardon, I cannot bring myself to address you as *Captain.* I know quite a lot about revenge. For instance, my cousin, a promising captain, was disgraced and stripped of command. Your doing, I believe. He would love to be here today to see this, but alas. I will only have the joy of telling him about it."

They bound his feet too, winding a rope around the mast and tying it to the manacles that they had not removed. Out of the corner of his eye, he saw the boatswain's mate, in a broad-brimmed hat with a ribbon and striped shirt, holding the "cat," a long-handled whip with several barbed lashes.

"Twenty lashes you gave him," Carter went on, his eyes deadly cold. "Twenty lashes to a sea captain of long experience in front of his men. He was court-martialed. Let me see, he was thrice disgraced—once before his men, once before the Admiralty, once before his family. So I believe thrice twenty should be adequate. Shall we throw in ten more just to soothe my temper? Very well. Osgood, seventy lashes."

The boatswain's mate blinked once. "Seventy, sir?"

"Have you grown hard of hearing, Osgood? Seventy. And do your duty, or take his place."

"Aye, sir."

James turned his face to the mast. He was no stranger to pain; a man did not fight pirates all his life without doing damage to himself. He was no stranger to the lash either. The pirate captain who had captured him twenty years ago had enjoyed wielding a whip. That captain had enjoyed other, more disgusting, pastimes too. James had gained his first taste of vengeance with that pirate captain.

Pembroke materialized near the mast just as the first stroke fell. James's skin was toughened by scouring sea winds, rendering the first stroke nearly painless. But he knew what would come. Stroke after stroke would lay open his back and the final ones would pile pain on top of pain. Seventy lashes could kill a man.

He looked into Pembroke's young eyes. "You're supposed to be looking after Diana."

Two. Three.

"I will look after her, sir," Pembroke said quietly.

"See that you do."

Six. Seven.

211

James flinched. He felt the sting now, each stroke a little hotter than the last. At ten, Pembroke requested a halt.

The mate immediately stopped, but the captain exploded in fury. "What are you doing, Lieutenant?"

Pembroke stepped forward with a wad of linen. James was sweating, droplets trickling into the slices on his back. They smarted and stung. Pembroke thrust the linen pad between James's teeth. He stepped back, out of the way of the lash.

The boatswain's mate hesitated. Carter snarled at him, "Keep going, damn you."

"Yes, sir."

Eleven. Twelve. Thirteen.

The last hit his skin where welts had already risen, and opened them. Fiery pain slithered over his back like sweat. Pembroke had been kind to give him the wad of linen. It would prevent James from screaming himself hoarse or biting through his own tongue when things got bad.

James wondered how the hell Pembroke had kept Diana inside his cabin. Locked the door? Chained her to the bed? Why couldn't they hear her screaming and railing?

May wind stung the opening welts. Blood dripped onto his skin.

Nineteen. Twenty.

James had ordered only twenty lashes for that damn fool British captain. The man began screaming at ten, even though only two stripes had gashed his skin. The beating had been meant to humiliate, not cripple. From the stripes on the backs of the other sailors, that captain had not been soft on his own men.

Twenty-four. Twenty-five.

This sailor was skilled. The whip whistled and landed square on James's back, the leather just thin enough to leave a slash. The sun was out today, the weather fine for May. The heat was nothing compared to what he'd grown up with in Charleston, but the sun found his bleeding back and added to the fire.

He closed his eyes. Slap, sting. Slap, sting. His back was raw. Maybe, he thought dimly, when I reach seventy lashes, I won't even feel it. I'll be in so much pain I won't notice any more.

Thirty-one. Thirty-two.

His mind drifted. He seemed to hear Diana's voice. "I am furious with you, James."

"When haven't you been, darlin'?"

He opened his eyes. Sweat blurred his vision, running together sun, mast, ship, Pembroke's face. He seemed to see Diana right in front of him, her fire-red hair stirring in the wind, her arms crossed over her lovely, lovely bosom. "You are wasting time."

His eyes drifted closed again. All at once, he was standing in a dark cave with Black Jack Mallory in front of him. Black Jack Mallory begged for his life, in genuine remorse for what he had done. James refused to listen. He shoved the pistol into Mallory's mouth, shooting him right through the head. Lieutenant Jack stared in horror as Mallory's blood spattered the lieutenant's pristine shirt.

And then back two years to a little boat in the North Sea, icy wind scrubbing his back. Another pirate sat before him, boasting of having caused the death of James's brother. James felt again the slim neck between his hands, the ugly crunch of bones under his palms. He remembered how his muscles had bunched as he'd flung the lifeless body into the waiting sea. His friend turned enemy, Grayson Finley, had looked on, silently condoning what James had done.

Oh, yes, Captain, I know all about revenge.

Forty-seven. Forty-eight.

Pain seared down his spine from his neck to his buttocks. His knees weakened, but he'd be damned if he'd fall in front of the captain.

"Had enough, boy?"

In his swimming memory, he watched not through his own eyes but as though he looked on from above. He saw the young, slim James Ardmore, green eyes wet with rage and fear, cowering in a corner of a captain's cabin, clad only in a pair of dirty breeches. The captain of the pirate ship, ropy muscles standing out all over his naked body, advanced on him, clutching the cat-o'-nine-tails in his white-knuckled fist.

"You have to earn your stripes, boy. I want stripes all over that pearly white skin of yours."

James flung up his arms to deflect the blows, but they rained down on him, lash after lash after stinging lash. His back was cut, washed with pain. He screamed, and found his mouth full of linen.

The pirate captain's eyes burned. "Pain will make you a man, lad. You'll like it." He reached for the waistband of James's breeches.

James jerked away, hating him and scared out of his wits at the same time. Until the pirate had taken him captive, James had known nothing but his polite upbringing. He'd learned to box and fight duels, of course, but he'd known nothing like this disgusting, perverted man determined to make James his slave in all ways.

The captain's mouth split in a leer. "Come 'ere, Yankee boy."

Rage flared through him, unfolding him, raising him

to his full height. The whip cut and hurt, but the ignorant insult gave him strength. "I am not a damn *Yankee!*" he screamed, the Southern words ringing in the small cabin. He struck out, and the captain fell.

Many hands and many punches had subdued him, and James watched as they threw the proud boy into a cage that was originally meant for exotic animals. He bled from his mouth, from one eye, from the cuts on his body. The captain snarled that James would be starved until he learned obedience.

Darkness fell, and James could see no more. And then he heard an unmistakable English, upper-class voice filled with mocking humor. A blond young man with deep blue eyes and muscled arms held the bars of the cage and peered inside. He blinked at James and grinned infectiously. "What the devil are you doing in there?" Later, when the ship had quieted for the night, the same blond lad smuggled James some food.

Hatred. He had never known such hatred. Hatred had carried him through the rest of his life. James saw that same grinning face between his hands, moments after he'd found Grayson Finley's sun-browned arm around the waist of the woman he'd loved. "I'll kill you for this, Finley."

Sara's startled face, her almond-shaped eyes, her beautiful Polynesian hair, shining black, loomed beside him. She looked surprised, but not ashamed. She'd turned her back, walked away. The woman he'd loved.

"Not love," Diana Worthing's voice said clearly. "Infatuation."

She glared at him with gray-blue eyes, furious with him as usual. Suddenly nothing else mattered. Nothing in his life mattered but the woman who shouted at him and threw bread at him and cursed herself for loving him. *This time, it is different.*

Sixty. Sixty-one.

The pain would not let him breathe. He gasped for air, but the linen in his mouth choked him. He sagged without knowing it, the ropes around his wrists taking his weight. He heard muffled, hoarse screams and realized they were his own.

He opened his eyes. Pembroke still stood there, his outline blurred by water and blood. The form suddenly solidified, but he wasn't Pembroke any longer. A tall young man, dark-haired and green eyed, studied him. "James, old man. What are you doing here?"

Through the raw pain, he remembered Paul and Honoria had called him "old man" when James had become head of the household. They'd played pranks on him and laughed at his rages. And he'd loved them with all his might.

"I failed," he said, his voice raw. "I did not keep my promise." He tried to find air. "I'm sorry."

Paul smiled, as though he had a secret and debated whether to tell James. "It doesn't matter, James. I'm with her now. That's better, isn't it?" He winked. "You'll understand someday."

"Paul—"

Paul Ardmore faded and was gone.

Sixty-nine. Seventy.

The whistle and crack of the whip ceased. The sudden absence of the noise burned James's ears. His legs were limp, his bare toes dragged on the boards. The slaps had stopped, but the pain did not diminish. It went on and on.

He heard Pembroke and the boatswain's mate start forward. Pembroke touched the ropes about his hands. If

Pembroke cut them, James would fall. He tried to turn his head, but every movement burned.

"No!" The captain's shout sounded almost in James's ear. "Leave him."

Pembroke looked at his superior officer, contempt plain in his eyes. "Should we not take him to the surgeon, sir?"

"No, Lieutenant. Let him think on his crimes and pray that his hanging comes soon."

Pembroke's mouth tightened. Too arrogant, James thought. Even with the might of his admiral father behind him, he would anger the wrong person someday, and that person would take his revenge. Revenge was such an easy disease to catch.

"Yes, sir," Pembroke said, disrespect in every word.

The boatswain's mate and the other sailors discreetly faded away. Captain Carter stood for a long time looking at James. Enjoying a good gloat, James thought dimly. James neither fought his bonds nor moved nor groaned. Carter should only enjoy the gloat so much.

At last Carter sauntered away, off to his duties of setting sail for Haven. James knew why the man left him there. Not so that James could reflect on his crimes, but so that Carter could return anytime and gloat some more. He could care less what happened inside James's head.

The ship moved, and the sun sank. The linen pad remained in James's mouth. He didn't mind. When he'd bit down in his agony, he'd felt, between its folds, something long, thin, and steely hard. Lieutenant Pembroke was slyer than he'd thought.

Diana was in full fury by the time Lieutenant Pembroke unlocked the door of his cabin and let her out.

The door had a real iron lock and a huge key that Pembroke had taken away with him. She'd shouted through the keyhole, promising her father would have him demoted. Pembroke had not seemed alarmed.

Locking her in had been the captain's order, of course. When Pembroke had told her of the captain's plan to have James flogged, she'd nearly gone wild with fear and rage. Pembroke had promised to do what he could, and had told her to stay put in the comfort of his cabin.

Not that Diana could have sat still. As soon as Pembroke had gone out, she'd slipped after him. Peering around the door that led to the deck, she'd had a clear view of the foremast and James tied to it, his muscular back gleaming in the dying sunshine. She'd watched, in stomach-churning horror, as they'd beaten him, stroke after stroke. His back had been bloodied, but he'd never once bowed his head.

She'd tried to rush forward, intending to snatch the whip from Osgood's hands and fling it into the sea. Two sailors had taken her firmly by the arms and pushed her back into the lieutenant's cabin, and Pembroke himself had locked the door.

When Pembroke let her out, she bathed him in a cold glare. "Where is he?"

"You are not to see him, Lady Worthing."

"He is alive, then." If James had died under the lash, the captain would no doubt have already dragged her to view his dead body.

Pembroke seemed to understand. "He is a strong man, my lady. He is hurt, but he will recover."

She pretended not to listen, even while her heart turned over. "I would like to see your captain if I cannot speak to James. I'd like to tell Captain Carter exactly what I think of him."

"Aye, my lady, I am to take you to the captain's cabin at once."

"Excellent." She played the freezing, haughty society lady to the hilt. "Lead me, please."

Pembroke did. He took her the five steps down the passage to the captain's door, knocked on it. Without waiting for answer, he opened the door, stepped aside to let her in, then closed it, leaving her alone.

She was not alone. A man, not Captain Carter, sat behind a table strewn with notes and charts. He wore civilian garb of black and buff breeches. His hair was blond, and he wore rather scraggly whiskers. The whiskers covered, she could see, a bent and twisted chin, where he'd been scarred by fire or gunshot.

Diana stared at him, speechless with horror. His hair had changed color, and his face was a parody of its former handsomeness, but Diana knew him.

She spun around, made it to the corner of the cabin, and was violently sick.

"Well, Diana," Sir Edward Worthing said coolly. "That happy to see me, are you?"

Chapter Seventeen

Her stomach turned and twisted. Sir Edward handed her a handkerchief. Diana pressed it numbly to her mouth.

"Not the way every husband wishes to be greeted by his wife," he said dryly.

His eyes were the same. Pale blue and mean. Edward had always been nasty, she understood that now. She'd been in love with him as a giddy girl, not understanding his true character. He was just mean enough to come back from the dead and ruin her life.

She wiped her lips and dropped the handkerchief to the floor. "I had been so relieved to be free of you, you see. This has come as a bit of a shock."

"You are free of me." Sir Edward lounged companionably against the desk. "I had our marriage annulled."

She felt a dart of illogical, annoyed rage. "Annulled? How? Did you tell them you were impotent?"

His fist caught her across the cheekbone before she was ready. She stumbled, hand to her face.

"You must always play the wench, mustn't you?" His companionable countenance went dark. "The annulment was my condition. The Admiralty wanted me to do delicate work for them. I had been listed among the dead—mistakenly—which they thought a perfect happenstance. So I have a new name and a new life, one not bound to you."

She was shaking all over. She wished she could stop. She did not like showing weakness to Sir Edward. But her limbs shook as though she had a palsy. "It must be difficult for you having to actually work instead of living on your glory. Although I suppose you still send subordinates to die and take the credit for what they do."

"I do not know what you mean," he said coldly. "I prefer this simple employment. The adulation had become cloying."

Diana snorted. "Spare me. You rejoiced in it. You merely want to hide your bent and ugly face from the world. You were so proud of your looks. And you had the gall to say that Isabeau shamed you!"

"Shut up. You never shut up. Carter was so pleased to tell me he'd found you with the American criminal. Tell me the truth. Are you Ardmore's lover?"

She raised her head defiantly. "I am."

"Proud of playing the whore, are you? He is going to die, Diana. Hanged, legs kicking, gasping for breath. Men soil themselves in their last struggles for life, did you know that? No dignity in it."

"My father will never let him hang."

"Your father has no say in the Admiralty anymore. He is an old man, and his career is over. The only reason you will not die as Ardmore's accomplice is because Carter runs scared of Admiral Pembroke. He was a fool to let Pembroke's brat on this ship, but he had no choice. Pembroke is protecting you. Are you his lover too?"

"Do not be vulgar," Diana said icily.

"You were always vulgar, my wife. Dressing like a tart and making trysts with every man in London. And then having the audacity to beg me to come to your bed. I was too disgusted."

"Perhaps disgust had nothing to do with it." She lifted her chin, realizing her new thought was probably right. "Perhaps you simply could not."

His answering blow knocked her to the floor. She picked herself up, secretly pleased. The great Sir Edward unable to perform in bed. No wonder he'd avoided his wife, blamed her. What shame!

"You have no right to strike me anymore, Edward, if we are not married."

Edward's face was white. "You are an accomplice to a criminal. That makes you a criminal yourself. The captain does not mind if I take out my wrath on a criminal."

She rubbed the side of her face, bruised by Edward's fist. "But James Ardmore might mind. He is not a man to anger."

Edward gave her an incredulous look. "Come with me, Diana." He grabbed her by the shoulder and steered her out of the room. He took her up on deck to the foremast.

The sun was sinking. The red and gold light fell fully on the bunched muscles of James's arms and on the blood that coated his back. He hung there, his legs collapsed, his wrists taking the strain of his body. His cheek rested against the mast, and his eyes were closed. No one had taken away the wad of linen Lieutenant Pembroke had stuffed into James's mouth. The wind stirred it and James's black hair.

"You see, Diana?" Edward crooned in her ear. "Here is your heroic James Ardmore. Just a man, beaten and subdued like a disobedient sailor."

James opened his eyes. His face was white and lined

with pain, but his green gaze was as cold as ever. There was nothing subdued about James Ardmore.

James let his gaze drift to Diana, rest on the bruises that stung her cheek and forehead. The light in his eyes went deadly. Even the haughty Sir Edward flinched a little under that gaze.

Diana reached for the linen pad, fearing it choked him. Sir Edward grabbed her wrist. "Leave it." He called out to Captain Carter. "I do not believe this man has learned his lesson, Captain. Perhaps twenty more lashes are called for."

A passing sailor looked at Sir Edward in amazement and dislike. Captain Carter strolled to them. "Do you think so? Very well then. Osgood!"

As the boatswain's mate approached, Diana flew at Sir Edward, clawed him. "No, damn you. Leave him be."

He seized her arms, cursed as her nails raked his skin. Captain Carter roared, "Pembroke, keep this hellion under control or I will lock her in irons!"

Pembroke hastened forward. Sir Edward threw Diana at him. She got in a few more good kicks before Lieutenant Pembroke, alarmed, caught her by the waist and swung her around. "It will be all right," he whispered into her ear.

"No, it will not. They will kill him." Her rage dissolved into tears. Pembroke led her gently away, just as she heard the evil hiss of the whip and the slap as it struck James's flesh.

She spent a miserable night on Lieutenant Pembroke's narrow bunk, staring at the boards just above her. Her breath hurt her, and she had no tears or anger left.

She listened to familiar sounds of a ship, creaking boards, wind snapping in sails, footsteps of officers overhead as they worked their watch. Pembroke tried to bring her supper of boiled beef, but she'd been unable to take a bite.

Edward, her hated husband, was alive. She believed him when he'd told her he'd had their marriage annulled, though she would certainly take trouble to ascertain this. Pembroke seemed to already know Edward's identity, the admiral's son in on the secret.

She'd gone to bed, exasperated, and Pembroke had locked the door. She could not sleep. Whenever she closed her eyes, she saw the whip falling on James's unprotected body and the blood on his back. She saw too, James raising his closed hands in Isabeau's sign, how he'd watched her with unmoving green eyes as he saw her understand. *I love you.*

Why had the blasted man waited this long to tell her? Why had he told her *now?*

Because he knew he would die. He knew that Carter would take him to London for his trial, conviction, and hanging. She opened her eyes, staring at the dark boards. One had split around a nail.

It would be unlike James Ardmore to submit so meekly. Very unlike him. Yet he'd known he would not have the chance to speak to Diana again, and he'd taken his only opportunity to tell her.

Her breathing came faster. He *wouldn't* submit meekly. Carter would never get James to London, would never make him face trial. James would never let him, and he knew it.

He'd sent the message to Diana not because he knew he would die, but because he had something up his sleeve. The damned man was planning something.

She sat up so fast that her forehead connected with the beam. She put her hand to her head in irritation.

He was planning to escape. How he'd manage it, she had no idea, but he was James Ardmore. He sank armed frigates and defeated pirates single-handedly. Captain Carter had put him in chains and thought himself safe. The bloody fool.

She swung down from the bunk. As soon as her feet touched the floor, she heard a commotion outside—angry voices, shouts, running footsteps. The square of Pembroke's window still showed black.

She banged on the door. "Let me out! What's happening?"

Her own cries were drowned by the furious shouts of the captain. He ran past her door, followed by several other men.

She had to beat on the door and demand Pembroke to open it for another half hour before the young lieutenant came. His eyes were round, the light of his lantern showing a pale face and shaking lips.

She clenched her fists. "What has happened?"

For answer, Pembroke took her wrist and half-dragged her out behind him.

A gray line of dawn just showed on the horizon. In the dim half-light, she saw the foremast. James no longer stood before it. She saw the ropes that had bound him, loose and cut, lying on the deck. Next to them lay a chain and two pairs of manacles, empty.

Of James Ardmore, there was no sign at all. Her former husband, Sir Edward Worthing, was missing as well.

One month later

Lady Whitney-Jones, wife of the seventh Baron Whitney-Jones, raised her plucked brows and gazed, aghast, across the dressmaker's parlor. What was the scandalous Lady Worthing and her decidedly odd daughter doing *here,* of all places? She ought to have had the decency to remain in hiding. To return to Mayfair and order fine gowns from Madam Aurora, cool as you please, was not to be borne.

Diana sensed these thoughts raging through the head of the utterly fashionable Lady Whitney-Jones as Diana fastened Isabeau's cloak. Lady Whitney-Jones's slightly protruding eyes followed Diana's every move, though she never once spoke.

Diana took Isabeau's hand. She gave the lady, who was now staring open-mouthed, a cool nod. "Good afternoon, Lady Whitney-Jones."

She walked resolutely past her and out the door before Lady Whitney-Jones could splutter a reply.

Outside, the June sunshine warmed the pavement of Oxford Street. London residents beamed at one another, happy for good weather at last. Diana spied her father's carriage a little way down the street. A tall man with brown-blond hair stood talking to the coachman. When he saw her approach, he turned and tipped his hat.

"Hallo, Diana. Your father asked if I would escort you home. So here I am."

"Lieutenant Jack." She took his outstretched hand. She had not seen him in some days because he'd taken lodgings near Whitehall and spent most of his time at the Admiralty now. "I suppose I should no longer call you that. You do have your own name, after all."

"I like Lieutenant Jack."

Though he had survived his ordeal on Haven, the surgeon having performed a miracle, Lieutenant Jack still wore a slightly haunted look, and the lines about his eyes had deepened. Upon awakening from the unnatural sleep caused by his head wound, he still had not remembered his own name. Diana had hoped that the trauma of the illness might have shocked him back into memory, but nothing had changed. Lieutenant Jack felt it keenly.

"Jack" was not his name. It was Richard Delacroix, as Lieutenant Pembroke had predicted. Lord Richard Delacroix, to be precise, brother to the Duke of Carlisle. He had been raised as a privileged son in Norfolk, then decided to try a career at sea. He'd joined as a midshipman and passed his examination, working himself up through the ranks to First Lieutenant. The Admiralty had considered giving him his own command. Now, of course, they hemmed and said they would wait and see what happened with his illness.

So Lieutenant Jack had a name and a family—and a wife. She lived in Norfolk with his son and daughter, and was currently looking after the children of his two brothers in London as well. Lieutenant Jack had not gone to see her. Diana had not asked him why.

"Jack seems more my own," he replied.

"I am honored to use it," Diana returned. She let him hand her into the carriage. He lifted Isabeau in beside her. She climbed happily on the seat next to her mother. Isabeau loved to shop.

Jack entered the carriage and took the opposite seat. The carriage started, taking them out of Oxford Street toward Mount Street where Admiral Lockwood's house lay.

As soon as they started, Diana's welcoming smile died. "Anything?"

"I am sorry, Diana. No."

Lieutenant Jack and her father had both busied themselves searching for clues to James Ardmore's whereabouts. After his escape from the ship, he had disappeared. No trace of him had been found on shore—

though Captain Carter had sent his marines to search. Carter had alerted his colleagues in Plymouth, one of whom had volunteered to take Diana and a surgeon back to Haven while Carter scoured the coast for James.

Sir Edward had been found very soon. He'd been robbed of everything including his clothes and his pistol and had been trussed up on a beach in his under-breeches. He'd fumed. Diana, for one, was relieved that James had not simply murdered Edward. He'd been angry enough to. He'd settled for humiliating the man. She imagined James had enjoyed it.

James himself remained elusive. Neither the Admiralty nor any of Diana's father's friends heard rumor of James's capture, his death, or his escape. Likewise, the *Argonaut*, James Ardmore's famous ship, had not been sighted in many months.

Diana vacillated between relief that no reports of his death had surfaced and burning fury. James had known exactly the right moment to escape. She suspected Lieutenant Pembroke had a hand in that escape, though the lieutenant looked just as surprised as his captain. Captain Carter had been enraged that he could not blame Diana for James's departure, but she had been firmly locked into Pembroke's cabin at the time.

She realized throughout those first sleepless nights that James would never have been captured in the first place if not for her. He could have easily gotten away from Carter's marines in the public house. He'd dropped his knife and let them bind him—for her. He'd chosen to escape the moment Diana could definitely not be accused of helping him.

A selfish woman might be pleased at his sacrifice. Diana only felt wretched.

At Lieutenant Jack's news, or lack of it, Diana

changed her mind and directed the coach to Whitehall. They descended in front of the columned façade of the Admiralty, and Jack led her and Isabeau inside. Her father had come here this morning to visit Admiral Pembroke. Diana had told her father about Edward and he had taxed Admiral Pembroke with it in private.

The admiral had confessed the truth of what Edward had told her. He had apologized to Diana most eloquently. She still was not certain how she felt about it. But her marriage had most certainly been annulled. As far as English law was concerned, Diana and Edward had never been married.

They found her father easily. He was standing on the marble stairs in conversation with Admiral Pembroke and a tall, broad-shouldered gentleman with a tail of long blond hair. As she approached her father, the blond gentleman glanced at her, scanned her with intensely blue eyes, then broke into a smile. The smile told her he liked what he saw, and that if they had not been in polite company, he'd say so.

She gave the blond man a cold look. His smile only widened. He could melt hearts with that smile. Not hers, of course. James had already shattered it.

"Diana," her father said warmly. "A pleasant surprise to see you, my dear. Your lordship, I would like to present my daughter, Lady Worthing. Diana, Viscount Stoke."

James's drawl rang in her ears, his voice soft and irritated. *The viscount she married was a grinning idiot called Grayson Finley. Once upon a time, he was a pirate.*

She stared at the viscount's blue eyes and long lashes before she remembered herself and took the hand he offered.

She found her fingers engulfed by a palm that was hard and calloused, just like James's. So like James's that her eyes grew momentarily moist.

He held her hand just a little too long. When he released it, he glanced at her out of the corner of his eye and lowered his eyelid in a brief wink.

He was one of the best, she remembered James saying. *I used to hunt him. Caught him a few times, but he always slipped from the noose.*

Grayson Finley, Viscount Stoke, was now walking about the Admiralty like he owned it and speaking goodnaturedly with admirals who would be more than happy to slap a pirate in chains. Impudent rogue.

Diana's father introduced Lieutenant Jack. "He is brother to the Duke of Carlisle, in truth. But he goes by Jack."

The viscount shook his hand. "We've met."

"Have we?" Jack answered vaguely. He hated this, Diana saw. People knowing and remembering things about him when he could remember nothing. Small wonder he put off going home to his wife. Not remembering her would be the cruelest blow of all.

"And Isabeau," the admiral continued. "My granddaughter." The viscount took Isabeau's small, and somewhat sticky, hand in his and raised it to his lips. "Hello, Miss Worthing."

Isabeau let out a muffled squeal. The viscount looked puzzled, and his face became blandly polite.

"She is deaf," Diana said, somewhat sharply. "She cannot speak."

The viscount squeezed Isabeau's hand again, then reached out and tugged gently at her braid. Isabeau laughed. The look the viscount turned on Diana held pure compassion.

"I was about to mention, Lockwood," Admiral Pembroke said, breaking the awkward moment, "Lord Stoke might be able to help you in your inquiries." He glanced about them and lowered his voice. "He used to know James Ardmore."

The smile instantly drained from the viscount's face. Diana saw in the blue of his eyes the ruthlessness, the raw intelligence, that had enabled him to elude James Ardmore, the best pirate hunter in the world.

"Why are you inquiring about him?" he asked in a clipped voice.

"He washed up on my island," Diana's father said pleasantly. "He was taken prisoner, then disappeared. Naturally we are curious."

This viscount glanced at Diana. "If he disappeared, then let him go. Likely you will never see him again."

Lieutenant Jack said, "There have been no reports that he has escaped to America. Or of his death."

"And there will not be. He comes and goes as he pleases. I suggest you do not waste your time."

"I owe him my life," Lieutenant Jack said, somewhat coldly. "I cannot simply dismiss him or his deeds."

"If he wants thanks," the viscount said, "he will turn up to receive it. Otherwise, mark my words, you will not see him." He bowed, his affable look returning. "Good afternoon, Admirals, Lieutenant, Lady Worthing. I am off to pack *again.* I am being sent to the Channel Islands for some reason known only to God and the Admiralty. You'd think they'd be finished with me after that month in Prussia. Bloody admirals adore keeping me from my wife and children."

He completed this gripe with a twinkle in his blue eyes, then he turned away and strolled up the stairs.

"Odd chap," Admiral Pembroke remarked. "But

damned useful. He found the French king when the man went missing, and he's turned up amazing intelligence on the French and their allies. He's had a dubious past, but the powers that be have decided to overlook it in return for his services." He shook his head. "One day, though, his lordship will chuck it all and hie back to his estate in Cornwall. He adores his wife and hates being parted from her."

So speaking, the admiral led her father and Lieutenant Jack down the stairs. Diana lingered. As soon as the others had strolled on, Diana quickly mounted the stairs after the viscount.

The viscount waited on the landing, peering out one of the wide windows to the flurried courtyard below.

Diana held tight to Isabeau's hand, but the little girl was mesmerized by the intricate ceiling above. "Do you know where he is?" she asked the viscount bluntly.

He raked his blue gaze up and down her again, as though he knew exactly what she and James had gotten up to on the island of Haven. "You are an extraordinarily beautiful woman, Lady Worthing. Precisely the sort of woman Ardmore and I would have fought over once upon a time. Fiercely."

"So you advise me to forget him, do you?"

"He is not one for sentimental good-byes."

"He told me you had been the finest of friends. And then the best of enemies. But it strikes me that you know him very little."

He studied her with narrowed eyes. "You are a fine woman, Lady Worthing. Far too good for the likes of James Ardmore." He took her hand. "Yes, we would certainly have fought over you."

"How is your wife, my lord?" Diana asked sweetly.

Lord Stoke suddenly smiled. It was like brilliant sunshine emerging after a week of rain. "Do you know Alexandra?" he asked, as though he were eager to talk about her.

"I met her once. She would likely not remember me."

"Anyone who has met you would remember you." He raised her hand briefly to his lips. "I will mention you when I write to her tonight."

"You are kind," Diana said. "Good afternoon, Lord Stoke."

He gave her another rakish look with those blue eyes, his lips once more curving into a melting smile. "Good afternoon, Lady Worthing."

As she turned away, she heard him add softly, "Damn, but we would have fought over you."

"Post has come, madam."

Admiral Lockwood's stiff-jointed housekeeper deposited Diana's letters in front of her plate.

The admiral had gone to breakfast with another acquaintance, and so she and Isabeau were alone at the table. Diana had planned to spend the morning catching up on correspondence. Not that she had much. Her father's oldest friends were the only people who would write to Diana Worthing.

She'd been toying with the idea of writing to James's sister, Honoria. She should tell Honoria that she'd met her brother, and that he'd disappeared. Or perhaps James was already safely in Charleston and his sister would consider her letter a vulgar intrusion. Diana sighed as she leafed through the post. She'd have no idea where to direct such a missive, anyway. James had not exactly given her his address.

She broke the seal and opened a heavy, cream-colored paper. The note was short and succinct, and at the bottom was a signature, "Yours most humbly, Alexandra Stoke."

Diana's heart squeezed. She lifted her gaze to the first line and read the letter again.

"It is with hesitation I direct this bold missive to you, Lady Worthing, but my husband wrote me of your meeting at the Admiralty, and several things that had puzzled me greatly suddenly made sense. Therefore, I resolved myself to approach you. I became acquainted with you three years ago at a gathering at Lady Featherstone's, where you were introduced to me by Admiral Hawes. You knew me as Mrs. Alastair, and I have since then become Lady Stoke. That explained, I believe I might have information you seek on a <u>mutual acquaintance</u>. If such a thing means anything to you, I would be delighted to have your company at the Stoke summer house, near Newquay, in Cornwall. P.S. If you happen to meet Lord Stoke before you depart London, please do not mention this letter to him. I will explain all when you arrive."

Diana read the short missive yet again, not quite certain she had read aright. Mutual acquaintance. Underlined.

Her heart raced. In the back of her mind, she dimly puzzled over the fact that Lady Stoke had wasted two sentences of the important letter assuring Diana that they had been introduced, and so writing to her was not a breach of etiquette. *Good Lord,* she thought, tossing down the letter and springing from her chair. As if that mattered compared to what else the letter implied.

She hurried to her father's study, Isabeau trailing her curiously. Diana pulled out maps, spreading them across the desk. She studied southern England and Cornwall. Newquay. Yes. It was on the coast, facing the Atlantic, about fifty miles or so straight across land from Plymouth. Much longer if one went around by ship. The entire area was rife with smugglers. *Let's just say we share a dislike of prowling English frigates.*

She closed her eyes. James had disappeared. Lord Stoke had just returned from Prussia, and now was being sent to the Channel Islands, without a break to go home. *Do not mention this letter to my husband,* Lady Stoke instructed. Lady Stoke's husband, James Ardmore's greatest rival. James Ardmore had spoken of Lady Stoke with familiarity and admiration.

Diana stood up quickly. Isabeau was looking interestedly at the map of Cornwall, but Diana took it from her and returned all the maps to their shelves. She wrote out a brief letter for her father, blotted it and placed it under his pen tray. Then she quickly packed belongings for herself and Isabeau and hired a chaise to take them to Cornwall.

Chapter Eighteen

Lady Stoke, formerly Alexandra Alastair, thumped her son down on the couch next to her.

"What have you been eating, Alex?" she said in good-humored exasperation. His entire face was covered in some sticky substance, and dirt clung to it. His twin sister Charlotte was still outside. No doubt she looked worse.

Alex and Charlotte had just celebrated their first birthday. Both were toddling about with alacrity and great speed. It took the combined effort of Alexandra, her stepdaughter Maggie, a nurse, the housekeeper, and two footmen to keep up with them. Grayson insisted that little Alex could already say "Papa," but even Alexandra, the most indulgent of mothers, could not make words from the stream of sounds emitted from either twin's mouth.

The little boy who lay upstairs in the nursery, four months old and growing rapidly, would soon be dashing about just like his brother and sister.

She settled Alex back on her knee, dimly wondering what was all over his little shirt, and pondered whether she'd been right to send for Lady Worthing. She wondered also if she'd been right to not inform Grayson. But when the green-eyed man had climbed into her carriage at the lonely turning of the road and collapsed at her feet, he'd told her plainly that if she wrote to her husband, he would not stay.

She'd known at once what he'd meant. *I need help, but I will not take it from Grayson Finley.*

He'd burned with fever and his back had been raw with oozing cuts. She had gotten him into bed with the help of her footmen and had sworn the household to secrecy.

For weeks he'd lain in her best upstairs guest chamber, sweating and shaking, moving in and out of fever. Some days he'd be lucid, questioning her in his slow drawl about the movements of the English fleet, smiling sarcastically when she refused to answer. Then he'd drift back into raving. He talked rapidly, eyes fever-bright or closed altogether.

Whatever he had been through, he would not tell her, even when he could speak. His back had been laid open by a whip, almost to the bone. Someone had beaten him most cruelly.

The wounds had sickened, settling the fever deep. The footmen kept him bathed and forced food and drink into his mouth. Alexandra nursed him the best she could. They'd had to cut off his filthy breeches, his only garment. Any nightshirt they put on him, he flung off in the fever-heat, so he lay naked, tangled in the sheets, sometimes throwing off the covers altogether.

It unnerved Alexandra a great deal, but she told herself that she was a matron with three children and had been married twice. She should feel only compassion and pity.

She sighed. With any other man, she would, but James Ardmore was different. He had been her husband's greatest enemy, and she'd been caught firmly between them two years ago. James had told her things he'd never told Grayson, and she thought that perhaps she understood James better than Grayson ever had.

Which was why she'd decided to write to Diana Worthing instead.

Maggie hurried into the room from the garden. She carried little Charlotte, who was, as Alexandra had suspected, even filthier than her brother. Charlotte was adventurous and, unfortunately, knew no fear.

Maggie looked agitated, but Alexandra took a moment, as always, to admire her. Maggie was Grayson's daughter by a Polynesian woman whom Grayson had met and married on the island of Tahiti. Maggie had inherited Sara's looks—black hair, almond-shaped brown eyes, round cheekbones, full red lips. But she had much of Grayson in her wide grin, the sparkle in her eye, and in her impetuous nature.

Alexandra had come to love the girl very much. At fourteen, Maggie was growing into a beautiful young woman. The young men of Newquay had begun to notice this fact as well. Grayson still thought of her as the little girl he'd rescued from Jamaica. Perhaps that was just as well for now. When he finally noticed the young men trying to dance attendance, country society would understand why everyone whispered that Lord Stoke used to be a pirate.

"Mama Alexandra," Maggie said now, brown eyes shining. "I think she's here."

Diana pried open her exhausted eyes as the carriage slowed and turned. She peered from the window as they swept along the half-mile drive through well-tended grounds. They rumbled over a three-arched bridge, and at last halted before a porticoed house that stretched out long wings like arms. It was late evening, but the June sun still shone strong across the park.

Diana ached in every bone, and her mouth was dry as dust. Four times today, the coachman had had to halt so that Diana could climb down and be sick. The sway of the coach had only aggravated her already weak stomach. She needed a bath, cool water, and a bed.

Four footmen emerged from the house, but Diana's hired coachman climbed down and opened the carriage door before any of the four could. One footman held a cushioned stool. He shot an annoyed glance at the coachman, shouldered him out of the way, and planted the stool just as Diana's foot came down.

"Stoke 'ouse, me lady," the coachman said in a thick Cockney accent.

The footmen gave him a frosty look. *We work for a viscount,* their cool faces said. *You, sir, are nobody here.*

Diana lifted Isabeau down, took her hand, and made her way past the stiff line of footmen to the open front door. Isabeau put her hand out and tugged the coattails of the last footman. He looked down, brows quivering. Isabeau gave him her friendliest grin. The footman, who looked to be about Diana's own age, at last softened into an answering grin. Then he looked about guiltily, as though ashamed he'd been caught out as a human being.

Footsteps echoed in the cavernous hall, and a woman emerged into the sunshine. Diana became suddenly conscious that she'd been traveling for twelve hours, that her hair was a mess, and that her dress, only a cotton day gown, was creased beyond repair. The lady who faced her wore elegant brown cashmere, a satin sash embroidered with pink roses, and a thin necklace of garnet about her slim throat. Her brown-red hair was smooth and sleek, every braided strand neatly in place.

Behind her stood an extraordinarily lovely girl. She had black, tumbled curls, exotic brown eyes, and skin the color of milky coffee. She held by each hand two small children with red-blond hair and the same blue eyes Diana had looked into at the Admiralty several days before.

Lady Stoke held out slim, white hands and clasped Diana's warmly. "Lady Worthing, please come in. You must be tired and hungry. I have prepared a supper for you, and a bed. You came a long way very quickly. You ought to have rested, my dear. . . ."

So babbling, Lady Stoke drew Diana into the cool, shadowed hall. The footmen pattered in behind them, shut the great door, and scattered to go about their duties. Isabeau strolled over to the children, put her hands behind her back, and examined them like she would a new specimen of shell.

Diana pulled her hands from Lady Stoke's. "Where is he?"

Lady Stoke looked slightly startled at her bluntness. "Upstairs. I must warn you, Lady Worthing, he is quite ill."

"He seemed a bit better this morning," the black-haired girl volunteered. "But he did not know us."

Diana's heart turned over. Her eyes burned, and her neck ached from holding up her head. "Take me to him."

She knew she was being appallingly rude, but politeness seemed not to matter. Lady Whitney-Jones knew every rule of politeness, and she was an empty-headed fool.

Lady Stoke seemed to understand. She slipped her hand under Diana's arm and led her up a wide marble staircase. On the first floor, they moved down a grand hallway to a double-doored room. Before they reached it, a tall, gray-haired woman emerged with a basin of water and dripping towels. "We've tried to settle him," she said. "But he's restless. If this fever don't break soon, my lady, I am afraid . . ."

Diana did not hear the rest of the sentence. She pushed past the woman and into the room.

James lay in the middle of a large bed in a vast, high-ceilinged room. A brocade canopy shaded him from the bright sunset pouring through the windows. He had obviously been tucked into the bed, but he'd pulled the sheets from his body. He sprawled on his side, his back to her, his right leg and half his backside exposed.

Across his back, nearly covering it, were broken, angry stripes, some scarring over, some still red and raw. His damp black hair brushed shoulders that were bruised and scarred.

A cry escaped Diana's lips. She was around the bed, kneeling on the chair beside it, before she even remembered moving. She brushed the hair from his face. His skin was white, pale under his tan, and burning hot.

Lady Stoke softly moved to the bed. She took hold of the sheet to adjust it. James's eyes shot open. The green burned fever-bright. He growled something and swung his fist at Lady Stoke. Diana sprang up and caught his hand just in time.

"James!" she said sharply.

She hoped that the sound of her voice would pull him awake, perhaps goad him to say something sarcastic, like of course she'd come in time to look at his naked backside. He only gave an irritated grunt, and fell swiftly back into stupefied slumber.

Diana's vision blurred so that his features dissolved. Lady Stoke straightened the sheet again, patient, and this time, James did not move.

Pattering feet approached. Diana wiped her wet eyes

as Isabeau stopped and gazed at the form on the bed. She shouted in joy, "Joo!"

She dashed around the bed and climbed up on the chair with Diana. "Ma!" she cried breathily. "Joo!" Isabeau reached out as though she'd embrace him, but Diana held her back. He was ill, perhaps dying, but still very strong. She could not risk him striking out again, catching Isabeau with his fist.

Isabeau signed frantically. "What is the matter with James, Mama? Is he ill?"

"He is very ill, darling," Diana told her.

"We should tell grandfather and Mrs. Pringle. He will make him better again. We must get a ship and take him back to Haven."

"We will. Soon."

Diana reached out and smoothed James's scorching brow. Then she leaned forward, heedless of danger, and pressed a kiss to his temple. James never moved.

"I suppose I've given myself away, rather," Diana said.

Lady Stoke regarded her over the rim of her teacup. "He has been calling for you."

Diana swallowed her tea, barely avoiding choking on it. She sat alone with Lady Stoke in the lady's private sitting room. The lovely Maggie had taken Isabeau to the nursery for tea with the other children. Diana had removed her jacket and smoothed her hair as best she could with hands that shook, but Lady Stoke insisted she have cakes and tea before changing her clothes and unpacking.

Lady Stoke clicked her delicate cup to her saucer and continued. "In his lucid moments, he pretends to not know what I am talking about when I ask him about you. Or he refuses to answer."

"Then he does not want me here," she said dully.

"He *does* want you here," Lady Stoke returned. "Else he'd not call out for you. I had no idea whom he meant by 'Diana' at first, of course. Then I received a letter from my husband who mentioned meeting Lady Worthing and her father, Admiral Lockwood, and that you had been asking about our mutual acquaintance. So I looked you up and discovered that, indeed, your Christian name was Diana. I wrote you, concluding that if my cryptic hints meant nothing to you, you'd simply burn the letter and dismiss me as an eccentric."

Diana's throat ached. "You asked me not to mention it to Lord Stoke if I encountered him again."

Her cheeks reddened. "James made me promise not to. He vowed he'd walk straight off into the blue just as he was if I did. You know James. He would do it."

"Yes, indeed he would. The wretch."

"Also, James Ardmore is rather a sore point between us. He and Grayson agreed to call a truce, but they still do not trust each other."

"So I gathered," Diana said dryly.

Lady Stoke pushed a plate across the tea table. "Please, have some seed cake. You are tired, and you must keep up your strength."

Diana knew the lady was right, and forced half a seed cake down. Under any other circumstance, she'd enjoy the honey sweetness and tart spices, but today the cake tasted like sand, and she felt her nausea rise.

"I know it is gossipy of me," Lady Stoke said, "but I simply must know how you met James Ardmore."

Diana let crumbs fall back onto the rose-patterned porcelain plate. "First, you must tell me what you intend to do. Patch him up and send him on his way? Or turn him over to the Admiralty?"

A smile hovered on Lady Stoke's mouth. "He has been

here some weeks. I have not mentioned that fact to the Admiralty. What I hoped is that *you* would have some idea what you wanted to do with him."

"And how did you know that my father and I would not betray him? If you wanted to protect him, you were courageous to send for me."

Lady Stoke's smile deepened. "Because he did not only call your name, Diana, my dear. He said many rather, er, *complimentary* things about you. A few times in his delirium, he mistook me for you. The things he told me quite made me blush."

Diana's face was already heating. "Oh."

Lady Stoke took another sip of tea. "So of course all this has made me very curious."

Diana studied the cooling liquid in her cup. An hour ago, she had not wanted to talk of James, wanting to keep what she'd had with him close in her heart. But Lady Stoke's presence was soothing, and Diana was so very tired. Keeping it locked inside was harder than anything she'd ever done.

She found herself talking, the words spilling from her mouth as though someone moved her lips for her. She poured out the tale to this elegant, slender woman, beginning with James's abduction of her a year before. Then flashing forward to this wild spring, when James had washed up on her father's island and nothing had been the same. She related everything, ending with James's escape from the frigate and his disappearance.

By the end of the tale, Lady Stoke was sitting on the couch with her, her arm about Diana's shoulders. Diana's tears wet Lady Stoke's lovely cashmere gown.

"You poor dear. You've been needing this rather badly, haven't you?"

"Forgive me," Diana said, but only because the words

seemed expected. She was not sorry to have told the tale.

"Not at all. We all need someone to talk to. When my own mother died, I had Lady Featherstone, her dearest friend. But she lives in Kent, and I sorely miss her."

"My mother died when I was seven," Diana said. "I had no one." She remembered the last time she and her mother had waved at the boat taking her father out to his frigate. She'd hated saying good-bye to him, but she'd always smiled, pretending cheerfulness, as her mother did. Not long after the ship had left harbor, her mother had caught a chill that had never gone away. A scant fortnight later, her mother lay dead.

"And you've had a difficult time of it, haven't you?" Lady Stoke lifted a lock of Diana's hair from her wet cheek. "I heard of your separation from your husband, of course. And about your daughter."

Diana conjured a wry smile. "Should you even receive me, Lady Stoke? I am too scandalous for words."

Lady Stoke smiled, and suddenly Diana understood why Lord Stoke had fallen in love with her. She radiated warmth and kindness and beauty. Her eyes were brown and green like a sun-dappled pond.

"Good heavens, if I worried so about convention, I would never have married Grayson! I am certainly talked about plenty, Diana, believe me. And please, I want you to call me Alexandra. Two ladies fool enough to fall in love with Grayson Finley and James Ardmore should be the best of friends."

Diana began to laugh. To herself she sounded a bit hysterical, but Lady Stoke did not seem to mind. She folded Diana into her arms, and Diana, for the first time since she'd seen James beaten and subdued, felt the slightest bit better.

Chapter Nineteen

James opened his eyes. He lay facedown, exhausted, every limb aching. He must still be on the white-sanded beach, lying next to an anonymous English lieutenant he'd pulled from the wreck of the frigate.

He smiled, his lips cracking. Any moment now, she'd appear, cotton skirt lifted by the wind, giving him a glimpse of those fine legs. Her red hair would tangle about her, and she'd exclaim, "James Ardmore. I never wanted to see *you* again."

Now how did he know that the woman who'd find him would be Diana Worthing?

Because he'd dreamed this before. He remembered the taste of sand in his mouth, the feel of the wind in his hair. He remembered the sound of her boots on rock, opening his eyes to see her bend over him. He would wake again later in a bed, and then Diana would come and touch him and rekindle the spark between them. They'd banter to hide their desires, sparring as only Diana Worthing could spar.

A sweet dream. He reached for it. He wanted it to go

on, to become a meeting in the sand outside the shallow caves, wanted Diana to throw her arms about his neck and breath into his mouth, "James. Kiss me."

The dream dissolved and his eyes flew open.

He lay facedown, his arms outstretched, but the white beneath him was linen sheets, not sand. He lay in a bedroom, a cool breeze issuing from dark windows. The bed was large, the sheets, sweet-smelling.

Was he home in Charleston? Would Honoria tap on his door and drawl in her haughty voice that he would miss his supper, and Mama would be mighty put out?

But the air was wrong for Charleston. It should feel mellow and warm and smell of orange blossom and peaches. The breeze that touched him was earthy and cool, overlaid with a tang of brine.

He opened his lips to tell Honoria he was getting up, but his voice did not work. He uncurled his fingers, one at a time, from the sheet, and pushed himself up.

He was not in his rooms in Charleston or in any house he recognized. Light from a guttering candle showed him a high ceiling painted and gilded. The same gilding repeated on the lavish doorframe. Brocade curtains, pushed back, hung on the bed, his sheets were finest linen.

A soft snore broke the silence. From a deep wingchair near the fireplace, two boots protruded. A head lolled forward, covered in a footman's wig, pushed askew.

James made no sound as he slid from the bed and stood up. He was naked, the cashmere carpet soft to his bare feet. He took a step forward and nearly fell. His legs were so weak they barely held him upright.

He knew he'd been sick, powerfully sick. He remembered snatches of coherency, people shoving burning liquid down his throat, several heavy gentlemen holding him down as he thrashed in fever agony. Where he was and how he came to be there was a mystery, but he knew he was in England. Even the gaudiest home in Charleston could not rival this one for ornament, and the footman's damn-fool livery could only be English.

He waited until his legs and feet would behave, and then he silently took up the nightshirt laid out on the chair next the bed and pulled it on. The nightshirt had been made for a broad-shouldered man, and fit him nicely.

He made his way quietly across the floor, then opened the door noiselessly and went out.

He stood on a wide, columned gallery that circled four walls of a huge staircase hall. Marble stairs spilled to a cavernous hall below, and an equally impressive set of stairs rose to floors above. Gods and goddesses frolicked in a frieze high above, most of them naked, most writhing in happy frenzy. The hall was lit by crystal sconces at intervals along the walls. Tall windows at the end of the hall let in a cool, night breeze.

A woman started up the stairs. James flattened himself behind the nearest column and watched. She ascended in graceful steps, one hand keeping a chocolate brown skirt out of her way, the other bearing a candle. The candle lit a face he knew, sweet-eyed, full-lipped, cream-skinned. Her dark hair burnished red under the sconce light.

Several things fell into place, and he knew where he must be. He slid from shadow to shadow until he reached the stairs. She gained the upper floor.

"Alexandra," he said softly.

She dropped the candle. It extinguished in a pool of wax on the carpet.

He covered her mouth before she could gasp. She

gazed at him with wide, brown eyes, bathing him in that reproachful look he so well remembered.

"Don't burn the house down, Alexandra," he said. He kept his hand on her lips, waiting until he was certain no one had heard this soft exchange. The hall remained still and empty. The open casement creaked a little in the wind.

He gave the vulgar goddesses another glance and slowly eased his fingers from Alexandra's mouth. "You should have married me when I asked you. My house is much more tasteful than this."

"Grayson's great-uncle built it," she answered, as though that excused the bad taste in painting. "What are you doing out of bed?"

Before he could stop her, she reached up and placed her hand on his forehead. She had cool, soft fingers. He remembered how he'd nearly fallen in love with her two years ago. That was, of course, before he'd met that witch of a woman, Diana Worthing.

"Your fever's broken," she announced in a happy whisper. "Thank heaven. But you should not be wandering about. You could so easily fall ill again. Back into bed with you."

"Tell me where I am first."

"I just did. In the house Grayson's great-uncle built. Grayson inherited it when he became Viscount."

"I meant where in England."

She reddened. "Oh. On the Cornwall coast." She hesitated. "Grayson has gone to the Channel Islands."

"Does he know I'm here?"

"No."

He reached out, smoothed the hair at her temple. "You're a fine lady, Alexandra."

She took one step back, away from his touch. "You ought to be in bed."

"You're probably right. I'm just a little tired of it right now." His limbs felt weak as a baby's, which didn't make his stomach any happier. "Does Finley like this monstrosity he's inherited?"

Alexandra relaxed into a smile that made her face radiant. "He hates it. We had planned a long sea voyage, but I—" She paused, blushed. "I have been in no condition for one."

"Henderson told me the happy news. He reads all the gossipy newspapers. So Finley has an heir, a spare, and two daughters. He has no cause to complain."

The smile turned shy. "He seems happy. Except . . ." She regarded him speculatively. "You left too quickly last time. He never had a chance to tell you the things he wanted to. Your rivalry should never have happened. You ought to be friends again."

"Don't try to play peacemaker, Alexandra. You love him, and I don't. We were never friends. Even in the beginning, we couldn't agree on anything. If he had a plan, I had to have a better one. If I found a diamond, he had to find a bigger one. When he found a beautiful woman . . ." He stopped. The obvious continuation, "I found one even better," struck him as a bit rude, so he changed his words. "It took me a long time to decide I should let him have her."

The image of Diana, her red hair down, her eyes heavy with desire, made his legs even weaker. He needed to get strong, fast, and sail back to Haven to find her. He needed to wrap himself around that woman, fall asleep inside her. He'd get well for that.

"Are you talking about Sara?"

He suppressed a snort. "I'm talking about you, lady. You deserve better than Grayson Finley."

"He has impeccable lineage," she answered, rather haughtily. She always did defend Finley's title and background. As though that made Grayson Finley lofty.

What Alexandra didn't know was that James had seen her husband at his very worst. He'd once watched Grayson board an innocent merchant vessel, hold a knife to the captain's throat, and cheerfully announce that he and his fellow pirates were plundering the vessel. He'd locked the captain into the hold and decided that the captain's young wife was worth knowing better. The young wife had agreed.

So James had supervised the loading of goods from the ship to the *Majesty* while Grayson disappeared into the captain's cabin. Grayson had reemerged only when the *Majesty* was pulling away. James remembered the look on the idiot's face when he'd vaulted across the widening gap of water, obviously pleased with himself. James told him he'd almost been left behind, which would have been fine with James. Grayson had just laughed at him.

James wondered how many of these stories Grayson had told his sweet young wife. James could give her an earful. Maybe that was why Grayson did not want him around, despite what Alexandra claimed.

He plucked the front of his nightshirt. "This is his, isn't it?"

"His are the only nightshirts that could fit you. It is of no matter. He never wears them." She stopped and turned a brilliant shade of red.

James suppressed a chuckle. He slid the nightshirt off over his head and, naked, thrust it into her startled hands. "Keep it. I will wear my own clothes."

She stared at him, mouth open, then suddenly hid her face in the nightshirt, ears and neck flaming. James turned and walked back toward his chamber, the cool air pleasing his hot skin.

She called after him, words muffled. "You were only wearing—uh—unmentionables, and they were ruined."

"Damn," he growled. She looked so funny, with her face buried in the nightshirt, determined not to look at his naked body. He watched her a moment, then turned and walked back into his bedchamber and closed the door.

He thought he heard the whisper of another door closing, the faint click of another latch. He listened a moment, but his body was tiring quickly, and he'd have to crawl into bed before he collapsed to the floor.

The footman was still snoring. James got into bed, pulled the sheet back over him, and fell sound asleep.

Diana could not sit. She paced the sitting room that faced the sea. The lowering clouds and gray ocean matched her mood.

James was awake and better, so Alexandra had told her. Two nights ago, he'd gotten out of bed, his fever broken, himself once more. Then he'd gone back to bed and slept an entire day and night. A natural sleep, Alexandra had assured her.

Indeed, when Diana had looked into the chamber, he'd been sleeping heavily, his head pillowed on his arm. Then this morning, he'd awakened and demanded breakfast. He'd eaten like a horse, then demanded more.

He had never once asked for Diana, not this morning, and not the night he'd talked to Alexandra. Diana had heard every word of conversation he'd had with Alexandra in the hall. Wakeful, she'd come alert at the sound of James's door opening. She'd pattered to her own door, looked out, seen him. Her heart had missed a beat. She'd been about to run to him, when she'd seen him approach Alexandra.

Their murmured exchange had come to her clearly across the high-ceilinged gallery. He'd reached out and touched Alexandra's hair.

Never once had he mentioned Diana, and Lady Stoke had not volunteered that Diana was in the house.

When James had pulled off the nightshirt, her heart had hammered so hard she thought she'd faint. Candlelight touched the hard muscles of his back, shadowed the sinews of his arms. She wanted him with a longing that maddened her. She needed those strong arms and legs around her, wanted his bruising kisses on her mouth.

She'd fought the impulse to dash to him, drag him back into her bedroom and make fierce love to him all night.

Alexandra had informed Diana only a few minutes ago that James had risen from his bed, dressed, and was coming downstairs.

"I did not tell him you were here," Alexandra said, her eyes sparkling. "I thought it would be a nice surprise."

Diana could not bring herself to inquire if he'd asked for her. So now she paced the sitting room, knees trembling, hands clenching and unclenching.

Isabeau resided happily upstairs in the nursery with Alexandra's children and Maggie. Isabeau had taken to the little ones, and they to her. They saw nothing wrong with Isabeau's sign language and had already picked up some of it. Maggie seemed to dote on them all, though she was far from being a docile child herself. Her father had been a pirate, her mother an exotic Polynesian woman.

She'd told Diana of the day her father had come for her. She'd looked up into the hard face and wild eyes of a pirate, and known he was her father. While he'd stared at her in amazement, she'd said, "Hello, are you my papa?" and put her arms about his neck.

Maggie had described how she and her father had traveled from Jamaica to England aboard the *Argonaut*, James Ardmore's ship. She spoke fondly of her friends, Ian O'Malley and Mr. Henderson, and hoped she could see them again. Knowing what she knew, Diana speculated on how much James Ardmore had enjoyed *that* voyage.

Alexandra instructed Maggie to keep the children busy while James made his first appearance downstairs. Diana wanted to send for Isabeau, so they could greet him together, but Alexandra smiled wisely, and forbade it.

The wind picked up. Diana wandered to the window, watching the whitecaps rise on the sea. A small fishing vessel, listing hard to starboard under the wind, hastened toward shore. She watched it, wishing she were out there battling wind and waves instead of listening to the clock tick in the stuffy sitting room.

"Hell," said a voice behind her.

She swung around. James stood just inside the doorway, watching her with no welcome on his face.

He wore clothes that must have belonged to the viscount: fine kid breeches, leather top boots, a frock coat, and linen shirt. He'd not donned a collar or cravat, but even so, the highly fashionable garb did not suit him. He'd bathed and shaved, and his dark hair, still damp, was pulled back into a tail.

They faced each other over the striped back of the

Sheraton sofa, he with a countenance as cool as only James Ardmore could make it, she with lips parted and her limbs cold.

"Why aren't you on Haven?" he demanded.

Typical of him. No inquiry about her health, her well-being. No rushing to her, gathering her in his arms, declaring he missed her.

"I have been in London," she said clearly. "We brought Lieutenant Jack back to England."

"He's recovered then."

"Mostly. He still has no memories. But he discovered he is the brother of a duke."

One eyebrow flickered. "Happy news for Jack."

"Not really. He seems rather unnerved by it all. He is married as well. Has children. Twins."

James slowly circled the sofa, never taking his eyes from her. "That must have been a blow. Full of surprises, isn't he?"

"So are you."

He regarded her steadily for a few moments, then turned and walked to the French windows. "Forgive me for starin'," he drawled. "I'm just not used to seeing you so—tidy."

He made it sound like an insult. Diana had put on her best morning gown, a pale cream, high-waisted cotton trimmed with black braid and tiny black buttons. The gown was long-sleeved, and left some of her bosom bare. She'd donned a cameo about her throat at Alexandra's insistence. Alexandra's lady's maid had swept Diana's unruly hair into a prim and sleek knot, somehow patting every hair into place.

"Of course I am tidy. The elegant Lady Stoke is to be thanked for that." Everything ran like clockwork under the eye of Alexandra.

"She is a fine lady," he said, almost absently. He leaned one hand on the window frame as he scanned the horizon. Outside, the lawn dipped to a low wall, along which was a walkway and benches so that someone on a Sunday stroll could rest and watch the sea.

Diana could not take her eyes off him. There he stood, long and tall with the tails of the frock coat hanging to his thighs. She wanted to go to him, and at the same time, balled her hands to keep from moving. Damn him, why didn't he say anything? He just stood, watching. The hand that supported him shook once.

"James—"

"Where is Henderson?" he interrupted.

"What?"

He gave her a weary look over his shoulder. "Henderson. My third in command. I asked where he was."

"I do not know, James. He is not hiding under the sofa."

He half turned and leaned against the doorframe. "We were supposed to rendezvous here if things went wrong. Best not tell Alexandra. She thinks I came here because in my heart I want to reconcile with her husband."

Diana felt familiar fury rising. "You chose *this* as your rendezvous? Why the devil should you? Certainly there must be safer places."

"Not if things are bad, like they are. I never meant to be ill. Nothing I could do but go to ground. I knew Alexandra wouldn't give me away. Neither will Finley. He owes me too much."

She clenched her hands. "You might have told me."

"I didn't exactly have a chance. When I was chained up on the frigate, I couldn't call out *meet me in Cornwall*. And you haven't told me why you're here yourself."

She blew out an exasperated breath. "Yes, I did. We took Lieutenant Jack to London."

"To London. Weeks and weeks ago. London's a long way from Cornwall."

"I was looking for you. Why the devil else would I come here?"

"And where is your charming father?"

"In London."

They watched each other again. His eyes were cold, assessing and unyielding. "You should have gone back to Haven. I'd have met you there."

"The last time I saw you, that horrible captain was flogging you. And then you disappeared. I had no idea if you were dead or alive, overboard or hiding. How could I go tamely back home not knowing what had happened to you?"

His eyes were like jade, cool and opaque, letting nothing through. "You had to know that if I was alive I'd come back."

"Oh, did I? How was I to assume that, Mr. Pirate Hunter? Just because I fell in love with you did not mean you were obliged to come back to me."

"I asked you to marry me, remember? Before we were so rudely interrupted."

"I am so sorry, James. I suppose the elegant Lady Stoke politely does everything Lord Stoke expects her to, but I am not the perfect Lady Stoke. I was never one to tamely obey orders."

James jerked the French door open. The fitful breeze gusted in, pulling Diana's hair from its carefully placed pins. "Let's walk."

Without waiting for Diana to answer, he seized her hand and dragged her out to the path that ran down to the sea wall.

He might have seemed weakened when he leaned against the door, and even now he did not walk steadily, but the pressure on her wrist was fierce, and his fingers bruised.

The clouds roiled overhead. "It is going to rain," Diana remarked.

"Good. Less chance someone will overhear us if we're going to yell at each other. And Alexandra does not obey Finley. She does whatever the hell she wants. That's why I like her."

He pulled her along the path. To their left, the sea rushed, breakers colliding with rocks. The path led around the house and up into a small wood, probably planted by the viscount's great-uncle. A little way under the trees stood a folly, columned and dome-roofed. Benches lined the inside. James pulled Diana down to one.

Trees creaked and groaned overhead. James released her, but they sat very close together on the bench, hips and legs touching. He smelled of the soap from his bath and the male scent that was purely his.

"Are we going to shout at each other now?" she asked nervously.

"I thought we had been."

He looked off into the trees. This close, she saw the pale, almost gray tinge to his skin. A few more lines were etched around his eyes. He was not well, or strong. They were sitting on this bench because he'd used up what strength he had walking out here.

"You should go back and rest," she said. She touched the sinewy hand that rested on his knee. "We can argue later."

He bathed her in a cold stare. "Don't fuss, Diana. You're as bad as Alexandra."

"Oh, do forgive me," she returned icily.

He said nothing for a moment. Then his gaze thawed the slightest bit. "You know why I like you? Because you don't cower and cringe, and you don't obey. I strike out at you, and you strike right back. And sometimes hold me at gunpoint." His amusement faded. "A man doesn't always like his lady to see him when he's not his best. It hurts his pride."

"Is that why you wanted me to remain on Haven? So you could mend?"

"Partly. But on second thought—"

She'd not thought he had the strength. He disproved it by scooping her up and abruptly depositing her on his knee. His hand pushed itself firmly between her thighs. "That's better," he said.

Diana's backside felt so good. He warmed his hands in the folds of her skirt and enjoyed studying her lips. They were red and full, and moisture waited for him just between them.

"What do you want to argue about?" she asked, her eyes still tight.

"Anything you want, darlin'."

He breathed in the fragrance of her hair, closed his eyes. Though the short walk had tired him to the point of queasiness, having his arms around her was already bringing back strength.

"James," she murmured. "We have to talk."

He pried his eyes open. When a woman said that, nothing good could come of it.

"What about? Your husband? And the little fact that he's still alive?"

She hesitated. "So you knew he was my husband."

"I guessed. I've never seen you look at anyone with

that much hatred, not even me. It poured out of you. Faked his own death, did he? Probably for some damn fool reason."

"The Admiralty wants him to be a spy or some such. They are fools." One strand of red hair broke the whiteness of her cheek. "Why did you kidnap him?"

"I had to. He caught me just as I'd unscrewed the manacles. It was that or kill him." He waited for her reaction. She gave none. She simply looked down at her clasped hands, her lashes hiding her eyes. "I thought maybe if I killed him, you wouldn't forgive me."

If she'd only look at him. When he'd awakened the night before, all he'd wanted was to get better and send for Diana. He wanted to hold her and kiss her and have everything simple. He should have known better. Things had never been simple between them. And now they were complicated as hell.

"You made a fool of him," she said softly.

"I couldn't help myself. I saw what he'd done to you. I hope he thought about it while he shivered on that beach." He paused. "And maybe I thought that if I made him look like a fool, I'd keep you from going back to him."

"I would not have gone back to him," she said in a low voice. "I could not in any case. He annulled the marriage."

"Did he?" A small weight lifted from his chest. "Well, I'm glad to hear that."

Her glance flicked to him, eyes dark blue and unhappy. She'd hated Sir Edward, but this annulment humiliated her. She'd been discarded, and to a proud woman like Diana, that must cut. She'd been married to Edward Worthing, slept with him, bore him a child. She'd had something with Sir Edward that she'd not had with

James, and Diana did not take things lightly. There was also the tricky question of what the annulment did to Isabeau's status. Diana must be fully aware of that.

Her voice was colorless. "So I am a widow in the eyes of the world, never married in the eyes of the law."

"You might have gone back to him if he'd asked you," he said quietly. "I've seen many happy reunions in my time."

Diana stared off into the woods. "Is that why you didn't want Alexandra to send for me?"

"I told you why. I needed to heal." He'd wanted to face her whole and strong, to sweep her into his arms and carry her off. As it was, he could barely keep his balance on the bench.

"You must have been in a bad way as you traveled here," she said. "And yet you did it. It's a long way from Plymouth."

"I knew Alexandra would help me."

She looked down again, guarding her eyes. He wasn't used to that. He was used to her glaring, washing him in bright anger. "So you are a free woman. I can only be happy about that."

"Not exactly free," she said with a touch of her usual acidity. "You are my lover, and you are very demanding."

He thought about the demands he'd made on her in the inn near Plymouth. And those she'd made on him. He started to get aroused. Again. Even in his weakened state of the last few days, his dreams of Diana had kept him almost permanently aroused.

"But you always get your own back, don't you, darlin'?" He wanted to break this spell, to nudge their banter back where it belonged. "Did you bring a pistol out here with you?"

She glanced at him sideways, surprised. "No."

"I thought you might point it at me and tell me to take down my breeches. You always enjoy that."

She at last looked at him fully. Her eyes were bleak. His stiff erection didn't like that one bit.

"I'll do something more shocking than that, James. I will tell you that you are going to become a papa."

Chapter Twenty

James nearly fell off the bench. His heart missed one, two, three beats. Then it started again with a vengeance. "Now how do you figure that?"

She gave him her usual scornful look. "I have been increasing before. I know how it feels. It is in the early days, but I am fairly certain." She made an irritated noise. "I am very ill in the mornings. Well, most of the day, really."

He studied the line of her hair, the fine bones of her face. She had vibrant, brutal beauty. The sight of Sir Edward Worthing's bruises upon her skin had beaten a primal rage through him. Sir Edward had sensed that, hence he'd ordered the second flogging.

James had barely felt it. When it was done, Captain Carter had ordered James lifted to his feet. He would have to remain there, he stipulated. If James fell, he'd be whipped again. James had felt only disgust at their stupid cruelty. He'd remained on his feet, just to spite them.

He'd used up his strength on that, which had left him barely any stamina to swim to shore. He still felt the dark water closing over him, the cold waves pulling him back, his lungs burning, his back searing like a lava flow. Hatred had kept him going. He was damned if he'd give the captain the satisfaction of pulling his dead body from the drink.

Sir Edward had fought him hard. On the beach, he'd scraped James's ribs with a knife before James had pulled it from him and turned the tables.

James said to Diana, "Remember when I told you that you'd never conceive with my seed?"

"Yes." She touched her hand to her abdomen with an expression that made the pain of the flogging nothing. "But one of those seeds has decided to take root."

His voice went hard. "Diana, I can't father children."

"I'd say you can."

Her unblinking blue gaze was hard to meet. "Let me tell you why I can't. I have been all over the world. To islands in the Pacific, all over Asia, and up and down the Atlantic. More than once. No woman has ever brought me a black-haired baby and told me I was its father. Very unusual for a sailor who's roamed the world for twenty years, wouldn't you say?"

"Perhaps they simply did not tell you," she argued. "Perhaps they either rid themselves of the inconvenient burden or contrived not to conceive in the first place. Vinegar-soaked sponges and so forth."

She looked so innocent and so utterly reasonable that it irritated him. "What do you know about that? I thought you had a proper upbringing."

"I am not a fool," she answered impatiently. "I traveled widely with my father as a girl and saw things that—well, that he would disapprove of. It was quite informative, really."

"Explains why your father's hair is gray," he muttered.

He wished he were not so ill. His mind didn't want to focus. He only wanted to sit in the cool shade and feel her backside on his knee and put his arms around her. He wanted to kiss her, to erase the pain inside him.

He supposed what she said could be true. But he remembered Sara, and every day of the two months he spent with her. They had coupled more hours of the day than they hadn't. If any woman would have conceived his child, it should have been Sara.

But she had not. She had waltzed from James to Grayson Finley, and then twelve years later, presented a child Grayson must have gotten on her right away. James had hoped at first that Maggie was his own, but one look at her had wiped out that hope. She looked like Grayson and talked like Grayson and grinned like Grayson.

"I don't want to discuss this right now, Diana," he said. "I'm still sick, remember?"

She flushed with her usual temper. "Well, I wish to discuss it. You can certainly sire children because you have sired one on me. Even when I told you I did not ever want another child." Her glare told him she blamed him completely. Never mind that she'd walked right into his room on Haven and started washing his naked body. And then when he'd told her to go, she'd taken off her nightdress and climbed onto the bed. His fault. Of course.

His own temper stirred. "You must know, Diana, that it could be your husband's child."

Her eyes widened like blue-gray twilight. She slid off his lap in a whirlwind, lips parting in outrage. "How could you think that, James? They were beating you to death just outside. What did you think, that I'd turned to the man I hated and beg him to comfort me? What do you take me for?"

Her glare could have burned down the folly. If she'd thought of kicking him, she'd have done it.

"I never said you'd gone willingly."

She stood, hands on hips, her glory-red hair falling from the neat bun, her white breasts pushing up the décolletage of her dress. "You understand nothing, James Ardmore. Sir Edward did not want me. Never wanted me. Not when we were married, not now."

Something burned through him. "So he didn't ask you. If he had, would you have gone?"

She hesitated. "Of course not."

Their gazes met. That tiniest hesitation made his stomach churn and made him want to swear hard. He should have stuck that knife into Sir Edward when he'd had the chance. He had to stop being kind.

She flushed. "If I had been younger, I would have gone. But not now. When I first married him, I was young and besotted. He soon disabused me of the notion that he wanted anything to do with me."

His hands hurt. They wanted to reach for her, touch the curve of her waist. His lap was colder without her. "Sometimes that young wanting stays with us. Even when we're older and know better."

"Well, it did not stay with me," she said sharply. "What about Alexandra?" Her face was rigid, but she was shaking.

"What about her?"

"You and she seem to share a fine friendship. When you were ill, you came to her. You told her not to mention your stay to her husband, and she agreed." She was breathing hard.

"I would not say we share a friendship. More an understanding."

"A great understanding. So much that you rip off your

nightshirt in front of her and wander away, not minding if she looks her fill."

"You saw that, did you?" He had been giddy with the fact that he could even walk upright. "You didn't bother to make yourself known. Did you look *your* fill?"

Her face flamed. He liked they way her eyes got all sparkly when she was embarrassed. "Yes, I did, if you want to know, you conceited man."

She was beautiful. He'd not had her for too long. His erection was pushing itself up, making its presence known. "Are we finished with this argument? I need you sitting back on my lap right now."

"We are not finished by a long way! Do you still believe I went to my husband?"

"No."

She shot him a suspicious look. "Do you really believe that, or are you just trying to get me to shut up?"

"I told you, darlin', nothing makes you shut up."

Her expression turned thoughtful. He took her hands, pulled her back to him. She was still shaking.

"Wait, James. What are we going to do about the child?"

"Think of a name for it and decide what color to paint the nursery."

She chewed her lower lip. "You want it, then?"

"I want its mama. When you deliver it, I'll probably want it too. I've never been a father, I don't really know what I'll feel like."

Diana settled back onto his lap, still stiff. Emotion of any kind so angered her. She was like a rigid sapling, afraid to bend any way in case she fell altogether.

"I should not have another child. I am an atrocious mother."

He slid his arm around her waist. "I don't agree."

Jennifer Ashley

"I told you. About Isabeau. How I was ready to abandon her."

"How old were you?"

"Twenty-one."

"Barely more than a child yourself. It's a hard thing to ask of a woman so young, to take care of a child the world thinks is marred. More so when they blame you."

"How could I have contemplated ever sending her away? The only explanation is that I am a rotten mother. I do not have the gift of motherhood."

He wanted to smile, but she looked so downcast. "Isabeau might debate that with you, Diana. She loves you with all her might."

"And I love her."

"Then what is the fuss? Isabeau won't let you be a rotten mother."

She gave him a hopeful glance from under her lashes. "Do you truly believe that, James? Or do you just want me to stop talking?"

"Both."

She reddened. "You really are the most—"

He put his fingers to her soft, full lips. "Let's not start the name calling, again. Let's enjoy being out here together."

She rested her head on his shoulder. Her fingers moved across his broad back, her touch light as drifting snowflakes. "I should not let myself be alone with you. I cannot be trusted."

"I am pleased to hear that."

She traced a line down his spine. He flinched, and she stopped.

"It's all right, darlin'. The pain's mostly gone. I'm a little stiff, that's all." He added, "That's not the only thing that's stiff."

He expected her to blush or grow angry. Instead she raised her head, stared down at him with gray-blue eyes that had darkened with desire.

In one swift move, she swung around on his lap, until she faced him, straddling him, her cream-colored skirt hiked up around her thighs. "You make me wicked, and I do not seem to care. Even when I'm angry at you."

"You were always wicked, Diana. And you'll always be angry with me."

She touched her lips to the bridge of his nose. Her cheeks were flushed, her lashes thick and curled. She kissed his eyelids, then her fingers went to the little black buttons on her bodice and started undoing them.

"Hmm," he said, trying to control his voice. "I thought those were only decorative."

She did not answer. The placket loosened, showing the lace of a pretty chemise beneath.

His heart beat hard. "Want me to help you?"

"No. You ripped it last time, and this gown was expensive."

Fair enough. He liked watching her anyway. The slim fingers opened the buttons, which looked like juicy little blackberries. He wanted to lean forward and taste one. There were about twenty buttons in all, and it took her a while to reach the end.

He was good and hard again by the time she parted the bodice and began untying the little bows that held the chemise closed. He could not remain still. He reached up and gently helped her reveal the wonders within.

Her skin, warm from the bodice, was flushed and damp. So easy to lean a little bit forward and lick the drops of perspiration from between her breasts.

Her fingers furrowed his hair. She tasted like honey and cinnamon, and like Diana.

271

She kissed his forehead, her breath hot on his skin. His legs were starting to shake. He laced his fingers beneath her buttocks, drew her closer. The bench beneath him was hard and cold. But her thighs were warm, and the skirt loose enough for him to snake his fingers under it.

His thumb found the curls between her legs. She made a noise of contentment. She was wet and sweet, and he rubbed his thumb through the moisture. He never found her anything but wet for him, his sweet Diana. Wicked and lovely woman.

"I wish I were a well man," he murmured. "I'd certainly like to make this more interesting."

Her eyes were heavy. "Should we go inside?"

"I think I can sit here a while."

"I do not want your fever to return."

"It's gone. I got well as soon as I saw you in the drawing room."

"I know, but . . ." She rested her hands on his shoulders as she thought a moment. She sent him a sly look, eyes all dark blue and roguish.

She slid from his lap and sank to her knees, using her skirt to pad the cold floor of the folly. His pulse speeded. Her bodice still gaped, breasts soft and exposed.

"I do not have a pistol with me," she said. "But I'd like you to unbutton your breeches. Of course, Alexandra might lend me one of her husband's pistols. I could go back to the house and ask her."

"You stay right here." He popped open the top button of the kid breeches. "I didn't tell you before," he said, opening the next one, "but if you had just asked me that day you told me to bare myself, even without the pistol, I probably would have done it."

She reddened. "I was not quite myself that day."

"Yes, you were. You were every bit yourself." He pulled open his breeches. His arousal thanked him. It had been getting tight in there.

Her hand, cool, closed around his shaft. She looked down at it a moment, then she gave a decided nod, leaned to his lap and closed her mouth around him.

He stifled a gasp. Lust burned through his veins, driving away the last dregs of the illness. Damn, if Alexandra had just let Diana crawl into bed with him, he'd have gotten better so much faster.

Faster, yes, did someone say faster?

Her tongue moved, and he rocked a little on the stone bench, his toes curling in Grayson Finley's slightly too-small boots. He wove his fingers through Diana's hair, loosening it from its bun. Why did she think it looked nice coiled up so tight? He wanted it flowing over his hands, falling about her hips, loose so he could drown in it.

His lips formed her name, his voice broke. The wind kicked up leaves, strewing them across the floor of the folly. Gusts of rain slanted through the trees, spattered hollowly on the roof.

Her mouth was hot and wet, her tongue, wicked. She had not done this before. She knew the theory, but not quite what to do. No matter. He'd teach her. What a joy to teach her and teach her and teach her.

She flicked her tongue all the way to his tight balls, then back again, circling around the fully aroused tip. He could not see her mouth, but he imagined her small white teeth, her red lips, playing with him. He drew in a long, dry breath. He couldn't stand this.

A smattering of rain blew into the folly. The cold droplets hit him and Diana. Diana gasped and jerked away.

James did not even notice the cold. He grabbed Diana's arms and hauled her upright. "I'm suddenly feeling much better," he said.

He lifted her, his arms shaking, pushing up her skirts and bringing her down to straddle him again. This time, his free-standing arousal snuggled right into her.

Her eyes widened. *Foolish woman, did you think you'd drive me wild and escape the frenzy yourself? No, no, Diana. You are going to enjoy this with me.* He rocked back, driving himself into her, feeling her close on him all the way. Muscles squeezed him, spiraling his frenzy higher.

He'd had women in his life with skills unimaginable, and Sara had been one of the best. But no other woman had made him feel like this, had made his desires and his heart get all mixed up and pour joy through him like he'd never known. And never mind her lack of skill. No, teaching her wouldn't be any problem at all.

She cried his name, eyes tightly closed, far gone in her climax. She squeezed him, her body unconsciously driving him further and further from sanity. He thrust hard into her, once, twice. Rain-drenched wind tore at her loosened hair and dragged it free of its confining pins.

And then it was over. He crushed her close while he spilled his seed, whispering into her hair. His legs were weak and shaking, and any moment he would fall off the bench.

It didn't matter. He'd fall with Diana, and he was certain they could find interesting things to do on the ground.

She rested her head on his shoulder, her warm hair drifting over his fingers. They had a lot of pain and a lot of things still between them. He was afraid, and she was afraid, and they had many walls to surmount. They still had a long way to go. But he thought perhaps they'd made the tiniest of tiny starts.

They spent the next week quietly, as James healed. Diana slept alone at night, but she lay awake imagining James in his huge bed, lying awake too. If she'd dared, she'd have crept around the gallery and into his chamber, but Alexandra's household seemingly never went to sleep. Footmen and maids patrolled the halls all hours of the day and night.

Diana had forgotten what it was like having servants constantly underfoot, gliding about in their business of running the house. Masters and mistresses might think the house theirs, but the servants knew better. Diana had grown used to waiting on herself and helping Mrs. Pringle, and found the servants bothersome. The ladies of society, including Alexandra, would faint in horror if they knew that Diana could peel potatoes and make beds like the best under-housemaid.

James had a slight relapse of his fever and returned to bed the morning after their time in the folly. Diana's heart squeezed in fear, and she spent an afternoon blaming herself for possibly killing him. But he threw off the fever quickly and growled at them to stop fussing.

The relapse seemed to close what they had opened. In the folly, they'd begun a kind of rapport, a sharing of hearts that she wanted to continue. But once recovered, James closed himself to her.

He had not again brought up the question of whether the child was his. He behaved as though he believed she had not gone to Edward, but she couldn't be certain because he refused to discuss it.

Diana watched him over the next several days in deep

frustration. He told her, in Alexandra's presence, that they would return to Charleston and marry when he was well, picking up her father along the way. He made no mention of how they would get there, where his ship was, or how he'd make the arrangements. So like a man, he simply announced it and expected her to obey.

She felt as though she were beating on a thick stone door. They had developed an affinity on Haven, arguing and making up and arguing again. They were both volatile people, but she had come to find enjoyment in their clashes. Now, he had turned cold, isolated. Alexandra watched them both worriedly, a pucker between her fine brows, but she made no move to help.

By the end of the week, James suggested he and Diana walk again to the folly. He chose the hour after the children's tea, when Alexandra lingered in the nursery. Diana strolled beside him to the woods, hoping they would begin more conversation about marriage, children, and Charleston. But when they reached the folly, she discovered that James had not brought her out here to talk.

During the next breathless two hours, James would discuss only whether another position he wanted to teach her was logistically possible. He found many varied and creative ways to make love on a stone bench, and he'd smuggled out some blankets to soften the floor.

They tangled together until they were weary. Then they dressed and made their exhausted way back to the house. Diana was too tired for conversation then, just like he'd known she would be. Bloody arrogant man.

She would have understood his need for silence—he had been powerfully ill after all—if he had not enjoyed so many private conversations with Alexandra. Where he shut Diana out, he opened himself to Alexandra in long, comfortable, earnest talks. Whenever Diana entered the room during these sessions, they would fall silent. Alexandra would quickly speak about something neutral, and James would again become a cold stone wall.

Diana tossed and turned at night, alone, frustrated beyond measure.

One evening before supper, she found James sitting easily in the drawing room balancing little Charlotte on his knee, having another of these interesting talks with Alexandra. The open windows showed a vast expanse of deep blue ocean, clear skies, and a stretch of golden sand beach. Londoners, amazed that the sun shone anywhere in England, were out strolling the far beaches and sailing little crafts all over the blue, blue sea.

This conversation was so intense that they did not halt when Diana walked into the room.

"We all need someone to hate, Alexandra," James was saying. "And your husband hates me."

"He does not," Alexandra answered, distressed. "I know what is in his heart. His compassion for you is boundless."

James's eyes turned hard. "The last thing I want is Grayson Finley's compassion. He has gall to pity me. I know things about him— But never mind, I'm not going to tell you. I'll be gone before he gets home anyway, and you can both feel sorry for me all you want."

Alexandra had looked up, seen Diana, and broken off. Neither would tell her what they had been talking about. Diana decided not to stamp away in a huff, but to sit down with the cup of tea Alexandra pressed on her. She busied herself teasing baby Robert with the end of the spoon to keep her anger at bay. Robert was happy at least. He shoved the spoon into his mouth and gnawed on it with two tiny teeth.

James just watched her. He seemed much stronger

physically now, almost at his normal strength. The bruises on her thighs attested to that. He'd taken her to the folly twice more, each time silencing her with brutal kisses that she did not struggle against. Now he drank his tea in silence. Alexandra darted a worried glance at him, but he only shook his head. Diana ground her teeth.

She had to wait until the next afternoon to confront him, when they again walked off to the woods, pretending to be nonchalant. Everyone in the house must know what they were doing out there. No one ever asked to walk along with them, and no stray child or gardener ever turned up at the folly to disturb them.

She had to wait longer because James started kissing her even before they'd reached the folly. His strength had certainly returned, she reflected, as his strong arm cradled her, protecting her from the stone floor, which was hard despite the blanket. His stamina had returned as well. He had great stamina.

The blasted man gave her no time to talk. By the time they lay quietly, with him stretched out on her, she was exhausted. The day had turned warm and lazy, and their clothes lay scattered about the folly. Cicadas sang in the trees, and birds chased each other in pursuit of what James and Diana had already found.

James dozed, his face in her shoulder, so it was Diana who was the first to see the man standing over them. His mane of blond hair moved in the summer breeze, but there was no laughter in his blue eyes, nor any humor in the pistol he held.

Chapter Twenty-one

At Diana's faint gasp, James woke fully. In one smooth movement, he rolled over, sat up, and pushed her behind him. She was never certain where he'd obtained the pistol or where he'd hidden it, but the next moment, he was pointing it straight at Grayson Finley.

Diana got her naked body as far behind James's as she could and peered over his shoulder. The two men eyed each other for a long, tense, silent moment.

Then Grayson rested his pistol's barrel back against his shoulder and took his finger from the trigger. "You're a bloody fool, Ardmore."

James did not relax. "Best get out, Finley, or your wife will be very unhappy with me."

Blue eyes flashed. "I came here to save your hide." His gaze dropped to James's body with ill-concealed annoyance. "Your bare hide." The gaze flicked to Diana, and his assessment became more approving. She tried to fold herself a little tighter.

James growled. "Keep your eyes to yourself."

Grayson did not obey. He looked over Diana, attempting to see as much as he could. "You are damned lucky Alexandra told me where you were. And what you were likely doing. A fine idea, the folly on a summer afternoon. I'll have to remember this."

"You'll remember better if you turn your back and walk away."

"James," Diana said nervously. "Perhaps you should not shoot him until he tells you what he's talking about."

"I like her," Grayson said calmly. "A very intelligent woman. While you were so sweetly dallying here—and I cannot blame you, James, she is extraordinarily beautiful and much too good for you. Anyway, while you were dallying, the Admiralty arrived in Newquay. They are scouring the grounds of my estate even now, looking for you."

Silence fell, except for the music of the excitable birds. Fury rose inside James, first at himself and then at Grayson, who kept looking at Diana. With interested, hungry eyes. "Are you saying you betrayed us?"

"Alexandra did," Grayson said quietly. "Through no fault of her own. She wrote to me about you and Lady Worthing. Unfortunately, the Admiralty is far from trusting me, no matter how much help I've given them. I'm still a pirate in their eyes, even if the Duke of St. Clair has made me his crony. So they read my post."

"Oh no," Diana breathed behind him. Her slim arms still circled his waist.

"Alexandra was wise enough not to actually pen your name. But with Admiral Lockwood's recent questions in London, then his daughter's quiet disappearance, and my past association with you, they put things together. That and the idiot Henderson took rooms in the Majestic hotel as he always does."

"Did they arrest him?" James asked tersely.

"Henderson vanished in the night. Have no idea where to. The Admiralty insisted that you were holding Alexandra hostage and that they accompany me down here to look for you. Alexandra has the sense to pretend you coerced her to silence, and everyone believes everything she says. So they are searching."

He felt Diana start to rise, unclothed and all. "Dear God, Isabeau is at the house."

Grayson's gaze rested on Diana again. "Alexandra and Maggie will keep her safe. Best you disappear, Ardmore. Quickly. Before they start wondering where I've been gone to so long."

James had already made up his mind. He distrusted Grayson with all his heart—in all matters except this one. Grayson had no love for the English Admiralty. They kept him dancing with promises of forgiveness for his pirate past, and he'd do anything to protect Maggie and his wife from disgrace and ignominy.

"Time to get dressed, Diana," he said. "If Henderson has left London, he'll be waiting for us on the *Argonaut*."

"I cannot leave." She got to her feet as James rose, keeping his body between herself and Grayson.

"You can and you must," Grayson replied, his eyes serious. "If you do not, they might arrest you and use you to bring him in."

She snatched her chemise from the bench and held it in front of her. "Are you mad? I cannot leave my child behind."

"Alexandra and I will hide her and get her to you. She will be perfectly safe, I promise you."

"Trust him on this, Diana," James said as he pulled on his breeches. "He's almost as good as I am."

Grayson ignored this. "Believe me, I am doing this for

your sake, Lady Worthing. Not his." He stopped as James took up the linen shirt. "Aren't those my clothes?"

"Picked out for me by your lovely wife," James said. "Hurry up, Diana. Finley, turn your back."

Grayson's idiotic grin broke out as he took one last sweeping glance at Diana. Then he turned on his heel and stared out at the woods.

James had to admit that watching Diana dress was enjoyable. She slid on the chemise, which hid her not at all. The thin folds moved enticingly as she leaned to pick up her dress. James shrugged on the coat, and then saw Grayson's blue eye watching over his shoulder.

"You look at her again, Finley, I'll shoot you."

Grayson took his time turning away. "Just admiring. You have commendable taste. She is delectable."

"You have your own."

Grayson glanced back again, but Diana was covered now, her back to them while she buttoned her bodice. Grayson took on the besotted look he always got when talking about Alexandra. "I know. I have the best of women."

"Not quite. I believe I have that claim."

Diana swung around, her bodice buttoned, her face flashing dangerous anger. "You speak as though Alexandra and I were race horses. She would not be pleased, I think." She sat down on the bench and wriggled her toes into her stockings. Both men watched her, mesmerized.

James heard sounds of movement in the woods. He hefted the pistol and grabbed Diana by the wrist.

An English voice, fresh from the back streets of London, called out, "This way, sir. Servant says there's a folly of some kind in the wood."

"Search over there, Sergeant," a well-bred voice answered. "I'll go 'round behind."

They were making unnecessary noise. Good. James could pinpoint exactly where they were.

James dragged Diana out of the folly and behind a tree. Grayson faded discreetly. James pocketed the pistol and removed a short knife he'd pilfered from Grayson's collection. A well-balanced knife that would make a silent, deadly weapon.

A man stepped into the folly. James watched him through the leaves. He could see only his dark blue coat and white trousers, the uniform of an anonymous officer. He steadied the knife. Diana breathed quietly behind him, stiff and tense.

The officer found the blanket. He paused, looked down at it for a long time. He looked up again, scanned the area, then made his way slowly out of the folly. He walked quietly, boots making little noise on the damp leaves.

He strolled unerringly to their hiding place, and stopped. James stepped from the shadows and swiftly brought the knife to rest at the hollow of the officer's throat.

Brown eyes regarded him calmly above the blade. He wore the uniform of a British naval officer, but James knew him better as Lieutenant Jack.

James kept the knife at his throat for a long time. Then he let his hand grow slack and lowered the blade. Lieutenant Jack returned his gaze silently. Then just as silently, turned his back and walked away.

In Alexandra's grandiose front hall, Diana caught Isabeau in a fierce embrace. "I was such a fool to leave you alone. I never will again, sweetheart, I promise."

Isabeau squirmed a bit, confused by Diana's rigor. The thought of leaving Isabeau to strangers indefinitely had frightened Diana badly. It was one thing to know her daughter was with her grandfather and Mrs. Pringle on Haven; abandoning her on the coast of England with naval men searching for them was something else.

"Good thing you did," Lord Stoke said. "Or they would have found you here with James."

"They would have found us in any case." James sounded irritated.

Lieutenant Jack had left them without a word. They'd heard him announce to the marine sergeant that he'd found no trace of them in or around the folly. She and James had waited in tense silence as Jack and the marine crunched away into the woods. A long time later, Lord Stoke had reappeared to tell them it was safe to return to the house.

"Only safe for so long," James said now. "They'll come back. They'll search the town and surrounding area for a while." His eyes were like green ice. "I seem to recall asking you not to write to your husband about me."

Alexandra drew herself up. "And I did not, until you were well. But I keep no secrets from him."

They gazed at each other meditatively. "Of course you don't," James said at last. "But I'd hoped to slip away quietly. Now we've got to evade a marine patrol."

Lord Stoke's eyes were quiet. "We'll come up with something."

They began planning. The rest of the afternoon and into supper, James and Lord Stoke came up with and discarded plans. Diana sensed that James wanted to do this on his own, as he did everything else, but he pretended to listen to Lord Stoke's ideas. Alexandra had no hesitation about throwing in her own contributions, and

Diana had never been shy about interrupting. A spirited, four-way argument ensued.

"The *Majesty* is the only real way out," Lord Stoke said much later that evening.

"And the way to your arrest," James retorted. "I don't mind so much seeing you on a prison hulk, but Alexandra might get mad at me."

Diana was exhausted. Her eyes felt as though fine grains of sand swam in them, and her back ached from the stone floor of the folly. James, the man who had battled fever and wounds from a flogging, downed brandy and paced the sitting room with perfect strength.

Alexandra mostly watched the two men. They were handsome specimens, worth watching. James, dark-haired, eyes like jade, his swarthy face strong; Grayson Finley, with his long mane of blond hair and blue eyes that could light up the room.

Alexandra had told her a little of the two men's history, how Grayson had long ago rescued James from a pirate ship then invited him to help take over a frigate. They'd succeeded in leading a mutiny, and two pirate legends had been born.

They looked like pirates. Diana could imagine them boarding a fallen ship, Grayson's hair glinting like sunshine, laughing as he made some quip; James quieter, his Southern drawl cutting with cynical coolness.

Somewhere along the way, the two pirate legends had turned enemies. Even now, Alexandra confessed she was not certain which way the balance swayed.

Diana sensed the tension between them as they discussed plans. James watched Grayson with narrow eyes, and Grayson's affable grin vanished whenever James drawled sarcasm at him, sarcasm that bit.

"My idea is the best," James said to Grayson now.

"It's something I would do, and it saves your pretty neck from the noose. You've got children to look after."

Grayson's friendliness had completely gone. He studied James with eyes as cold as James's own. "I do not want Alexandra caught up in your schemes. I remember what happened last time."

The two men shared a long look. James said, "I remember your hands around my neck often enough. I think you got your revenge."

"Not even close, Ardmore." Grayson's voice went soft, purring. "Not even close."

They eyed each other like dogs circling, hackles raised. Alexandra looked uncomfortable. Diana wanted to leap up and demand they tell her exactly what they were talking about. Bloody men. "May we keep to the point? James must escape. His plan is audacious enough to work. We must do something."

"I agree," Alexandra said in her quiet voice.

Grayson swung to her. "You agree?" His face was still, waiting for something.

"I think that's settled," James said.

"No," Grayson said sharply. "I do not want Alexandra in it. I will go along with it, but not her."

"She has to." James had an odd light in his eye. "No one will believe it unless she plays along. You stand on precarious ground, old friend. The Admiralty might seem in awe of your title, but they're not happy about all that fun you used to have in the Pacific. I could give them a whole long list of your activities. I bet they don't even know most of them."

"Don't threaten me, James."

"Not a threat. I'm just pointing out where you stand. One hint that you helped me, and they'll start coming after you for all the rest."

They faced each other, blue gaze meeting green, each knowing more about the other than anyone else in the world.

Finally, Grayson let out his breath. "All right. Damn you. I'll contact Jacobs, tell him what to expect." He glared at James. "But if you so much as scratch the varnish, I will come after you. That ship is Maggie's legacy. I want it in one piece for her."

"I know how to sail a ship, Finley. You taught me, remember?"

Grayson growled and said nothing.

They broke and went up to bed after that, but Diana could not sleep. She went to the nursery to look in on Isabeau. The little girl slept on her cot, one fist resting on the pillow beside her. Diana pressed a kiss to her forehead. Isabeau had taught her all about love and caring, and about courage. She could not imagine life without her.

She touched her hand to her abdomen. She hoped that something equally as precious would happen with her next child, and that she would not make the blunders she'd made with Isabeau.

She left the nursery and wandered back downstairs. James would be sleeping in his room, but she hesitated to go to him. He had never once continued any discussion with her about marrying or going to Charleston, but he assumed she would accompany him on this escape. His coolness unnerved her.

The Stoke house was gloriously ornamented. All the gold and silver furnishings flashed under the candlelight in the hall, a bit overwhelming. A servant, ever wakeful, sprang to attention at the bottom of the stairs, ready to offer her a glass of water, a cushion, a full feast, whatever she wanted. She nodded to him and continued to the drawing room, thinking to find a stray book to read and ease her mind.

She found the viscount there instead. He stared moodily at the fire, his blond hair bright in the gloom. She made to tiptoe away, but he saw her.

"Lady Worthing," he said. He beckoned to her. "Come and sit down."

She took the offered chair, not because she was naturally obedient, but because she was curious to know what he wanted to say.

For a long time, he simply looked her over, but his gaze held no flirtation this time. She saw in his eyes assessing intelligence, usually hidden behind his affable, outrageous pirate persona.

"In London," he began, "I told you to forget about James Ardmore. And then I find you here very much with him." His eyes twinkled. "In my folly."

Her face grew hot. "I beg your pardon about that, but—"

"You are not sorry. You are in love. But you really ought to know what you're getting yourself into."

Diana made an irritated noise. "I know already. He is exasperating and high-handed and bad-tempered. But then, so am I."

He grinned. "I like you, Lady Worthing. You have fire and courage. You just might be what he needs. That, and you are damn beautiful. How did he get so lucky?"

Her face heated still more. "Your observation is unseemly."

"But right on the mark. Men must fall over when you walk down the street. You only have to quirk your finger and they all fall in line, don't they? I wager Charleston men will be no different."

She thought of the ballrooms of London, the parade

of her admirers, their empty flattery, their indecent suggestions. She certainly did not want that to start again. But then, she had been married to Sir Edward Worthing, a man who had ignored her. When she was married to James Ardmore, things might be very different.

"James does not really want to go to Charleston. He is taking me there because that is the only safe place we can marry."

"I know."

She looked at him in surprise. "You do?"

He nodded. "James used to love Charleston. He's very proud of it. When he first took me there, he showed me every corner of it. The people of Charleston love him back. They worship the Ardmores. His sister, Honoria, is a beautiful woman. Fine-mannered and as arrogant as he is. She has every lady of Charleston society wrapped around her fingers. No one makes a social move without the approval of Honoria Ardmore. Her power would frighten you."

"It already frightens me. What will she make of me, I wonder?"

Grayson gave her another assessing look. "Once she discovers you have a backbone, and that you tamed her hopeless older brother, I predict she'll take to you. She'll have someone to complain about James with if nothing else."

She regarded the fire thoughtfully. "Is it because of Honoria that he does not want to return? He speaks of her with affection. She sounds like a formidable woman, but he likes formidable women."

"He and Honoria don't get on, but only because they are too much alike. No, he does not want to return to Charleston because of Paul."

"I see." She chewed on her lower lip.

"Do you?" Grayson said. "He blames himself for Paul's death. James had gone off after some pirates who were terrorizing the Carolina coast, and Paul decided to go on a rampage of his own." His grin turned rueful. "James does not entirely blame himself. He also blames me. Paul was doing his best to kill me when he died. I lived. Paul didn't."

Diana digested this in silence. She could never get complete stories from James, and piecing things together frustrated her. "I know he grieves still," she said. She looked up at Grayson. "What can I do? I want to help him, but he will not let me. I do not know if I can, in any case."

"I think if anyone can, it's you. I've seen James Ardmore angry, I've seen him dangerous, I even knew him when he was young and pigheaded and mostly happy. But I have never seen him like this. It's like he's come back to life. He is not hiding in his cold shell any longer. He's snarling at me and staring at you like he wants to eat you up."

She looked at him in trepidation. "Do you mean that this is *not* his cold shell?"

The viscount leaned over and took her hand. He had large, brown, scarred hands, like James's. "Not by a long shot. You're waking him up. Whatever it is you are doing, keep doing it."

She watched his fingers trace hers a moment. "You are fond of him, aren't you?"

Grayson looked embarrassed. "I would not say *fond*. But we shared a past and a friendship. I am not entirely blameless in what happened between us. He intimidated me, and I loved to put one over on him. It was like shooting an arrow into a bear's foot. Yes, I hurt him, but I mostly made him angry."

Diana smiled at the image. James's sudden temper and ruthless retaliation were very like that.

She sensed it now as James leaned over the backs of their chairs. His hands gripped the upholstery until his fingers went white. "Finley," he said, his green eyes like ice. "What the hell are you doing?"

Grayson looked up at him, his blue eyes going cool and wary. "Sorry, Ardmore," he said. "Habit."

"Not this time, Finley," James returned. "This is different."

Grayson looked at him sharply. They seemed to be continuing a conversation they'd begun years ago, one that didn't include Diana.

They looked at each other for a long time. Then Grayson said, "You're right, old friend." He withdrew his hand from Diana's.

In the small hours of the morning, Diana roused Isabeau and prepared her to leave.

She had packed everything before putting Isabeau to bed, and now they gathered in the downstairs hall with James, Alexandra, Grayson, and Maggie.

The hall was surprisingly free of servants, and no lights flickered in the sconces. Grayson still fumed over James's plan, but he had made the necessary arrangements. James had worked everything out, Diana had no doubt. He was a man who planned contingencies for everything.

Alexandra, obligingly, provided the rope.

Grayson snarled and swore until James gagged him, not gently. Grayson glared at him over the white linen.

Alexandra and Diana bound Maggie's hands. Maggie insisted the bonds be tighter than Diana wanted because

291

that would be more believable. She even volunteered to wear a gag, to Grayson's obvious fury.

Diana had thought James would order her to truss Alexandra, but James insisted on doing it himself. As James tied Alexandra's wrists behind her back, he leaned forward and said, sotto voce, "Just like old times, isn't it, Alexandra?"

And Lady Stoke blushed.

After that, he took Diana's hand and led her and Isabeau into the night. They reached a rowboat hidden under the shadow of a wharf, and James rowed them across the black sea, stars in a riot of light above them. Diana glared at him all the way to the ship, but James offered no explanation and no time to talk.

Very soon, they pulled up alongside a three-masted ship. The *Majesty* in all her glory.

James climbed on board like he owned it. Once upon a time, he had owned part of it. Mr. Jacobs, the young first officer, eyed him askance as Grayson had. Mr. Jacobs's beautiful wife, however, welcomed Alexandra and Isabeau and made them comfortable while the men readied the ship to sail to the rendezvous point.

Diana had no time to question James, or to argue with him, or do anything but give him looks that boded him no good. But she swore in her heart that sooner or later, the two of them would have a long talk. A very long talk.

Chapter Twenty-two

The Ardmore house in Charleston astonished Diana. Graceful and white, it rose four stories from the street, each floor replete with a lacy white balcony. It resembled nothing less than a bride in finery, a flirtatious bride who smiled and beckoned and dared you to discover her secrets.

A sumptuous wrought-iron gate set in the wall opened to a courtyard paved with gold and white tiles. A small fountain bubbled away, surrounded by summer geraniums. A wide black door, topped by a graceful fanlight stood closed at the top of a short, curved flight of stairs.

Houses in London sported anonymous façades, revealing the riches inside to only a very few. This house tantalized with tall windows coy with lace curtains, balconies strung with bougainvillea and wicker chairs placed so that a sitter could enjoy the cool courtyard.

Diana had been warm since the *Argonaut* had entered Charleston Harbor. Her father had mopped his brow as their hired carriage made its way to the Battery and

Meeting Street. Isabeau, on the other hand, had found everything delightful, and Diana herself had gaped like a tourist.

She had supposed that James would take them all to a hotel and approach his home alone, but he commanded the coachman to drive them straight to the Ardmore house. They all came, including Mr. Henderson and Ian O'Malley. She wondered, as they crowded into the court-yard, whether James had brought them all to remind his sister that he was indeed master of this house.

The door opened slowly as James climbed the front stairs. A tall man in butler's clothes with a coal black face and gray-white hair stared down at them. His smooth face was as dignified as an English butler's, probably more so, but Diana saw a flash of joy in his dark eyes.

"Mr. James." The man greeted him with barely a tremor in his voice. "I've informed Miss Honoria of your arrival."

He opened the door wide and ushered James inside. He stood aside deferentially for the lot of them, but his eyes were only for James.

The inside of the house was even more stunning than the outside. The walls were painted a light yellow, as though sunshine had been swallowed and dispersed. A black and yellow floor cloth led through another set of double doors to a wide hall housing a magnificent stair-case. The stairs swept upward without obvious support, twisting from ground to first floor, and from first to second, and on up without end.

Isabeau eyed the staircase speculatively, and Diana knew it would be only a matter of time before Isabeau's little backside was dusting the railing.

"You have a fine home, James," Admiral Lockwood

said, admiring the paintings that lined the hall.

The butler intoned in a soft, musical accent, "The original house was built in 1778 by Mr. James's grandfather. In 1795, Mr. James's father had it repaired and expanded, adding the formal rooms in the back of the house."

James was peering up the staircase. "Never mind, Daniel. You can give the tour later. Is Honoria still showing it off on Saturday afternoons?"

"Miss Honoria likes to keep on the tradition," Daniel answered.

"Like I thought." Footsteps sounded on the stairs above, and James's face became as neutral as a blank sheet of paper. He folded his arms and stood at the bottom of the staircase while his sister descended.

Diana recognized her easily from the portraits in James's cabin. Black curling hair, a round face and pointed chin, a Grecian nose, and eyes as green as James's own. In the portrait, she had been smiling. Now lines about her eyes attested to the unhappiness she'd experienced since the picture had been painted. Her resemblance to James was striking, even to the faint air of scorn. If Diana had encountered the woman anywhere in the world, she would have known at once she was James Ardmore's sister.

Honoria Ardmore swept her gaze over the assemblage below her. Her gaze lingered on Diana, as though curious but refusing to betray herself. Her dark green gown suited her coloring, but it was subdued and elegantly plain, the garb of a woman who had given up the dreams of a girl.

"James," she said. Her voice was like his, low, contralto, lilting with Southern gentility. "You should have sent word. It isn't fair to Cook that you have such bad manners."

James's expression did not change. "I would have arrived before the message."

"You are always in a hurry. Would it hurt you for once to be courteous?"

Behind Diana, Mr. Henderson murmured, "Is it not touching? They have not seen each other in four years."

Honoria's chill gaze flicked to Henderson, bathing him in scorn worthy of her brother. "Please, Daniel, show our guests to the drawing room. Bring them refreshments. I imagine they are all hot and weary if they have been following James."

Daniel snapped to attention without losing his dignity. He began to motion with his white-gloved hand.

"By the way, Honoria," James said, "I'm getting married. To Lady Worthing, here. I thought we could do it in a couple of weeks. You can fix up a fine wedding if you like."

Honoria's coldness vanished like ice warmed by the June sun. "A couple of weeks? James Ardmore, I can't prepare a wedding in a couple of weeks!"

"Why not? It doesn't have to be a grand affair. Just something small with family and friends."

Honoria stared at him in horror. Diana's irritation rose as well. "James, for heaven's sake, I haven't even got a gown. It will take a least a month to plan any sort of affair, and even then it would be thrown together. You cannot expect the people of Charleston to drop everything and attend your wedding with only a few weeks' notice."

"Really, James," Honoria said. "We need at least two *months*. You are the most thoughtless, arrogant man I've ever known!"

James gave Diana a look that was almost smug. "I knew you two would get along." He started up the stairs, passing the outraged Honoria. "You'll like her, Honoria, she has a fine pedigree. Diana, why don't you make the introductions?"

He kept walking, up the stairs and out of sight, damn the man. Honoria glared after him. "Really, James. I can take your coming and going without a word, but I cannot countenance your being rude!"

James said nothing, but a whistled tune drifted down to them.

James stood in his own bedchamber, and the memories came.

He had grown up in this room. He'd lain on the tester bed recovering from boyhood injuries incurred from climbing or riding or exploring where he shouldn't. In this room, he'd asked his father what it was like to fall in love and whether lying with a woman was as enjoyable as he'd heard. In this room too, he'd lain awake, eyes burning, the night his parents succumbed to illness and died—together, as they had done everything else.

The memories came, and strangely, they did not hurt. He'd avoided this house, and this room, ever since he'd taken up his career as pirate, then pirate hunter. His cabin aboard the *Argonaut* was his sanctuary now, the place he'd occupied much of his adult life.

But this room held him too. The brocade curtains had been updated as others wore thin, and chairs that he had broken had been replaced, but the chamber was much the same as when he'd woken every morning to the smell of bacon and hominy and cornbread, the sound of his mother's lilting voice, his father's answering baritone.

These memories had no part of James Ardmore the famous pirate hunter. And yet, they *were* him, down to the core of him.

He'd wanted to face the room alone, without Diana. He would bring her up later, when the dust of his memories had settled. If he brought her upstairs after everyone went to sleep, perhaps they could consecrate the room with new, happier memories. The taste of her lips would be fine, her body soft beneath him.

He'd known that the best way to get Honoria to accept Diana was to unite them in annoyance against him. Honoria would want the wedding of the season. The wedding of the head of the Ardmore household was no small event. His ploy had worked from the sound of things below.

He departed the room and made for the bedchamber at the head of the stairs. His footsteps slowed. Facing his own boyhood memories was one thing, but *this* he'd truly been dreading. Diana had suspected, but he had not known how to explain to her just what was wrong.

So he was alone to face his demons. He could avoid it, could walk downstairs and be part of the warmth again. Diana would look at him with her gray-blue eyes, and he'd feel fires in his soul. But he'd put it off too long.

He opened the door of the bedchamber at the head of the stairs and walked inside.

The room faced the courtyard, and a small balcony opened from the double French doors. The walls had been painted a light green, the cornice lined with a relief of classical Greek figures planting and harvesting crops. The bed was covered in ivory damask matching the curtains, and a fine oriental rug covered the floor. The room was elegant, painstakingly neat, and anonymous.

"Honoria," James said. Then his voice shook the walls. "Honoria!"

From below, he heard her say, "Your pardon," in a voice of strained politeness, then her slippers whispering on the stairs.

James waited in the middle of the room. She stopped on the threshold, her eyes cool. She neither asked why he'd called nor berated him for his lack of manners.

"What have you done?" he demanded.

"I felt the need for another guest room. The others are rather small."

He swept a delicate porcelain figurine to the floor with a crash. "A guest room for whom? How many guests do you entertain in my absence?"

"Hardly any. I spend every Christmas alone, unless friends who pity me allow me to share in their celebrations."

He was too angry to let her goad him into guilt. He'd tried to spend Christmas with her several times, and they only had quarreled. Likely she had a better time with her sympathetic friends.

"What did you do with his things?" he asked tersely.

"Put them in the attic. Don't worry, James, I did not sell them or anything vulgar like that."

"Put them in the attic? Why didn't you put *my* things in the attic if you wanted another guest room? You know I wouldn't give a damn."

"Because you were more likely to come home."

They regarded each other for a long moment. Outside, bees droned in the flowers, and far below, Isabeau laughed.

"So you took away everything," James said. "Everything that would remind us of him. I know it hurts. Why

299

do you think I stay away? But I never expected you'd erase him altogether."

Honoria swung on him, fists clenched. "You at least have the luxury of going away! How do you think I feel, living here day after day and year after year, knowing he will never come home? With his trinkets still scattered about the tables, waiting for him? You were never close to Paul like I was, so don't you dare talk about how his absence hurts you."

"*I* was never close to him?" he thundered, incredulous. "I sailed with him, fought beside him. I held him when he died, for Christ's sake."

"But you weren't beside him when he was shot. If you had been, maybe you would have been shot instead. I would gladly have thrown away all *your* things!"

She knew how to cut deep. James's greatest regret, the one that gnawed at him in the dark of the night, was that he had departed to pursue that privateer and decided to meet up with Paul later. Paul had chased and attacked the *Majesty* and Grayson Finley, a foolhardy choice that James would have talked him out of.

But Paul, crazed with his pursuit of revenge, had determined to wipe out every pirate, especially the notorious Grayson Finley. He'd rammed the *Majesty*, shot Grayson almost at once, then was struck by another bullet. He'd stayed alive long enough for Ian O'Malley to get him back to James, so that Paul could die while James held him.

"We were much closer," Honoria was saying. "He lived here with me when you abandoned us. I knew his wife, helped deliver her children. Where were you? Tearing about the world with your friends, turning up every once in a while with your foolish gifts and tall stories. Where were you when Paul's wife was killed, and I stayed with him and kept him from taking his own life? Why were you not practicing law in Charleston, living here with us, watching out for us like you were supposed to?"

"I'd have been no good at law, Honoria," he ground out. "I am good at pirate hunting."

"Your own form of law. Of course, James Ardmore cannot bow to anyone else's rules! Good luck to Lady Worthing making you conform to them. Or have you brought her here to settle down, to stay in Charleston, to live like a real family?"

"Yes," he barked.

"The poor thing. What has she ever done to you?"

"We are going to live here. Like a family. This is my house, Honoria, and if I want Paul's things in his room, then I want them there."

"Why?" she flashed. "You have not walked into this room in seven years. Seven! What are you afraid of?"

"I at least thought that when I wanted to remember him, I could."

Her green eyes were wet, luminous. "This is not *your* house, James. Your name may be on the deed, but this house is mine. I lived here when everyone else left it behind. I have kept it alive. You walked out and never came back." Tears tumbled down her face.

"Hell and damnation."

"I hate you, James. I am all alone, and it's your fault."

Diana hurried into the room. She closed the door, crossed the carpet, and gathered Honoria into her arms. His haughty sister actually put her head down on Diana's shoulder.

James looked on, hurting and numb. He hated coming home.

"You are the most unfeeling man I know," Diana said in a clear voice.

"For God's sake, Diana."

She gave him her familiar glare. "You are more interested in ghosts than you are in the people around you, James Ardmore. Do you think your brother is any less special because his things are in the attic? Of course not." She smoothed back Honoria's hair. "I believe any sister who has put up with you all these years deserves a commendation!"

"This isn't a game, Diana," he said, gritting his teeth.

"Neither is life, James."

She was so haughtily beautiful. He'd thought so the first time he'd seen her. He knew that whether he won or lost every argument with her, his heart would stop whenever she walked into a room.

Honoria glared at him from Diana's shoulder. Diana shot him a look that made him highly suspicious. "I know exactly how to make him sorry," she announced. "Should the oldest son of one of Charleston's first families not have the best wedding of the century? He is a hero. I am certain people would come from miles around to attend such a gathering."

Honoria wiped her eyes with the heel of her hand. Her face had taken on a light of hope. "Yes, we'll have the ceremony in the Episcopal church. You are Church of England, and Mama raised us to be Episcopalian. She'd like that. We'll decorate with orange blossom and pink roses. We'll have Madame Madeline do your gown. She is the best in Charleston. White and pink, yes, that will make a lovely theme, with perhaps some yellow thrown in."

Diana's eyes gleamed in triumph. "And we will plan a banquet for after, perhaps a ball." She looked at him critically. "James will have to wear a cravat. And a hat. Perhaps Mr. Henderson can suggest something."

She looked so lovely and so happy planning his doom that he did not have the heart to get angry again. "You're lucky I love you so much, Diana."

Honoria lifted her head, throwing off her melancholy. "I must see to hiring the musicians and planning decorations for the ballroom. You really ought to have sent word, James. I could have had half the plans in place by now."

She left the room, frowning over the details. Diana closed the door again. Silence fell.

James sank onto the cushioned bench at the foot of the bed. This room had once been a mess with Paul's things, and then Paul's children's things. Model ships and animals from the garden and lengths of string had given way to hair ribbons, building blocks, and dolls. Now it was blank, empty.

Diana looked at him. "Do you want me to go?"

"No."

She came to him, her gown rustling in a way that made him think of her legs underneath. Her long, elegant legs.

"I did not mean you should forget him entirely," she told him.

He reached out, traced his finger across her abdomen. Inside her lay his son or daughter. He still could not quite believe it. But he knew the child was his. If it weren't, Diana would have looked him in the face and told him the truth.

"I was supposed to look after him," he said slowly. "And I didn't when it was most important."

A note of anger entered her voice. "You cannot know that. He might have died just the same. You might not have been able to stop him."

"Maybe. We'll never know, will we?" He clasped her hand. "See, I thought, Diana, that if I killed Black Jack Mallory, that would make everything all right." He met her blue scrutiny. "But sittin' in this room, I know it wouldn't. Even if I'd shot Mallory, right in front of your father, everything wouldn't have been all right." He paused. "What I'm trying to face is that my promise to Paul made me everything I am."

"A legend," she said softly.

He made a derisive snort. "The legend never existed. Now the promise is gone. Where does that leave me?"

She took both his hands, settled herself on his knee. She'd made a habit of that. All the way across the Atlantic, they'd sat on a bench on the quarterdeck every morning this way, her on his lap, his arm around her waist, while they watched the sunrise.

"Remember when we came across the privateers sacking the merchant ships four days out of Haven?" she asked.

He and Diana had been sitting just like this, enjoying the cool air of the morning. On the horizon, they'd seen a plume of smoke, which could only mean one thing. James had given command to change course for it.

They found a French privateer that had just burned one English merchantman and was about to board the other. James's flag, plain midnight blue with one slash of gold from corner to corner, was hoisted in the stern. The privateer ran up a flurry of flags in return, signaling James that he could join them and have a half share of the plunder. James responded by firing all guns.

The privateer fired back. A gunner fell, wounded. Diana, the reckless woman, ran and took his place. Her bright hair had flashed in the sun, and her cries had joined the shouts of victory when the privateer at last surrendered.

The captain, a Frenchman of fastidious arrogance, presented James the letters of marque he'd obtained from Napoleon himself. James had burnt them, just to show him what he thought of Napoleon Bonaparte's signature.

James had taken the captain prisoner, as well as the surviving crew, knowing he'd be kinder to them than the angry merchants. When he returned to the *Argonaut*, the crew cheered. Diana cheered with them, waving the gun's ramrod alarmingly and clapping the shoulders of the other sailors.

He was going to marry her. God help him.

James and Diana had stood together on the quarterdeck, his arm about her waist, as the *Argonaut* circled in a victory lap (Ian O'Malley's idea). The merchant crew cheered them. Henderson had raised his cutlass in acknowledgment, the blade flashing as bright as Diana's hair.

Now in the quiet upstairs chamber of the Charleston house, Diana said, "That had nothing to do with Paul, or your promise. You enjoyed rousting those pirates. You were happy. You *laughed.*"

He relived the taste of triumph, and better, the savage kiss he'd bestowed on Diana. "It had its moments," he admitted.

"*That* is what you are, James. An avenger. You like it. You began pirate hunting before your brother died, and you would have carried it on regardless. I believe your promise was only your excuse. Do you not see?"

Her warmth was distracting. The Charleston climate made her perspire, and he turned his head to kiss the dampness between her breasts.

He thought about the years he and Ian O'Malley had

torn up the seas, riding recklessly against ships that out-
gunned them, taunting frigates, chasing pirates to their
doom. He had been all over the world and sailed every
water. He'd known stinking ports and exotic islands and
the sweet peace of coming home.

He'd been ruthless and cruel, compassionate when
needed. He'd saved the lives of beleaguered crews, then
sailed away without acknowledgment, leaving the rescued to write yet another verse of the ballad.

Diana was right. He loved it.

He looked at her. "I really am a ruthless bastard, aren't
I?"

"I have always said so."

He pulled her closer. "I just told Honoria I was here
to settle down."

"I see no reason she cannot join us on the *Argonaut*.
She would like Haven."

"Oh, so we are going back to Haven, are we?"

"Of course. It is my home. We should spend the sum-
mers there and the winters here. And you can pirate hunt
to your heart's content."

He kissed the corner of her smile. "Well, you have
everything worked out real nice."

"You need someone to work things out for you, James.
Besides pirate hunting I mean. You're good at that."

He stopped her talking in his favorite way, something
else he was good at. When she emerged from the kiss,
her eyes sparkled.

He slid her from his knee and patted her on the backside. "Why don't you go help Honoria with the wedding.
She's probably got the guest list already worked out and
is planning what they all should wear."

Diana smiled, and his heart turned over. She'd
wormed her way into his life, all right. On the ship, when

he'd put his arm around Diana as they sailed past the grateful merchantman, it had felt so right. Like he'd been missing something all these years.

Of course, he'd had to haul her back by her fine backside when she'd tried to board the privateer with the others. They needed to have a little talk about that.

Back on Haven, when he'd faced Black Jack Mallory, the living people he'd cared about had suddenly become more important than long-ago promises about violence and death. Much more. He'd known the truth in his heart, and so had shot his pistol into the gray-blue waters instead of into Black Jack, and had walked away.

It all still mattered. Paul mattered. Diana mattered. But James's promises, like his anger and hatred, were of the past. Diana and their child were about now. They were about love, and now, and the future.

She kissed his brow, her scent soothing him, and glided from the room. Her smile as she departed was a bit smug.

He gave the closed door a smug smile of his own. Let Diana and his sister plan a fine wedding and a grand ball that people would talk over for generations to come. Let Diana plan their lives after that all she wanted. Because while Diana had her revenge planning the wedding, James would have his planning the wedding night.

Chapter Twenty-three

It was over. The last guest had faded into the night, and the wilted garlands had fallen. Ian O'Malley found Isabeau curled up under the violinist's chair, and Honoria carried her off to bed.

Diana's father had met up with cronies he'd known from his long career, and he'd returned home with one elderly gentleman of Tradd Street, where he'd stay the night to talk over old times.

Honoria had had her grand wedding. James—peculiarly, Diana thought—had not fussed. He'd looked extraordinarily handsome in a black suit with a cutaway frock coat and tails. He'd worn a cravat, stark white against his brown skin, and his hair had been trimmed and bound in a tail. He'd not looked himself, but when she'd entered the church and seen his tall, muscular body filling out the well-fitting suit, she'd felt a bit weak in the knees.

Honoria had made a lovely bridesmaid in cream-colored silk. Diana had made her wear the lighter color; Honoria had at first planned something dark and unobtrusive. Isabeau, likewise dressed in finery, had strewn flowers everywhere, enjoying herself hugely. Ian O'Malley had looked after her, just as he had on the *Argonaut*.

Honoria had been most pleased with Diana's lineage and had made certain that everyone from Charleston to Savannah knew about it. An English lady, widow of a knighted naval captain, daughter of an admiral whose family name went back generations, was well worth boasting about. Discreetly, of course. Honoria Ardmore would never openly boast about anything. But people heard the news, and they talked, and they approved.

At the altar, James had looked as calm and cool as when giving routine orders on the deck of his ship. Diana had shaken all over. Memories of her first wedding had been pressed into the oblivion of bad memories of Edward, but the sight of the priest in his robes and her father waiting to walk her down the aisle for the second time in her life momentarily panicked her. She'd wanted to turn and run as fast as her feet would carry her.

But it was James waiting for her, not Sir Edward Worthing. James who was a true hero, not Edward who was a sham. James waited for her with his warm green eyes and wicked smile, looking rather like he was planning something.

When she'd placed her hand on his strong, calloused palm, her panic had vanished. She suddenly regretted her silliness over planning the wedding. They'd have to wait through a long banquet and ball before she and James could be alone together.

When he slid the cool gold ring that had belonged to his mother onto Diana's finger, she regretted the banquet even more. And when he leaned down to brush her lips with his, all too briefly, she longed for him to simply lift her over his shoulder and run away with her back to the *Argonaut*.

This did not happen, of course. She lived through the dinner and the innumerable toasts, kept a smile pasted on her face while Charleston's finest citizens congratulated her and James. James sat through it all with a relaxed manner and a neutral expression, while below the tablecloth, his foot tangled with hers in intimate and suggestive ways.

Diana was positively rigid with nerves by the time they entered his upstairs bedroom, at last alone.

The Ardmore staff had prepared a meal for them and left it under silver trays, just in case they should be famished in the few hours between the banquet and the lavish breakfast that would begin at nine.

James insisted that they partake, lest they hurt the cook's feelings. She'd been cooking for the Ardmores since he was a baby, he said. She'd never forgive him if they didn't send back clean plates.

Diana forced down the crab bisque, soft rolls that he called biscuits, slabs of ham, and boiled hominy. James ate contentedly, as though he'd looked forward to this meal all day. She dragged her spoon through her soup and watched him warily. He seemed much too capitulating.

"Tell me, Diana," he said, fishing up a bit of ham and biscuit. "What do you want to ask me?"

She blinked. One wisp of dark hair had escaped his queue and drifted across his cheek. His loosened cravat revealed a triangle of swarthy throat that she kept imagining touching with her tongue.

"I beg your pardon?"

He took a leisurely bite, his lashes hiding his eyes. "You have been watching me like you were making a

311

bet with yourself about something. Like you've been wanting to ask me something for quite some time. Except we've been too busy to be alone together, what with traveling from England and planning the wedding, and me not wanting to soil your reputation."

He knew, bloody wretch. She glared at him. True, she had wanted to ask him since she'd heard the murmured words in Lord Stoke's house and seen Lady Stoke blush. She'd wanted to know, and she hadn't wanted to know. She certainly had not wanted to bring it up now, during their wedding dinner.

He glanced up, his expression composed, his eyes cool. He already knew the question.

Well, he'd better hope, for his sake, that she liked his answer. She stirred her soup again and set down the spoon.

"Very well," she said. "Since you bring it up, what exactly is Lady Stoke to you?"

He started just the slightest bit. His gaze dropped as though he found his biscuits interesting.

Aha, she thought. Not what you were expecting. Which made her wonder very much what he *had* been expecting.

He answered, "I really don't want to talk about Finley and his wife on my wedding night."

"That means there is something to talk about."

He buttered another biscuit. "I believe this is why Ian O'Malley avoids serious involvement with ladies. They ask too many awkward questions at the damnedest times."

"I believe you wanted me to ask it."

"I've changed my mind."

She glared. "James Ardmore, if you do not want your

cook's fine soup all over your new suit, you will answer the question."

"Threatening me?" he asked mildly. "And I've just become your lord and master. You are supposed to submit and obey your husband."

Her snort rang across the room. She swore she saw his mouth twitch before he became absorbed in eating his biscuit.

"Were you two lovers?"

There, she'd said it. She did not want to know, and yet, she had to know. He'd gone to Alexandra when he'd needed help, not the mighty Lord Stoke. He'd told Alexandra to keep it silent from her husband, and Alexandra had done it. He'd trusted Alexandra and known he could trust her. That trust spoke of an intimacy that even Diana might not yet have with him.

"No," he said. "Never even once."

He stopped pretending to eat. He watched her over the domed silver plate between them, the one that contained the mounded slabs of ham.

She relaxed the slightest bit. But that still did not explain what he'd said to Alexandra when he fitted the ropes about her wrists. Her breath came fast. "You told her, 'It's just like old times.' What the devil did you mean by that?"

He fingered the stem of his wine glass. The candlelight threw a ruby-red shadow onto the tablecloth. "Do you really want to know?"

"Yes." She didn't. "I truly wish to know."

"All right." He took a sip of wine, returned the goblet carefully to the table. "I abducted her."

Her heart pounded. "Well, that is your usual style."

"I abducted her, stripped her naked, put her in chains, and used her to exact revenge on Grayson Finley."

He picked up his glass again, calmly took another sip of wine, set the glass back down.

She gaped. He just looked at her, like he did such things every day and she shouldn't be surprised. She swallowed, only her throat was too dry, and it turned to a cough. "Why?"

For a moment, she thought he would not tell her. She thought he'd go cold again, bottle it up, and let it stand between them the rest of their lives.

He shrugged, ever so slightly. "I blamed Finley for Paul's death, whether or not his hand actually pulled the trigger. I would have done anything to get back at him for that, including stealing the woman he loved. If Alexandra had not been who she was, I would have ruined her and broken Finley's heart. I would have wrecked both their lives and pulled them down into my misery." He reached forward, touched the thick gold band around her finger. "There's a world of hurting inside the Ardmores. You only have to look at us to see it. I've decided it's time to change that."

She looked at his calloused hand, scarred with years of fighting and surviving. He'd saved people's lives and taken other lives. He'd known quiet happiness in this house, and he'd known heartache she could barely comprehend.

Her chest felt tight. "I am glad you chose me to help you change it."

"I damn well didn't choose you, Diana. You sprang into my life like a comet and destroyed every preconception I ever had. It's like holding a wildcat by the tail. I don't dare let go."

"That is not very flattering, James."

"But true. I knew you were a wild one the minute I found you tearing up my cabin after I abducted you.

Despite your title and your daddy being so famous, I knew you weren't anything like a proper young lady. But that's fine. I don't like proper young ladies."

A drop of wine lingered on his lips. She wanted to lean over the table, platter of ham and all, and lick it off.

She made herself sit still. "Back to Alexandra, since you have so neatly turned the discussion. Why did you let her go? Did she tell you to go to the devil?"

"No. She was prepared to martyr herself to save Finley's neck. She was besotted with her pirate next door, and she'd have done anything to keep him safe, including marrying me."

Diana sprang to her feet. The table rocked and the soup swayed dangerously. "You asked her to *marry* you?"

"I thought it the surest way to hurt Finley. I would let him live, and let him suffer."

"And she said yes?"

"She did. But I don't think I would have enjoyed it much. She'd have played the sacrificial lamb to the hilt. I'd have gotten tired of that real fast."

She'd caught up her napkin when she'd jumped up, and now she clenched it hard in her fist. "I assume Alexandra came to her senses and turned you down?"

"No. I came to mine." He watched her calmly, but a wary light burned in his green eyes. "They were so sickening about each other that I couldn't stand it anymore."

"Sickening?" She twisted the napkin.

"Ready to die for each other. It got a bit cloying at the end. I decided to stop playing the villain and let true love take its course. Very romantic of me, I thought."

He had the gall to take another drink of wine, as though he'd been the hero of the piece.

"Romantic?" Diana seethed. "You are the most un-

romantic man I have ever had the misfortune to meet!"

"Lower your voice, Diana. People are trying to sleep."

"How romantic is it to simply take what you want? *You* decide to let Alexandra and Lord Stoke be together because you couldn't intimidate her to your side. You wanted to question me about my father, so you simply absconded with me. You brought me here because it would be more convenient for you than dodging the Royal Navy to corner me."

"You must admit," he said, in that annoying, cool way, "that my house is much more pleasant than a village tavern or the drenched caves on Haven. A proper bed after a proper meal. I thought you'd like that."

She snatched up a buttered biscuit. "Do *not* tell me I should be grateful!"

He came alert, dangerous. "Don't you dare throw that biscuit at me, Diana."

"Tell me this, then, if you want to save your wretched suit. Did you love her?"

"No."

"You sound certain."

"I am certain. I didn't love any woman until she threw bread at me in a wayside inn. Not that I want her to do it again. It's bad manners. My sister would be shocked."

Diana refused to let him distract her. "You and Alexandra seem very fond of one another."

"I admire her. And I respect her. It isn't every woman who stands up to me and tells me where I've gone wrong. Especially when I've just locked her in chains. She was scared to death of me, but that didn't stop her from telling me exactly what she thought."

"You have not shown much respect for *me.*"

"You are still alive," he pointed out. "I think that means I highly respect you."

"You arrogant, infuriating, bloody blackguard! I cannot believe I let myself fall in love with you. I could be living peacefully with my father on Haven, but instead I let you drag me halfway across the world and help you hunt pirates and watch men I am supposed to respect beat you until it nearly killed me and then I thought you dead for days and days. What kind of a life will I have with you? Madness, that's what I'll have. And all because I was stupid enough to fall in love with you."

"But I'm damn glad you did."

She stopped. For some reason the gentleness of the reply, the warm light in his eyes, made her more furious than ever.

She let fly the biscuit, then the other half of it, then the half-eaten bowl of soup. He rose even as the missiles hit him. The bisque landed with a liquid *splat* all over his black cashmere frock coat and fine silk waistcoat.

"Diana." His voice was very, very soft, at its most dangerous. "I can't let you get away with that."

She took a nervous step back. "Your sister would be upset if anything happened to this dress, James."

"Then you'd better take it off."

She'd seen that look in his eyes before, right before he planned to mince up a few pirates. "I think I will just keep it on."

He took a step toward her. "I'll do it for you."

"No, no." Her hands flew to the hooks, started unfastening them. "You'll rip it to shreds."

"That was the idea."

She undid the hooks quickly, knowing that if she lingered, he'd grow impatient and rip it off her anyway. She slid the warm silk down her body and folded it carefully away into the armoire. His shirts and coats hung there, smelling of wool and cotton and James.

By the time she turned around again, he had armed himself. She shrieked, but it was too late.

Buttered hominy made a good weapon. It splattered across her shoulders. He laughed, then blinked and cursed when she returned fire with a ladle full of bisque. The ham made a satisfying noise when it hit him too.

The battle did not last long. Within seconds, he'd seized her wrists and shoved her to the bed. She found herself flat on her back on a soft featherbed with his weight on top of her.

He took her mouth in brutal kisses, pinned her wrists above her head.

"I love you, Diana," he said hoarsely. "I never thought I could love this much. It hurts me how much I love you. No one in my life has ever made me this—"

His hands burned and his lips bruised her. She thrust her knee between his, laced her foot around his muscled calf. "Yes?" she asked, pretending innocence.

"This angry. And happy. All at the same time. Demon woman." His eyes sparkled. "You have grits in your hair."

She laughed. She stroked her tongue across his cheek, where the crab bisque lingered. "You taste good."

"You taste better." He demonstrated how much he liked her taste. "Damn but I love you, Diana." He kissed her again, this time gently. "You brought me home."

She touched his hair. "We're getting maudlin, Captain Ardmore. I think we should get on with making love."

"I must agree with you, Mrs. Ardmore."

"I think we should make love until we're worn out. But it will be morning soon. They'll expect us for breakfast."

His smile warmed the night. "Then we'd better get a move on."

He seized the placket of her chemise and ripped it from neck to waist. He leaned down and licked her breasts, his hot touch blazing to life the fires he'd already stirred.

She laughed, loving him, put her arms about him and drew him down to her.

Epilogue

"There is a new Ardmore in the world, Alexandra. God help us all."

"Yes, Grayson. A handsome baby boy."

Grayson Finley looked across the sitting room at his wife. He'd been reading a letter written to them both by Diana Worthing, now Diana Ardmore.

Alexandra lounged on the end of the divan, leaning against its curled arm and staring into the fire. Her red-brown curls had escaped their pins, and she stretched in a relaxed, contented way.

It was dark. The sound of the sea entered the windows, along with the cooling spring breeze. Alexandra seemed very distracted this evening, ever since she'd read Diana's letter.

Well, his old friend and enemy had certainly come up smelling of roses. Diana Worthing, a fiery redhead with enough heat in her eyes to burn down whole villages, would certainly keep him jumping. And warm. And happy. Ardmore was no easy man, but she looked like she'd be up to the challenge.

He and Ardmore had shared bad blood and anger and even hatred, but he wished the man well. And, if Diana kept Ardmore as busy as Grayson suspected she would, then Ardmore would stay the hell away from Alexandra.

He folded the letter, dropped it beside him on the desk. "What are you thinking about, sweetheart?"

She turned to him, smiling a smile that could still turn his bones to water. "I was gloating, rather."

"About what?" Not that he was interested in conversation. The Admiralty had kept him away from her far too much in this past year. He had spoken to the Duke of St. Clair, told the man it had to stop. *I want to be with my wife,* he'd told the very proper duke. He did not add, *I want to be with her in my bed and on the floor and in the garden and out in the woods in the folly.* They had put Ardmore's idea to the test many times, and he and Alexandra quite enjoyed it.

"I told James that he would find someone for himself," Alexandra said dreamily. "Someone on the wide seas meant for him. I never dreamed at the time that Diana Worthing was right in London with us. Of course, she was married to Sir Edward, then. But to think she and James met soon after that, and then she was waiting for him on Haven. Very romantic, I think. No wonder they fell in love. I am very pleased with myself."

Grayson grinned. His wife was fond of believing that her good wishes rubbed off on everyone. But she was a person who genuinely wished others to be happy. Perhaps that was one reason he loved her.

Her look turned pensive. "I only wish—"

He rose, strolled toward her. He had thrown off his

Lord Stoke garb and returned to the comfortable open shirt and buff breeches of the pirate Grayson Finley. Alexandra's gaze ran up and down him in a satisfying way. He never got tired of her looking at him. "Wish what, my love?"

"I wish that you and he could be reconciled."

Her old argument. He started to shake his head and tell her that such a thing could never happen, then he stopped. "We *are* reconciled, Alexandra. He has his life, and I have mine, and we each respect that. If he needed my help, he knows I'd give it. If I needed his help, I know—" He broke off. "No, I don't know if he'd give it. He's an unpredictable bastard."

"Well, now he's married and in love. I wish him well."

"So do I." He gave a silent salute to the west windows. James was somewhere out there. In Charleston. Or at least, that's what everyone thought. With Ardmore, who knew?

"Grayson."

The tone of her voice made his rising arousal dance a little more. "Yes, Alexandra?"

"The little ones are all tucked up in the nursery."

"I know. I said good night to them. So did you."

"Maggie has gone to bed," she continued.

"Yes, I kissed her good night too."

"The servants have gone to their rooms, as well."

"I wish them pleasant dreams."

She rose from the divan, moved softly to meet him. "I think no one will enter this room until daybreak."

"I believe," Grayson said, breathing the fragrance of her hair. "That you are correct."

As he bent to take her lips, he thought he heard a voice

in the recesses of his mind. A cool, drawling, sarcastic voice with a heavy Charleston accent.

"Finley, you are damn luckier than you ever deserved."

Grayson silently agreed with him.

The Pirate Next Door

JENNIFER ASHLEY

What is a proper English lady to do when a pirate moves next door? Add the newly titled viscount to her list of possible suitors? Take his wildly eccentric young daughter under her wing? Let the outlandish rogue kiss her with wild abandon?

As everyday etiquette offers no guidance, Alexandra Alastair simply sets aside her tea and follows her instincts—whether that involves rescuing her new neighbor from hanging, fending off pirate hunters, plotting against aristocratic spies, or succumbing to a little passionate plundering. Forget propriety! No challenge is too great and no pleasure too wicked, for Grayson Finley promises the adventure of a lifetime.